CW01511158

A Spring Fling at Hotel Mayfair

By Elizabeth Holland

Copyright © 2023 Elizabeth Holland

All rights reserved

The characters and events portrayed in this book are fictitious. Any similarity to real persons, living or dead, is coincidental and not intended by the author.

No part of this book may be reproduced, or stored in a retrieval system, or transmitted in any form or by any means, electronic, mechanical, photocopying, recording, or otherwise, without express written permission of the publisher.

Cover design: Elizabeth Holland in collaboration with Dawn Cox Photography

Elizabeth Holland is a writer of romance novels. She enjoys the escapism of picking up a book and losing herself in a new world. Elizabeth is a keen advocate for mental health and often speaks out about her own struggles. She writes to escape her own thoughts. When Elizabeth isn't writing, she's usually outside walking the dog. Her favourite walks are when it's cold and rainy, so she can work on her next plot.

THANK YOU

Before we begin, I must say thank you to Deborah, Rosemary, and Nicole.

Without you, this book wouldn't be the escape I envisioned.

AUTHOR'S NOTE

Dear reader,

Thank you for picking up A Spring
Fling at Hotel Mayfair.

I hope you enjoy your stay.

The hotel is set in London but is entirely fictional.

It's a haven amongst a bustling city
for you to check in to.

Lots of love,

Elizabeth
xxx

This book is for those of you still searching for your place in the world.

CHAPTER ONE

The kitchen was in darkness as Carrie walked in. The squeak of her rubber shoes echoed throughout the unoccupied room. She flicked on the overhead lights and suppressed a shiver. The cold morning air crept through the old windows on the far wall. Once the ovens switched on, the draughty windows were a blessing, but at this time of the morning, she wished they were modern and doubled-glazed. She zipped her fleece up and turned to her morning routine. It was her favourite time of day when the castle was still asleep, and she had the kitchen to herself. Today, the usual fizz of excitement was absent. Truthfully, over the last few weeks, the fire within her had been smothered. Today, she resented getting up in the pitch black and shivering until the kitchen warmed up. The loneliness of the castle was seeping into her soul. Endless nature surrounded the castle. There were fields, streams, and towering mountains as far as the eye could see. Usually, it felt exhilarating to be surrounded by so much grandeur in the heart of the Scottish Highlands. However, lately, Carrie felt the endless fields and isolation were slowly suffocating her, leaving her lifeless. She craved the hustle and bustle of a city. And the excitement of not knowing what every day would bring.

Ignoring her growing unease, Carrie pulled out all the ingredients to make miniature tarts for today's dessert menu. She cleared her mind and mixed the ingredients. Cracking the eggs into the bowl, Carrie marvelled at the perfect round yolk. They were collected last night just before she went to bed. She rolled the dough out and pressed it into a tin then slid it into the oven. Baking was her meditation. It cleared her mind of the endless stream of doubts swirling inside her head.

With the tart shells baking, Carrie went over to the fancy coffee machine Lachlan had insisted on installing. She hadn't touched it since scalding herself on the first day.

"Morning!" Eve called as she walked into the kitchen, stretching her arms above her head.

"You're up early," Carrie commented. Usually, she'd be on her fourth instant coffee by the time Eve padded into the kitchen. They were always the first two awake and working, both early risers, and enjoyed the quietness of the castle before the staff arrived. Then the kitchen would transform into a working kitchen, preparing for paying customers.

"Let me do that," Eve said, watching Carrie's attempt to froth the milk. "You clean up that puddle of milk, and I'll make us both coffee."

Once they had their drinks, Carrie started the next item on her list of things to do. She needed to bake the bread for the day. Silence shrouded the kitchen as both women flitted around, preparing for the day ahead. Carrie tried to silence the thoughts flying around her head, but they only seemed to get louder. She pounded her clenched fists against the dough. Despite the continuous movement, her frustration wasn't abating. Baking was no longer providing her with its usual solace.

"What's wrong?" Eve asked. She'd been watching Carrie for the last five minutes.

"Nothing," Carrie snapped, continuing to pound the dough.

"Carrie, you've been aggressively kneading that dough for the last five minutes." Eve turned to stir the pot on the industrial-size stove.

"I'm sorry," Carrie said, allowing her fists to come to a stop. She rested them on the bench and took a deep breath.

Eve turned the heat off and took the pot off of the stove. "What's wrong?" she asked, moving to Carrie's workspace.

"I feel like I'm suffocating." Carrie leaned against the workbench and ran a finger through the flour, creating a path from one side to the other.

"Is it being here, in Lachlan's castle? Do you want to go home? If you want to move back in with

3

your grandmother and commute, we'd be okay with that." Carrie's grandmother lived close by on the grounds of the castle owned by Lachlan's parents. "I know your gran still works at the McLeod's Castle. We'd miss you, Carrie, but we'd understand if you wanted to go back." Eve reached out to take Carrie's hand in hers. They'd been working together in Lachlan's new restaurant for the past three months, and their friendship had solidified. Growing up, Carrie had been a bit of a loner. Eve was her first close friend outside of the McLeod family.

"No, I love the restaurant. I love my job. I just want more. My brief relationship with Rhys sparked something inside of me. I have this longing to share my life with someone, to make memories with them and to always have someone in my corner. Those few months dating Rhys gave me hope. I loved being part of a couple, but now it's just me again." She shrugged her shoulders and stared at Eve's grip on her hand.

"Rhys really liked you, but his job means he can't stay in one place for too long. Your relationship was too new for him to commit to giving up his career."

"I know, but nobody ever stays here, Eve. Sometimes, I think about my year in London, and I miss it. I want to spend a week having a different cuisine from around the world for dinner. Imagine walking into a clothes shop and buying something other than a fleece. Or ordering something online and for it to arrive the next day! To drink fancy cocktails not made by us, with questionable music blaring out so loudly we can't hear each other speak. Instead, I'm tucked up in bed by nine. At the weekend, I'm sitting drinking tea with my grandmother. It's not that I don't love it, Eve. I need a change before I become set in my ways. If I continue like this, my work will become my entire life. There's a fire in me, and right now, being here, I feel as though it's being extinguished."

"Carrie, you know we love you. But if you feel the nee—is that smoke?" cried Eve, letting go of Carrie's hand and running to the oven with smoke escaping from the closed door.

"Oh, my tarts!" Carrie cried and ran to where Eve was trying to pull the smoking tin from the oven, coughing as the acrid smoke filled her lungs.

"Carrie, they're burnt to a crisp!" Eve exclaimed, staring down at what was once a tart shell.

"That was supposed to be for today's dessert special," groaned Carrie. She used a knife to scratch off the charred crust. It was no good. The underneath was just as burnt. Her eyes stung from the smoke as she scrubbed at them, trying to hold back tears.

"It's not like you to be so absentminded."

"I'm sorry." Carrie stared down at her hands, unable to meet her best friend's gaze.

"Come on, let's get some fresh air in."

They opened the windows and used tea towels to encourage the smoke out of the kitchen before the smoke alarms went off. It was still eerily quiet, and the sun was only just rising. The chilly early-morning air flowed into the room, sending a shiver down Carrie's spine. It was early April, but the temperatures were low, nestled in the hills of the Scottish Highlands.

"Where's Lachlan?" asked Carrie. Normally, he'd have joined them by now.

"Last night's guests were awkward, and he was up late with them, so I told him to have a lie-in, and I'd help with prep today," Eve explained.

"Is he enjoying having his restaurant up here?" Carrie asked. The last few months had been a whirlwind, and Carrie hadn't had time to ask Lachlan how he was enjoying living his dream.

Lachlan had only opened his new restaurant in January after restoring the castle. He'd worked his way up and proven himself in the culinary world, and now he was an award-winning chef with a Michelin-star restaurant in London. He had fallen in love with Eve two Christmases ago when she came to work as a private chef at his parents' castle. Eve had been grossly unprepared for the role, but Lachlan, Carrie, and Carrie's grandmother, Alice, had all helped her to find her feet. Eventually, they'd fallen in love, and Lachlan had begged Eve to move up to Scotland with him when he opened his restaurant at the castle he had bought and renovated.

"He's loving it. It's his dream. Carrie, stop trying to change the subject. You're not behaving like yourself. How can we help you?" Eve cast a worried glance in Carrie's direction.

"I think I need to get away from here for a while. A change of scenery and a chance to spread my wings." Admitting it out loud was painful. She loved her life here in Scotland, but right now, she felt as though she were being pulled in two. Scotland was increasingly feeling like a reminder of what she didn't have.

"Why don't you take some time away? I'm sure we can pull together without you. The restaurant is still finding its feet, and we've been playing it safe with the dessert menu since you don't have an assistant yet. A well-rounded pastry chef could step in. Lachlan can always step in when needed." Eve drummed her fingers on her mug. Carrie had been refining Lachlan's baking skills over the last few months.

"Are you sure?" Carrie's voice perked up at the thought of escaping for a few months and going somewhere to indulge in new things and meet new people.

"I'll need to talk with Lachlan, but I can't see why he'd disagree. You could probably go back to his restaurant in London and work there for a bit. After all, you trained there."

"I think I want something completely new."

"What about the agency I used that got me the job at the castle? I still have the number somewhere." Eve pulled out her phone while Carrie stared out the window and watched as the sun rose in the sky. "Here it is, *Peace, Joy and Love Catering Company*. I'll forward you the email with their contact details. Why don't you see if they have any temporary roles that would suit you?" Eve's eyes glistened as their plan came together.

"Thank you, Eve." Carrie felt excitement fizzle through her body. There was a chance she might get to go in search of a new adventure. Carrie knew she would always return, but watching Lachlan fulfil his dreams with Eve by his side had awakened something inside of her. It reminded her she had dreams to chase.

"You'll have to tell Alice before she hears it from someone else. She'll miss you." Eve reminded her.

"I know. Let me contact the agency first. They might have nothing that suits me. There's no point worrying Gran over nothing."

"Are they almost ready?" Lachlan was hovering around the workstation where Carrie was filling profiteroles with a whisky-infused cream. It had been a special request from a customer celebrating a milestone birthday.

"Almost," whispered Carrie, concentrating on piping the right amount of filling so it wouldn't all ooze out as somebody bit into it.

"Eve mentioned you might like some time off to travel?" Lachlan kept his voice low so nobody could overhear their conversation.

"Lachlan, I'm trying to concentrate."

"Carrie, you and I know you could fill these with your eyes shut. If you need the time off, you can have it. You've lost your spark lately. I understand sometimes you need to get away and refill your creativity. Just let me know when you'll be gone and when you'll be back. You're always welcome to return to my restaurant in Mayfair. I know Belle would love to have you back as part of the pastry team." With a smile, he walked away, leaving her to mull over his words.

Continuing to fill the last few weightless balls of choux pastry, Carrie thought about Eve and Lachlan's advice. They both supported her decision to get away for a while. Carrie cursed as her hand slipped on the piping bag, and a blob of cream fell on her foot.

"Let me take those for you. I don't think we need anymore." Eve swooped in and took the platter of profiteroles out to the restaurant before Carrie could protest. "Take your lunch break!" Eve called over her shoulder.

With a cup of tea in her travel mug in one hand and a croissant in the other, Carrie left the kitchen through the back door, which led to the kitchen garden. She'd pulled on one of the staff puffer jackets and a pair of Wellington boots. The sun was shining, but it was yet to warm up. She took the path through the kitchen garden, marvelling at how vibrant the spring greens looked under the glow of the early afternoon sun. Slowly, she meandered down to the little jetty and sat on the bench beside it. The water was flowing rapidly, and the sound filled Carrie's ears. Nature surrounded her with stunning views, yet she was craving something different. She pulled the top of her travel mug off and watched as the steam rose into the air and floated in the same direction the water was running. Carrie took a sip and picked at the croissant in her other hand. There was no point in putting it off any longer. She pulled her phone from her pocket and saw a message from Eve with the website for *Peace, Joy and Love Catering Company*. Carrie broke off a piece of croissant and popped it into her mouth, allowing the flaky pastry to melt as her phone slowly loaded the page.

There were three hundred job vacancies on the website. However, as Carrie used the filters to find the adverts which suited her skills, they rapidly dwindled. She finished the croissant as she read the last few job descriptions. Each one was looking for a chef proficient in savoury cuisine and pastry. At the bottom of the page, Carrie spotted a message from the company encouraging people to get in touch if there was nothing that suited their skill set. With nothing to lose, Carrie quickly typed out an email telling them about her training and her experience. She emphasised she was a pastry chef trained by a French patisserie master.

Carrie stepped back into the kitchen to find the atmosphere had changed. Lunch service had ended, and everyone had relaxed now the rush was over. "How was your break?" Eve gave her a knowing look.

"They had nothing that suited me." She shrugged her shoulders, trying to mask her disappointment.

"I can put some feelers out?" Lachlan had overheard their conversation.

"It's okay. I've emailed the agency. I'll see what they come back with. You've helped me so much, Lachlan. I really appreciate everything you've done, but I feel as though I need to do this for myself. This break needs to be all about me. I've lost myself in the grandeur and excitement of the castle, but it's not my journey. It's yours and Eve's, and it's time I found my own."

Eve wrapped an arm around Carrie's shoulder and pulled her against her side. "We'll be here waiting for you when you return," she promised.

CHAPTER TWO

Carrie's phone vibrated on the bedside table. She groaned and sat up in bed, with the duvet wrapped around her. Her alarm had already gone off twice, and she'd ignored it. Usually, Carrie was up before the sun, but today she wanted to stay snuggled under her duvet and hide from the world. Her phone kept vibrating, so she picked it up, and through bleary, tired eyes, saw it wasn't her alarm. It was a phone call.

"Hello?" she answered.

"Ms. Mackenzie? It's Sarah from *Peace, Joy and Love Catering Company.* I'm just calling about the message you sent us yesterday." The words took a moment to pierce through Carrie's sleepiness.

"Hello, Sarah. Sorry, I didn't expect to hear from you so quickly." Or so early. Carrie's voice was thick with sleep, but she felt wide awake, waiting to hear what the woman had to say.

"It's unusual for us to get back to a query this quickly, but we've just had a position come in that would suit you."

Silence hung in the air as Carrie tried to find the words to respond.

"Ms. Mackenzie, are you still there?" Sarah asked.

"Yes, sorry. I'd love to hear more about the position." Carrie swung her legs off the bed and reached for the unopened post on her bedside table. She flipped an envelope over and took a pen from the pot on the window ledge, ready to scribble any details Sarah gave her, not trusting her memory to retain the information.

With a few illegible scrawls, Carrie stared wide-eyed at what she'd written. With the envelope grasped between her shaking fingers, the only two words she could make out were *Hotel Mayfair*. Carrie said goodbye and hung up. Almost immediately, it vibrated in her hand. She dropped the envelope and watched as it floated to the floor. Her phone continued to buzz, reminding her that if she didn't get up in the next three minutes, then her entire schedule would be behind.

Unsure how, Carrie stumbled through her morning routine and soon found herself standing in the kitchen, kneading more dough with the ovens whirring away in the background. Mindlessly, she added butter to her dough, folded it, rolled it out, and then repeated the process.

"What are you making?" Eve asked, causing

Carrie to jump.

"Sorry, I was lost in my thoughts. I'm just making some croissants." Carrie shrugged. There were chocolate brioches left over for the staff breakfast, but she'd needed something to keep her busy while she sifted through her thoughts.

"I'll make coffee while you finish them, then we can sit down, and you can tell me what's on your mind." Eve was studying Carrie's expression. Carrie nodded and started cutting strips of dough before rolling it into the typical croissant shape.

With steaming cups of coffee and warm buttered toast, Carrie followed Eve into the castle's grand drawing room. They were restoring it to its original beauty and planned to open a boutique hotel. For now, the opulent rooms were at their disposal. Today, they sat on either side of the vast mahogany coffee table and sank into the dark velvet sofas. Carrie took a bite of toast and clasped her mug of coffee in the other hand.

"What's going on? You seemed okay when you finished work last night." Eve jumped straight in, wanting to know what was wrong.

"I woke up to a call from *Peace, Joy and Love Catering Company*." Carrie paused and took a sip of the scalding coffee. She swallowed it quickly and winced as it burnt the back of her throat. "They called to tell me a position has opened up that would be perfect for me." Carrie took a deep breath, wondering what to say next. If she said it out loud, then there was no going back.

Eve sat forward in the chair. "Really? What position?" she asked.

"There's a temporary role in a London hotel for a pastry chef. They've just lost their pastry chef. Sarah said they have a pastry team responsible for the hotel's desserts, but they're looking for someone with patisserie skills. The hotel's known for hosting beautiful weddings, so they need someone confident in baking and decorating wedding cakes and anything else that the bride might demand. There's also a high-profile wedding at the end of the summer that they need me for." Carrie took a deep breath, having not paused for breath throughout the entire explanation.

"Carrie, that sounds perfect. When would they want you to start?" Excitement danced in Eve's eyes.

"Next week. I'll be focused on afternoon teas and the odd birthday cake day-to-day, but they really want me for weddings. I could be back in Scotland by July."

"It sounds like everything you wanted. A new challenge in a city. And if it all goes wrong, you know Lachlan will have you back at his Mayfair restaurant in a shot. Or you can just come home."

"This feels right, Eve. I want to wake up not knowing how every second of my day is going to be spent. I love my routine here, but my soul feels restless, and I can't ignore this pull to London. It feels as though something is waiting for me there. How do I ignore that, Eve? I can't. If I do, it's something I'll always regret." Carrie paused for a breath. "When I lost my parents, I promised myself I'd live my life with no regrets. They passed when I was young and they always put themselves first. I want a chance to live my life before I settle down. This is my chance to follow my heart, to have my adventure. Just like you did when you came to Scotland. You're happy here with Lachlan. I know you don't miss anything about London or your old life. One day I hope I have that feeling; to find my home in someone else. I can't just sit around waiting for my life to come knocking. I have to find it for myself." Carrie looked up to meet Eve's eyes for the first time. She could barely make out her friend's smile through her misted eyes.

"Four months in London sounds just what you need, Carrie. This opportunity is too good for you to miss out on it. Have you accepted?"

Carrie nodded. "I accepted immediately. The position was too perfect to be anything but fate." She let out a wistful sigh.

"I'll miss you. Promise me you'll send me lots of pictures and keep me updated on how it's going."

"I'll miss you, Eve. But I promise I'm coming back. We'll be back to our early morning routine before you even notice I'm missing."

"All you have to do now is tell Alice." Eve raised her eyebrows at the prospect.

Carrie winced at the thought. She would miss her grandmother, but she knew she had to follow her heart. "I'll go over this afternoon to tell her,"

Carrie voiced her plans, knowing Eve would ensure she did.

"I'll pack you a basket to bring, and you can have lunch with Alice." Eve stood and took her half-drunk cup of coffee with her to pack a selection of goodies for Carrie to take with her.

Carrie felt the nerves bubble in the pit of her stomach as she drove towards The McLeod Castle. It was a route she was familiar with, having grown up on the castle grounds. Her memories were etched into every inch of the surroundings. Carrie sniffed and turned her attention back to the road. Scotland had her heart, and it would always be her home, but she needed to spread her wings again before she settled. Besides, as she'd pointed out to Eve, she'd be home before anyone missed her.

In the distance, the castle rose against the grey skies. It was drizzly and Carrie could feel her red curls becoming frizzier as the damp air clung to them. She turned into the castle's driveway. Alice would be in the kitchen, cooking for the impending arrival of Alexander and Isla. They were coming up to celebrate their recent engagement. Carrie dug her fingernails into her palm as she climbed out of the car. It would be another occasion she missed, but she couldn't stick around for everyone else.

"What a lovely surprise!" Alice called from the front door. She must have heard the car coming down the drive.

"Hello." Carrie smiled and hugged her grandmother before retrieving the hamper of food from the back of the car.

Alice led the way down to the kitchen, where the familiar and comforting smell of her cooking filled Carrie's nostrils. "What's going on?" Alice asked.

Carrie put the hamper on the kitchen table before taking a deep breath. Eve had tied a tartan bow around the handles, which Carrie threaded through her fingers.

"Carrie? You're worrying me. Let me put the kettle on." Alice bustled over to the kettle, switched it on, and pulled out two mugs.

She made them each a mug of sweet tea while Carrie unpacked the food. Eve had packed them an afternoon tea. There were little finger sandwiches made from the soft white bread Carrie had baked fresh that morning. Cucumber and cream cheese filled some and smoked salmon and cream cheese filled the others. Inside a tin box were orange and whisky-infused scones with a pot of clotted cream. Hidden at the bottom of the basket were two of Carrie's signature shortbreads, which she had developed for Lachlan's restaurant. They were ginger and raspberry with brown sugar to counter the tartness of the fruit. Each biscuit melted in the mouth.

"Tell me what's wrong," Alice insisted. She poured a splash of milk into each of their teas.

"I'm going to London for a few months." Carrie picked up a cucumber and cream cheese finger and nibbled on it as she waited for Alice to process the news. Silence hung in the air as Alice took a sip from her mug.

"Will you be working in London?" she asked. Her tone was level, not giving away her thoughts.

"Yes, I've been offered a temporary position at a London hotel. They need a new patisserie chef in the build-up to a high-profile wedding. I'd be covering afternoon teas and a handful of weddings. They only need me until July."

"Good. I'll need you back in time to start preparations for Alexander and Isla's August wedding." Alice pulled out a scone and pulled it apart with her fingers. Carrie watched in silence as she spread her homemade jam and lashings of clotted cream onto it.

"Is that all you have to say?" Carrie wondered.

"I think it's a good thing, Carrie. You've not been yourself for a while. It's clear you're feeling restless. We both know it's a fantastic and exciting opportunity for you. Enjoy your time, Carrie. You're young. The castles will still be here when you return."

Not realising just how much her grandmother's approval meant to her, Carrie felt a weight lifted from her shoulders.

"Where will you be living?" Alice asked.

"They're providing accommodation. I think it's just a room in the hotel, but it's one less expense."

Carrie shrugged. She was grateful that it was one less thing she had to worry about arranging.

"I'll get Eve and Lachlan to help me with my emails, and you can send me some pictures." Alice beamed at Carrie.

"Thank you, Gran. For everything."

"Your mum couldn't settle here until she'd seen the world. Then she met your father, and they travelled together. Her heart was never truly here, Carrie." Alice's eyes had glazed over.

"Maybe my mother should have settled before deciding to have a child." Carrie bit back. She loved her parents, but she couldn't forgive them for leaving her behind and going travelling.

"I'm sorry, Carrie. I always tried to do my best."

"It's not you, Gran. You did your best, but I deserved better from them. They prioritised their wanderlust over their child. Then they died, and I never had the chance to get to know them. Never had the chance to make memories with them. I don't want to repeat their mistakes. This longing inside of me, I want to satisfy it before I settle down. I know my heart is here, but it feels as though only half of it is here. I need to find the other half."

Alice squeezed her hand and poured them another cup of tea. "Carrie, you may have a burning desire for adventure, but you're nothing like your mother," she reassured her.

"Thank you. I love it here, Gran. But I feel as though I'm living in the shadow of their death.

I need to explore, to find myself. Then I can come home."

"I understand." Alice smiled before dropping Carrie's hand to smother another scone in cream.

CHAPTER THREE

Carrie reluctantly pushed the soft duvet off and allowed her bare toes to touch the glacial floorboards below. She pulled on her fluffy dressing gown, which she'd left at the end of her bed the previous evening. The cold was seeping through to her bones, and she knew she needed to pull on layers of clothes before her teeth started chattering. She pulled on a pair of fluffy socks to protect her toes from the floorboards. Her small bedroom in the castle had been one of the first rooms Eve had renovated. Eve and Lachlan had offered Carrie a bedroom in their apartment, but she had refused, wanting her own space. It was a decision she regretted every morning when she had to prise herself out of bed and away from her heated blanket.

Carrie glanced at her watch. She didn't have long until she needed to leave. Unsure what to wear for the journey, she opted for comfort and sentiment. Carrie pulled a knitted mustard-coloured jumper from her small wardrobe. It clashed something rotten with her bright red corkscrew curls, but it was once her grandfather's. For weeks after his death, she'd pulled it on and snuggled into the oversized jumper as the smell of her grandfather wrapped around her. It was like he was beside her, pulling her into one of his bear hugs. Eventually, she conceded it needed to be washed. Yet, to this day, she could still faintly smell his aftershave and the sharp tang of oil from where he'd been busy working on their old Land Rover. Carrie couldn't think of anything better than to feel her grandfather was by her side today as she embarked on her new adventure.

With a last look at her little bedroom in the castle's eaves, she grabbed her suitcase and rolled it down the hallway to the newly installed lift. "Goodbye room," she whispered as the lift doors shut, and she descended. It was goodbye for now, not forever.

Lachlan was standing in the foyer waiting for her, his own suitcase propped up against one of the plush new sofas.

"You ready?" he asked.

"Yes, let's go." With a yawn, Carrie took the coffee he offered her in a flask and wheeled her suitcase to the door. Lachlan had to be at his restaurant in Mayfair for an annual meeting with his suppliers, so he had offered to drive her down with him. It would be a long journey, but Carrie was grateful not to be doing it alone. Lachlan held the castle's door open for Carrie and followed her outside. The sun hadn't risen yet, and a thick mist shrouded everything as far as Carrie could see.

Lachlan's car was fancy. She climbed inside the driver's side and switched on her heated seat, waiting for the warmth to loosen her tightly wound muscles. Lachlan settled into the passenger seat beside her.

"Thanks for offering to do some of the driving. It'll halve the journey time," he said. It was a twelve-hour drive to central London, and Carrie had offered to split the driving with Lachlan so they wouldn't have to stop somewhere on the way. They'd agreed she would drive first while Lachlan slept for a little longer. Then they would swap. Although Carrie had made it very clear, she had no intention of driving around central London in Lachlan's tank of a car.

"Are you sure that's the right address?" asked Lachlan for what felt like the thousandth time.

"It's the one they sent me in the email," Carrie replied, speaking slowly to keep her frustration at bay.

"Well, something must be wrong, because the postcode keeps leading us to this dead end." Lachlan sighed and rubbed the palm of his hands against his eyes. Carrie could tell he was becoming increasingly annoyed by the Scottish edge his accent had acquired over the last hour. They were both tired and hungry. The journey had taken longer than planned due to traffic and comfort breaks. It was almost midnight, and they were driving around Mayfair, lost. The postcode was wrong and the hotel's name took them to the wrong hotel.

"I'll just get out and find my way on foot. You head to your flat and get your head down. You've got a long day ahead of you tomorrow." Carrie went to undo her seat belt, but Lachlan reached out to stop her.

"Carrie, I'm not just leaving you by the side of a road in central London at midnight. Asides from anything else, Eve would never speak to me again." Lachlan had tried to persuade Carrie to stay at his flat tonight, and then he'd help her find the hotel in the daylight. However, she'd refused. Insisting they were expecting her today, so today was when she'd arrive. Although, technically, it was past midnight.

"Hold on. The hotel must have a website. Let me see what their address is on there." Carrie tapped the keys on her phone and waited as the website loaded. Not much thought had gone into the hotel's name. It was simply *Hotel Mayfair*. "Here, the postcode is wrong. That should be a four." Carrie entered the updated postcode into the car's SatNav. Lachlan didn't comment.

They soon pulled up outside a smart-looking townhouse. There were marble arches on either side of the porch with the name *Hotel Mayfair* in swirly letters above. A man dressed in a smart black coat and matching hat stepped forward and opened Carrie's door for her. She thanked him and turned back to Lachlan. "Thank you for coming with me." Carrie swallowed as she felt her emotions creeping up on her. Having Lachlan beside her was like having a piece of home by her side. Once he drove off, she'd be on her own.

"Good luck, Carrie. Remember, you can always come home. You're also always welcome at my restaurant. I know everyone would love to see you. Your food will be on the house. I'll miss you." He leant across the car and pulled her into a hug. Carrie hugged him back and felt a tear slip from her eye. She was excited about her new adventure, but it didn't make leaving home any easier. She'd grown up with Lachlan, and he was like an older brother to her.

"Thank you. I'll be home before you even notice I'm gone." She shot him a small smile.

"I doubt that. Right, get going. Send Eve regular updates, or she'll force me to drive back to check you're okay."

"I promise. Goodbye." With a wave, Carrie jumped out of the car and went around to the boot to pull her suitcase out. The doorman walked to the boot with her and took the suitcase.

"I'll leave this at reception for you. Take your time." He tilted his hat and made his way inside the hotel.

Carrie waited until Lachlan had turned the

corner before she turned her attention back to the hotel. This was her home for the next four months. Before she could have second thoughts about her decision, she forced her feet to move and walked through the fancy revolving doorway and into the reception area. The first thing she noticed was the smell. The sweet scent of lilies filled the air, and as Carrie turned on the spot, she saw vases filled with flowers on every available surface. It was over the top and indulgent, but the smell was simply divine. Her boots squeaked against the white marble floor, and she noticed the empty brilliant-white sofas. A glance at her watch told her it was almost one in the morning. Now she was inside, she could see that the outside was deceiving and the hotel actually sprawled across many townhouses. She blinked and looked around for the reception desk, hoping someone could help her.

Straight in front of her was a marble counter with a computer on top. A small silver plaque read 'reception'. Carrie tiptoed her way towards it. Each step she took seemed deafeningly loud in a space that should be buzzing with activity and chatter.

"Can I help you?" The clipped tone of a man came from behind the reception counter. Carrie jumped. She'd thought she was alone. Had he been watching her the entire time?

"Sorry, I'm Carr— "

"I know who you are," he interrupted her. Carrie came to a stop at the counter and took in the man's appearance. His sandy-coloured hair looked overdue a cut. It flopped across his forehead as he studied something on the computer. He ran a hand through it, pushing it back. He glanced up at her, and his striking blue eyes met hers. It was as though he could see into the very depths of her soul. Swaying, she reached out to steady herself and tore her eyes from his.

"You're very late," he commented, tapping away at the keys on his keyboard.

"How do you know who I am?" asked Carrie, her senses finally returning to her.

"We don't get very many Scottish redheads turning up in the early hours of the morning," he quipped. "Also, I saw your picture on your application."

"Oh," Carrie whispered, staring down at her feet. She'd forgotten her application had included a picture of herself.

"At least you're here now." He attempted a smile, but it looked closer to a grimace.

"I'm not usually this late. There was just a lot of traffic on the roads. Then the agency had put the wrong postcode on the email."

"Yes, well, here's your key. Do you need help with your bag?" He gestured to the side where the doorman had left her suitcase.

"I'm fine, thank you."

He reeled off directions to her room, and Carrie just nodded. Truthfully, she'd zoned out as soon as he'd finished telling her to get into the lift. Hopefully, there'd be signs telling her where the rooms were. Instead, she was examining the dark shadows underneath his startling eyes. There must be a story behind his tired appearance, and she wanted to know what it was, even if it wasn't any of her business.

"Thank you," she called with a wave and walked over to the lift, pulling her suitcase behind her. Someone cleared their throat.

"It's those lifts." He pointed to the ones on the other side of the reception area.

"Thank you! I'm always getting my left and rights mixed up," Carrie joked, trying to move the attention away from her flaming red cheeks.

With her back turned towards the grumpy man, Carrie waited for the correct lift to arrive. She thought she remembered him saying something about floor three. The lift was as sumptuous as the reception area. The thick cream carpet almost sparkled in the bright spotlights above. Carrie pulled her suitcase in and pressed floor three. As the doors closed, she chanced a glance towards the man at the reception desk. He was sitting down, frowning at the computer screen. The doors closed, and Carrie returned her attention to the hunt for her room. She looked down at the keycard he'd handed her. It had the number thirty-three written on it in swirly gold writing. At least she knew which number to look for.

As Carrie emerged from the lift, she noticed the luxurious carpet covering the hallway. The walls were painted in the same cream colour, and gold frames housed pictures of London throughout the years. An enormous, floor-to-ceiling window was at the opposite end of the hallway. During the day, it would let in the rich sunlight. Now, all Carrie could see was the darkness of the night and a few flickering street lights below. She looked at the door closest to her. She needed to keep going to find her room. Carrie made her way down the corridor to the end and glanced out the window. She could see for miles across London. Thirty-three was the very last room.

The door bleeped as the keycard unlocked it, and Carrie swung it open. She gasped as she looked around at the space in front of her. Someone had made a mistake. It couldn't be her room. She'd walked into an entrance hall with marble black-and-white tiles on the floor, white panelled walls, and a huge marble console in the middle with a towering vase of lilies on the top. Carrie's eyes widened as she saw an archway which led into a sitting room. She left her suitcase by the door and went to explore. The living room seamlessly transitioned into a dark wooden floor with cream wallpaper adorned with green ferns. Imposing green sofas were on each side of a glass coffee table, with a stack of patisserie books in the middle. Carrie sat down and giggled as she sank into the chair. She looked up at the monumental chandelier and felt her stomach flip. There must have been a mix-up. Surely they didn't mean to put her in this room? She was here to bake, not to enjoy the luxuries of a five-star London hotel.

With some effort, Carrie stood up from the

chair and went to look at the bathroom and bedroom before calling down to reception to ask if they could send up the correct keycard. She mentally chastised herself for not listening to the man at reception. Carrie stuck her head inside the door to the bathroom and gasped. The same marble tiles as the entrance hall covered the floor and walls of the bathroom. His and Hers marble sinks were on the right, with a claw foot bath opposite. On the back wall was a walk-in shower large enough for several people. Carrie felt her face flush as her heart hammered in her chest. She really ought to stop snooping and rectify the mistake.

In her search for a phone, Carrie found the bedroom with its white panelled walls and a king-size bed piled high with neutral-coloured cushions. All she wanted was to throw herself onto the bed and sink into it. Instead, she sought the phone on the bedside table. There was a code beside it telling her how to contact reception.

It rang twice before there was an answer. "*Hotel Mayfair*. Lucas speaking, how may I help you?" Carrie cringed as she realised it was the same man who had checked her in.

"Hi! I'm so sorry. It's Carrie. The redhead Scottish woman you just checked in." She paused for a moment, waiting for him to confirm he remembered her.

"How can I help you?" His tone was polite, but Carrie could hear a hint of irritation in his voice.

"I'm so sorry to bother you, but I think there

might have been a mistake with my room?"

"There's no mistake."

"Are you sure? It seems very luxurious for a pastry chef." Carrie pressed. She didn't want to settle in just to move in the morning.

"The hotel owner appreciates you stepping in and helping until we find a permanent pastry chef. They wanted to show you their appreciation by housing you in one of our prestigious suites. Besides, aren't you a fancy pastry chef?" His tone suggested speaking to her was the very last thing he felt like doing.

"I'm trained in patisserie," explained Carrie, ignoring the thinly veiled dig. "Thanks for clearing that up for me."

"You're very welcome. I'll have a member of the kitchen team bring breakfast to your room tomorrow. They'll give you directions to the kitchen, and you can pop in and get settled before you officially start." He hung up before Carrie could say anymore. She glared at the phone before putting it down. If she'd known arriving late would prompt such an attitude, she would have stayed at Lachlan's and checked in tomorrow. It would do no good going over it. She was here now.

Carrie wandered over to the windows and looked out at London. Even in the dark, it looked exciting, with endless lights twinkling and the faint hum of cars. She was finally here in London. Carrie let out a little squeak of excitement. She pulled out her phone and took some pictures of her room, and sent them into a group chat with Eve and Lachlan. As she looked longingly towards the vast bed, a yawn captured her. The view was stunning, but Carrie wanted to jump in the shower and snuggle into the mountain of pillows and cushions.

CHAPTER FOUR

A persistent knocking on her door woke Carrie the following morning. She squinted as she took in her surroundings. Last night she'd fallen into bed after showering and had forgotten to close the curtains, so the bright light shone through, and she could hear the buzz of London below. The knocking continued, reminding Carrie why she had woken. She pulled on the soft hotel robe from the foot of the bed, where she'd thrown it last night, and went to see who was at the door. Perhaps they'd finally realised she was in the wrong room.

Carrie peeked through the spyhole to see who was on the other side, aware she was wearing just a dressing gown, and her curly hair was sticking out in all directions. On the other side stood a young woman with a breakfast trolley beside her. Carrie's stomach rumbled, reminding her she'd missed dinner last night. She opened the door with a welcoming smile on her face. After all, this woman was probably one of her colleagues.

"I have your breakfast," the sandy-haired girl announced. A man stood beside her, whom Carrie hadn't noticed through the spyhole. He gave Carrie a polite nod and pushed the trolley over the threshold.

Carrie watched opened-mouthed as the woman directed the breakfast tray into the sitting room and pointed to how it should be laid out on the coffee table. Carrie's mouth shut with a snap as she remembered she was in the doorway of her room in a bathrobe while guests walked down the hallway. A small child ran to look out the window, and Carrie jumped backwards, closing the door before she could be spotted.

"This looks delicious," Carrie commented as her eyes wandered over the spread. She couldn't eat half of this.

"I've bought us tea. You can leave now." The young woman instructed the man who had pushed the trolley. She then pointed to a teapot and sat down on the sofa. Carrie raised her eyebrow but didn't comment on the woman's decision to join her. She thanked the man, who insisted he could leave without her help.

"I'll pour the tea." Carrie arranged her dressing gown and poured them each a cup of tea. "I'm Carrie." She held her hand out.

"My name's Lily and I have Down's syndrome." Lily shook her hand and beamed at her. The woman's statement left Carrie speechless. "My brother says I'm not supposed to tell people like that." Lily continued to pour milk and sugar into her tea.

"It's lovely to meet you, Lily. Well, you've shared something about yourself. I should probably tell you about me. I'm a pastry chef from Scotland, hence the hair and funny accent, and I'm trained in patisserie." Carrie smiled, already feeling at ease in Lily's company, despite her turning up at the door and inviting herself in for breakfast.

"Can you make shortbread?" asked Lily, her brows knitted together. Her shrewd blue eyes looked Carrie up and down from behind her glasses.

"I can. Do you like it?" Carrie stirred her tea and glanced at the food, wondering what to pick first. The yoghurt and granola tempted her, but the perfectly round, white, crusted rolls looked mouthwateringly delicious.

"I love shortbread." Lily beamed.

"I'll make some for you today if I can get into the kitchen."

"There's just us in today. The old assistant left with the chef, so until my brother can hire someone new, I'm helping. If you'll have me?" For the first time since stepping through the door, Lily's confident smile faltered.

"Thank you, Lily. I'm going to need someone to show me around later, and of course, I'd love all the help I can get. Do you know the kitchens well?"

"I know everyone here. The last pastry chef didn't want me around, so I worked with Jamal for a while. But I really want to learn how to make desserts." Lily reached forward and took a roll, cutting it in half before smothering it in strawberry jam. Carrie reached out for a roll and did the same.

"I'd love to teach you. These are amazing," Carrie sighed, biting into the soft white bread. The crust was crispy, giving way to the fluffiest bread.

"I helped make them this morning," Lily commented.

"You made these?" Carrie spluttered. Lily had made it seem like she was stuck with her as an assistant.

"Yes. With Jamal. They're easy to make. I'll give you the recipe if you like." Lily shrugged her shoulders and reached for another roll.

Carrie blinked and took another bite. She hadn't expected her first morning in London to be so overwhelming. As Carrie sipped her tea, there was another knock at the door. She frowned and went to answer it, still in just her dressing gown.

"Hello, sorry to disturb you, but I was wondering if you had an over-enthusiastic assistant sitting in your bedroom enjoying breakfast with you?" A woman stood dressed in a smart black shirt and matching tailored trousers.

"I do," Carrie trailed off.

"I'm so sorry. I gave her strict instructions to serve you breakfast and leave you to settle in." She let out a sigh. "I'm Camille, the head waitress." She held out her hand for Carrie to shake.

"Lovely to meet you, Camille. I'm Carrie." She

shook her hand and stood aside. "Come in."

Camille followed Carrie to the sitting room, where Lily was sheepishly spooning granola and yoghurt into her mouth.

"She couldn't eat breakfast alone," Lily defended herself. Camille crossed her arms, her gaze not wavering from Lily. Carrie looked between the two women, unsure what to say or do. "And I wanted to make sure she was nice."

Camille's resolve softened. "Lily, you can meet Carrie later. Let her enjoy her breakfast and get ready in her own time." Camille kept her eyes focused on Lily as she stood up and picked up another roll, stuffing it in her pocket.

"Sorry, Carrie," mumbled Lily as she trailed past her.

"I'll come and see you in the kitchen later. We'll make some shortbread." Carrie smiled after her. She already liked Lily and could see she would make work enjoyable.

"See you soon." Lily waved and walked out of the room.

"I'm sorry," Camille apologised.

"No bother. It was a nice chance to get to know my assistant. She's an amazing baker.

"She is. Lily came in early and persuaded the sous chef to help her bake them for you. Ever since we discovered we were getting a new pastry chef, she's been excited. You don't start work until tomorrow, but you're welcome to visit the kitchens today to familiarise yourself."

"Thank you, Camille. I'll see you soon." Carrie walked Camille to the door and breathed a sigh of relief at being alone again.

She returned to the spread of food and dished herself up a bowl of granola and yoghurt. It wasn't as comforting as her grandmother's oats, but it tasted good. Excitement was fizzing away inside Carrie. She was looking forward to meeting the kitchen team. As she finished her last mouthful of yoghurt, her phone rang from the bedside table. She ran to get it before it went to voicemail.

"Are you missing me yet?" Eve's voice called down the phone. Carrie laughed and sat down on the bed so she could look out the window. She watched as a woman walked up to the hotel holding a little girl's hand. The child was staring up at the hotel in wonder, eyes wide and looking everywhere. Carrie could only imagine the pure joy on the little girl's face as she sat in the luxurious dining room as waiters carried over cake stands overflowing with sweet treats. Not that Carrie had even had the chance to explore the dining room yet.

"Carrie? Are you there?" Eve's voice pulled her back from her daydreams.

"Yes. Sorry, I got distracted looking out the window."

"You didn't answer my question. Are you missing me?"

"I've not really had the time." Carrie launched into a retelling of her morning so far.

"It sounds like Lily will keep you on your

toes." Eve chuckled.

"I think this is just what I needed." Carrie sighed in contentment.

"Good, just don't forget about us." Eve's voice held an edge of sadness.

"I'll always come home, Eve."

"Enjoy your adventure and bring home lots of yummy recipes."

They said their goodbyes, and Carrie put the phone down. There was a prickly feeling inside her. The beginnings of homesickness. She was comfortable at home, too comfortable, but she still missed it. Life was continuing at the castle, and it was continuing without her. Before she could delve further into those thoughts, Carrie forced herself into the shower. She had a kitchen to explore, an assistant to get to know, and shortbread to bake.

Once showered and dressed in a pair of jeans and a long sleeve t-shirt, Carrie slid her room key into her back pocket and went in search of the kitchens. She went down to the reception, hoping there might be a staff entrance somewhere, but if there was, it was very well hidden. With nothing else to do, she made her way to the reception desk, where the same man from last night was checking in an older couple. Carrie stood in line, trying to look anywhere but at the man. She seemed to recall he had introduced himself as Lucas when she'd rung down to reception. Despite the purple marks under his eyes, he still looked very handsome. Carrie shook her head, sending those thoughts scuttling away. She'd already embarrassed herself last night. She couldn't do it again today.

The couple trailed off to the lifts, and Carrie stepped forward. "Morning!" she called.

"Miss Mackenzie, good morning. How may I help you?" He smiled at her, but something about it looked forced. Carrie suspected he hadn't been home to bed.

"Have you been home yet?" asked Carrie. Her eyes widened as she realised the words had slipped right out of her mouth. She hadn't meant to say them out loud.

"No, I haven't. I'm afraid we're rather understaffed at the moment." He cleared his throat and looked up at her. Carrie found herself exploring his eyes. Underneath the tiredness, there was a little twinkle. "Miss Mackenzie?" he prompted.

"Sorry. I'm looking for the kitchens," she said, keeping her reply short, not wanting to blurt out her thoughts. He reeled off instructions on how to get to the staff staircase and where to go from there. Carrie did her best to concentrate on what he was saying, rather than the way his eyes creased at the edges as he smiled at her.

"Do you think you can remember that?" he teased. "You're not going to get in the wrong lift, are you?"

Carrie felt a blush spread across her face. She

ELIZABETH HOLLAND

looked down, allowing her hair to fall to hide it. "I was tired last night after a long journey. Thank you for your directions. I hope I don't see you later." She gave him a wave and turned to leave.

"You hope you don't see me?" he questioned.

Letting out an internal groan, Carrie spun around to face him again. "I really didn't mean it like that. I just meant I hope you go home soon to get some rest."

"I'll be here until seven." He smiled at her before turning his attention to the next person in the queue. Carrie walked away from the reception desk in a daze, her mind replaying his smile. Somehow, she remembered his directions, and she soon pushed through a door and into a bustling kitchen. All thoughts of the handsome man at reception escaped her.

"Carrie, there you are!" Camille gripped her hand and led her towards the back of the kitchen. Carrie noticed Camille's black hair was pulled back into a neat bun. She ought to do the same with hers. Grabbing a hair tie from her wrist, she pulled her hair into something that resembled a messy bun.

"This place is like a maze!" Carrie gasped as they turned a corner and another set of workbenches lay ahead of them.

"I know. Here you are, you have your own work area. Only one oven, I'm afraid." Camille shrugged her shoulders. Carrie felt her jaw drop. Just one oven. She was used to having full use of all the ovens at the castle. Her morning routine meant she

42

was awake early enough to bake everything for the day before the savoury chefs took over.

"I'm sure I can adapt."

"Who's this?" A man's head popped around the corner.

"Jamal, this is our new patisserie chef. Carrie, this is Jamal, one of our sous chefs." Camille made the introductions.

"Patisserie chef?" asked Jamal.

"I'm a fancy pastry chef," explained Carrie.

"She was trained by a fancy French patisserie master," Lily chimed in. She walked straight over and hugged Carrie. With everyone staring at her, Lily shrugged and said, "I Googled her."

"Why does Lily get to meet everybody before me?" Jamal pouted.

"Right, Jamal, back to work. I'll leave Lily to show you around. She knows this area better than I do. Give me a shout if you need anything."

Carrie waved goodbye to Jamal and Camille before turning her attention to Lily. "Did you still want to make shortbread?" she asked.

"Yes, please. I'll show you where the pantry is." Lily started walking before she'd even finished her sentence. She led Carrie into the giant cold storage with endless rows of ingredients. "Follow me," instructed Lily.

They walked to the far back, where an aisle of fridges towered above them with the words 'pastry' scrawled on a piece of paper stuck up at the end. The edges of the paper were tatty, and the 'r' looked as though it had faded with time. Carrie's footsteps could just be heard above the whirring of the fridges.

"Here's a basket." Lily handed her a wicker basket big enough to pile high the ingredients for their bake.

"Thank you, Lily." Carrie smiled, taking it from her and filling it with butter, flour, and sugar.

"The last pastry chef didn't like the baskets. They were my idea." Lily looked down at her feet.

"I love the idea! This means we can carry more ingredients back to the kitchen with us. Do you want to make plain shortbread, or shall we put a twist on it?"

"Plain, please. Are you ready?" Lily glanced at the overfilled basket.

"Yes, come on, let's get baking!"

Carrie had been baking shortbread with her grandmother before she could even speak, so it was an easy bake but made all the more fun by Lily's presence. She was knowledgeable and helpful, but from a few things she had said, Carrie suspected the previous pastry chefs hadn't been very encouraging towards her.

As the shortbread baked, Carrie made them both a cup of tea to enjoy with the buttery biscuits. "How long have you been here?" she said, making conversation as the tea brewed.

"Three years. I started when I was sixteen."

"That's a long time."

"The first pastry chef was okay, but the last one wasn't very nice. She'd just send me to fetch

A SPRING FLING AT HOTEL MAYFAIR

things, so I ended up working with Jamal instead."

"Would you like to learn some patisserie?" Carrie asked. She'd watched as Lily pushed the flour and butter through her fingers to make a crumb.

"Yes, please." Lily beamed.

Carrie pulled the hot biscuits out of the oven, swatting Lily's hand away as she went to grab one. "Lily, they'll be molten hot!" Carrie exclaimed.

"Sorry, I forget." Lily backed up and sat on the wooden stool by the kettle.

"It's okay." Carrie smiled reassuringly while making a mental note to always remind Lily of how hot things were.

Once the biscuits had cooled, they ate them and washed them down with cups of tea. Lily declared they were the best she had ever tasted and decided her input had made them so. Carrie had just smiled and agreed with her.

"I'm going to take some to my favourite people. See you later, Carrie." Lily walked off with a plateful before Carrie had the chance to respond.

Revelling in her own company, Carrie sipped her tea and pulled out her phone to snap a picture of the shortbread for Eve and Lachlan. Lachlan's reply was almost instant, telling her he was going home in a couple of days and inviting her to have dinner with him at his restaurant tomorrow evening. Carrie immediately accepted, looking forward to seeing everyone from her time training there.

45

The day had passed quickly. Lily didn't return, but Camille popped by to see how Carrie was settling in. She'd made Camille a drink while she was on a break, and the two had chatted about the service the following day. The rest of the kitchen bustled around her, but Carrie felt as though she were hidden away in her little warren. Camille took Carrie to the staffroom where lunch was served daily. It looked to be a spread of salads and jacket potatoes today. Once she'd said goodbye to Camille, Carrie returned to the cold storage and pulled out the ingredients to make a couple of chocolate cakes. She baked and iced them before depositing them in the staffroom. Wide eyes watched as she walked in with two towering cakes, one in each hand. A chorus of 'thank yous' followed her out the door as enormous slabs were already being cut.

"Take some home if I've baked too much!" she called back. It was clear the hotel was understaffed, but she didn't want to risk them running out of cake.

It was early evening, and Carrie called it a day. She went to her room to shower and change, deciding to pop out for dinner.

As she wandered through the reception area, Carrie couldn't help but glance over at the desk, hoping to glimpse Lucas. However, he wasn't there. Instead, a short woman with brown, spiky hair welcomed guests with a bright smile. Disappointed, Carrie made her way towards the grand doors.

"Miss Mackenzie?" called a voice from behind. Carrie froze, instantly knowing whose voice it was. How had she not spotted him?

"You can call me Carrie." She turned around to smile at him. "It's Lucas, right?"

"Yes, sorry, have I not introduced myself properly?" He caught up with her. Carrie was surprised to see how tall he was. He towered above her. "I'm Lucas Raven, the hotel manager."

"Lovely to officially meet you." Carrie reached out to shake his outstretched hand. His hand engulfed hers as he gave it a firm shake, but all Carrie could focus on was the feel of his skin against hers. She chose that moment to look up at him and found his gaze on her. Their eyes locked. Her heart rate picked up, and her hand tingled from his touch. There was a glint in his eye as he squeezed her hand before dropping it. Missing the thrill that had washed over her, Carrie clasped her hands behind her back so she didn't reach for his hand again.

Her gaze was focused on his sparkling blue eyes as his soft London accent filled her ears. "Are you okay?" he asked.

"Yes, sorry. It's been a long couple of days."

"How has your day been? Have you met everyone? Has anyone given you a tour of the kitchens?

"It's been great, thank you. I've met Camille and Lily. They've shown me around and introduced me to everyone."

"Brilliant," his voice trailed off as he glanced at a message on his phone.

"You're obviously busy," Carrie said, wanting to escape from this awkward exchange. She kept finding herself staring into his eyes, unable to ignore her physical attraction to him.

"Sorry. The hotel's understaffed, and I'm overworked." He put his phone in his pocket and returned his attention to her.

"No bother. That's why I'm here."

"Indeed. I'm looking forward to trying some more of your bakes."

"Thank you." Before Carrie could ask his opinion on her chocolate cake, a loud clatter sounded as china shattered against the marble floor. The sound set Carrie's teeth on edge. She looked over to see a child standing surrounded by shards of china. The child's face was quivering, about to burst into tears.

"I need to go. Bye Carrie!" he called. Lucas was already halfway across the room. Carrie stood on the spot, looking after him. She watched as his tall frame swooped down to check on the child. Carrie shook her head and tore her eyes away from the scene. Lucas was busy enough, without her lusting after him. She'd never felt so thrown by someone's appearance before. Normally, Carrie would have said she was far more attracted to someone's personality than their looks. However, Lucas Raven was proving her wrong. She knew nothing about his personality, and yet she was very much attracted to him.

Forcing herself to move, Carrie stepped outside onto the busy London street. She felt a rush of unseasonably warm air wash over her. Well, it was warm compared to what she was used to. The road had transformed into a bustling hub of tourists and people were going about their daily life. In the early hours of the morning, it had been quiet. But now, Carrie knew it had just been waiting to wake from its slumber. With a quick look left and right, she crossed to the other side of the road and wound her way through the busy streets of Mayfair to Oxford Street. She only had a couple of hours until sunset and she wanted to make the most of it. The hustle and bustle of countless people was a shock to her system. Although she'd been expecting it, her memories had dulled how overwhelming it could be. Carrie shook her head and reminded herself that this was what she wanted. She wanted to lose herself in a crowd of unknown faces. At least, Carrie thought that was what she wanted it. But alone, surrounded by the crowds of London, she felt a yearning for the familiarity of home and her loved ones. It all seemed very far away.

"Will you move!" shouted an angry voice from behind. Carrie jumped and realised she'd come to a halt in the middle of the pavement. Shoulders slammed into her as people walked around her. She mumbled an apology to nobody in particular and forced her feet to keep moving amongst the sea of bodies. The sun was quickly setting and Carrie's stomach rumbled, reminding her she hadn't eaten anything since the shortbread she'd had with Lily. With a destination in mind, Carrie picked up her feet and made her way down Regent Street before taking a side street. She reached the little square where there was a hub of excitement with the courtyard filled with tables from various restaurants. A mixture of scents filled Carrie's nostrils, but she'd already made up her mind about where she wanted to eat. There was a table set for two outside Pizza Pilgrims, by the edge of the courtyard. Carrie sauntered over and sat down, claiming the table before anyone else could. Her stomach rumbled as she took a menu from atop the gingham tablecloth and attempted to decide what to order.

"Can I take your order?" said the bored voice of a waiter.

"What would you recommend?" Carrie asked, unable to decide.

"The eight cheese is a particular favourite of mine. You can also get a pesto dip, which helps with the creaminess of the cheeses."

"That sounds wonderful. I'll have that, please." Carrie smiled and handed over her menu.

"And to drink?"

Carrie sighed. She'd become so caught up in the food she hadn't even considered what to order to drink.

"I can recommend the Amalfi Lemonade," suggested the waiter.

"Perfect. Thank you." Carrie smiled at him

and turned her attention to her surroundings as he went inside to place her order. She loved the vibrancy of London. Here she was, sitting in the busy city centre and she had the taste of Italy on her doorstep. It was worlds apart from her home. Carrie settled back into her seat and enjoyed the moment before the chaos tomorrow brought with it. Her first day baking for the hotel would be chaotic. She really should have used today to get ahead of herself. Instead, she'd enjoyed getting to know the people she would be working with. Carrie let out a contented sigh, wrapped her coat a little tighter around herself, and enjoyed the London evening with great food and her own company. The food was as mouthwateringly delicious as the waiter had promised. Once she'd eaten, Carrie strolled down Bond Street, popping into a few shops as she went. The night sky had rolled in, but with the shops still open and the bustling crowds, Carrie didn't feel like calling it in a night. Instead, she wandered into an All Bar One and ordered herself an espresso martini, reasoning that she needed the caffeine boost for the short walk back to the hotel. People in suits stood and sat around tables, all speaking a little too loudly. Carrie sipped her cocktail and sank back into her chair. There was nothing to rush back to the hotel for, so she could sip her drink and watch those around her.

CHAPTER FIVE

Carrie didn't need an alarm to wake her up. She'd had an awful night's sleep, tossing and turning, worrying about the day ahead. With a glance at the clock on the bedside table, Carrie gave up on sleep and swung her legs off the bed. She showered and dressed in black leggings and a matching black top. Last night, Carrie laid out her clothes and put her chef's coat in her backpack. She thought it wouldn't be appropriate to wear it down to the kitchen in case she bumped into guests in the hallway. With her hair tightly secured in a bun, Carrie swung the bag over her shoulder, picked up her keycard, and went down to the kitchen. As she pushed through the swinging door and the familiar buzz of ovens whirring and conversation flowing hit her, she felt her nerves ease.

With her chef's coat neatly thrown over the stool in her workplace, Carrie went to the staffroom to discover if breakfast was available. The room was empty, but there was a bowl of fresh fruit, a loaf of bread, and a pot of yoghurt on the side. It wasn't quite the breakfast she'd grown accustomed to at the castle, but it was better than nothing. She padded over to the coffee machine in the corner and pressed the buttons to make a flat white with an extra shot of coffee.

"Morning, Carrie," called a voice from behind her.

Carrie jumped and blushed as she let out a small squeak. "Lucas, hello." She turned around and smiled at him.

"Your first official day. Are you nervous?" He walked over to put his mug in the sink, leaving him in touching distance.

"No. I don't really get nervous." That was a lie. Her hands were clammy, and her stomach was doing somersaults. She didn't know whether it was his proximity or her first day.

"That's good." His smile sent a flash of warmth through Carrie.

"You look as though you've had a good night's sleep," commented Carrie. Thankfully, she stopped speaking before she could voice her internal monologue. Her mind had wandered to whether his sleep had been alone or snuggled up to someone.

"I finished work early to go to a fundraising event. It was a great night and finished early, so I got home at a reasonable time."

"What were you raising funds for?"

Carrie watched as he opened his mouth to answer before his eyes flickered to behind her. "Your coffee is overflowing," he said, but his words didn't register. "Carrie, the coffee!" His tone was harsher this time, forcing her to focus on the words.

"Oh!" she cried, spinning to face the machine. Coffee was spilling over from her cup and into the drip tray. She reached out to grab the overflowing cup and hissed as the coffee splashed up and scalded her.

"Here, let me." Lucas stepped in to switch the machine off. He poured some coffee into the drip tray, wiped the cup, and handed it to Carrie. "Did you not read the sign?" he asked.

Carrie shook her head and glanced at a piece of paper taped to the wall. It was directly above the machine and informed everyone the coffee machine was broken and had to be switched off at the plug. She busied herself with adding sugar to her drink.

"Anyway, no harm done." He took the drip tray to the sink and washed it out. "How's your burn?"

Carrie looked at her fingers. They were red and throbbing, but she was no stranger to a burn. "I'll live." She shrugged.

"Are you sure? Do you want me to look at it? I've recently done my first aid refresher, so I'm qualified." He reached out as though he were about to take her hand in his.

"Honestly, I'm fine." Carrie kept her hands firmly at her sides. Just the idea of him touching her made her heart thunder. "I'm so sorry. I've not even started work, and I'm already causing chaos."

"No, it's my fault. I've been meaning to ask maintenance to look, but I keep forgetting."

"You seem pretty busy," Carrie commented, remembering he had been working at reception when she checked in and was still there the following morning.

"We're having some staffing issues." He rubbed a hand across his eyes. The twinkle had extinguished, and for a brief second, she felt she could see the man behind the smile.

Instinctively, Carrie reached out and touched his arm. His tired eyes looked up at her, a smile buried deep within them. As their eyes met, she felt the room around her melt away. Her physical attraction towards him was only growing as she spoke to him. He was thoughtful, caring, and hardworking.

Footsteps pounded the corridor, nearing the staff room. Lucas looked away, taking the mixture of emotions he'd stirred up inside her with him. His expression hardened as he continued to step backwards, increasing the space between them. "Anyway, our staffing problems aren't your problem. Lily should be along shortly. I hope your first day goes well." He gave her a wave and walked out of the room.

Carrie slumped against the worktop and let out the breath she'd been holding. "You're a fool, Carrie Mackenzie," she whispered, followed by a groan. Carrie sipped her coffee, and the door swung open, and some of the kitchen team trailed in, looking for their breakfast. She smiled and introduced herself before she slipped out of the room and returned to her work area.

"I've just burned myself on the coffee machine," Carrie told Lily as she walked into her workstation.

"I'm always burning myself. Here's breakfast." Lily handed her a napkin with something wrapped up inside it.

Carrie unwrapped the napkin, and her mouth watered as the smell of a bacon sandwich hit her. "Where did you get this from?" she asked, having spotted only yoghurt and fruit in the staff room.

"It's all about who you know." Lily grinned and tapped her nose, unwilling to give up her secrets.

"I could kiss you right now, Lily. I needed this." Carrie sighed.

"I've had defence classes in case strangers try to kiss me."

Carrie glanced over at Lily and saw she was being serious. She suppressed a smile. "Thank you for the warning, Lily. Right, let's get to work. What are we baking today?"

"So, how was your first day?" Lachlan asked as Carrie sat down. She'd stepped inside the restaurant, and her former colleagues enveloped her in a rush of excitement. They all wanted to catch up and offer congratulations on her new role. Lachlan had smiled at her from a table by the front window and patiently waited while she said hello to everyone.

"It was good. Not what I was expecting." It surprised Carrie to discover how relieved she was to see a familiar face.

"In what way?" Lachlan poured her a glass of wine as he waited for her answer.

"There just doesn't seem like a lot for me to do." Carrie shrugged, trying to push away the disappointment she was feeling. She'd spent the day preparing a handful of afternoon teas, which was something she could do with her eyes closed.

"Have you spoken to anyone about it?"

"The head waitress, Camille, told me I'd be busier once I'd had my first meeting with the wedding planner. There'll be cake-tasting events for the couples, and I'll be required to make lots of samples in the lead-up to the weddings. Then there's *the* wedding. The one they hired me specifically for, but everyone's remaining very tightlipped about it. I suppose I'll find out more tomorrow when I meet with the wedding planner."

"It's your first day. They're probably just easing you in. You'll find yourself rushed off your feet by the end of the week. What are the people like?"

Carrie's cheeks flamed red as Lucas's face popped into her head at the mention of her new colleagues. Lachlan spotted it and raised his eyebrows. "Should I be threatening someone not to break your heart?" he said, puffing out his chest.

A giggle escaped Carrie as she snapped an olive breadstick in two and popped a piece into her mouth. "No. I just made a bit of a fool of myself in front of the hotel manager. Everyone seems lovely, and I even have an assistant. She's called Lily. I don't think the pastry chef before me treated her very well. It's got me thinking about us introducing a scheme for young people at the castle. I'd like to train them and give them a step up, as you did for me. It's even something we could introduce into the hotel side, too. The options are endless. We'd pay them just like any other member of staff." Carrie stopped to take a breath and sipped her wine as she watched Lachlan process everything. His eyes lit up, and she could see he was forming a plan.

"Carrie, your heart never fails to amaze me. It sounds like an amazing scheme to train others and grow our workforce. We're going to be busy with the hotel while you're gone, so why don't we put your idea on the back burner until you're home? Then you can set it all up. It'll give you something to dive into when you come home."

"That sounds perfect." Carrie relaxed back into her chair.

A waiter brought their food over. They hadn't had to order. Everyone already knew their order. Everything looked, smelt, and tasted divine. As they ate, Carrie told Lachlan about the afternoon teas she'd made that day. Her favourite had been the petit fours, covered in pastel fondant, with delicate flowers iced on the top. She'd had to double the recipe after Lily had eaten too many. They were a deviation from the existing afternoon tea menu, but Carrie couldn't put out food that didn't look and taste amazing.

As the waiter took away their empty plates, Carrie jumped when someone tapped on the window. She turned to see Lily beaming in at her, waving. Carrie couldn't help but smile back and wave.

"That's Lily," she said to a confused Lachlan.

"Ahh. It's nice to see you're already making friends," Lachlan commented as he watched Lily walk by. Lucas and Camille accompanied her. They both smiled at Carrie as they passed.

"They must be heading in the same direction. I think Camille said she lives near London Bridge."

"Dessert?" Lachlan asked. Carrie nodded and called the waiter over to ask for her favourite strawberry Millefeuille, which she knew Belle would have made as soon as she heard Carrie was coming in for dinner.

"Shall we finish dinner with a wee dram?" asked Carrie.

"Of course. Let's toast to home." Lachlan went to grab a couple of glasses from the bar and poured two measures of whisky.

"To home," Carrie echoed his words. As she tipped the amber liquid back, she felt a sudden longing for her grandmother's embrace. She hadn't missed home this much when she was last in London. Something deep down inside of Carrie told her this was the last time she would embark on such an adventure. She was eager to enjoy everything London offered, but she couldn't ignore the way home called to her.

Lachlan insisted on walking Carrie back to the hotel. It wasn't far, but it was nighttime, and she was rather tipsy.

"Are you okay from here?" Lachlan asked as they reached the doors to the hotel.

"Lachlan, I'm not that drunk." Carrie put her hands on her hips.

"I know. I'm leaving first thing in the morning. Are you going to be okay?"

Carrie gulped. Having Lachlan around the corner had been like a comfort blanket. After tomorrow, she'd be alone.

"I'll be fine." She took a deep breath and smiled up at him.

"Okay. Call us if you need anything. I'll get Alexander to send the helicopter if you want to come home." He pulled her into a hug.

"Thanks, Lachlan. Send Eve my love. I'll be home before you know it." She put on a brave smile as she watched him walk into the night.

"Are you okay, miss?" a voice said from behind her. Carrie whirled around to see the doorman standing, holding the door open for her.

"Yes, sorry. I was in my own little world. I'm

Carrie, the new pastry chef."

"Ah, yes. The girl who completed her training under a patisserie master. I'm Bill."

"Who—?"

Bill interrupted Carrie's question with a simple answer. "Lily," he said. They both rolled their eyes and smiled.

"Well, it's lovely to meet you, Bill. Goodnight."

CHAPTER SIX

"Shouldn't you be in your meeting?" asked Lily.

"What?" Carrie whirled around, careful not to burn herself on the tray of choux buns she'd just pulled from the oven.

"In the tulip meeting room with Rachel." Lily reached out for a choux bun, but Carrie pulled them away before she could burn herself.

"Who's Rachel?" Carrie asked. She pulled out a Tupperware box filled with choux buns she'd baked and filled earlier that morning. Grabbing a plate, she handed one to Lily.

"The events planner." Lily smiled at her and walked off with her choux bun, humming as she went. Carrie wanted to cry out in frustration. She had another fifty choux buns to bake and fill, and she was only now finding out her meeting with Rachel was this morning. Carrie had assumed the meeting was in the afternoon since nobody had told her otherwise. Flour covered Carrie's leggings, but there was nothing she could do about it. Deciding to keep her chef's coat on, she grabbed two choux buns filled with a fresh cream and raspberry mix, placed them on pretty plates, and took a tray by the kitchen entrance.

"Where are you off to?" Jamal asked, watching her balance the tray as she pushed open the heavy door leading to the staff corridor, which wound its way around the back of the hotel.

"I have a meeting with the events planner." Carrie shot him a harassed smile.

"Good luck!" Jamal held open the door for her.

"Actually, Jamal, do you know where the Tulip meeting room is?" Carrie didn't even know where she was going. Jamal chuckled and suggested he walk with her in case she needed any more doors opened. He was young and enthusiastic, but Carrie could already tell his passion didn't lie in cooking. It was a means to an end for him.

"Here we are," he announced with a flourish, pointing towards a door, much like Carrie's bedroom door, with a small plaque with 'Tulip' written in the hotel's signature swirly writing.

"Thank you so much, Jamal!" She smiled and watched as he walked off. With a deep breath, Carrie knocked on the door.

The door opened, and a woman in her mid-forties stood in a matching burgundy suit, glaring at her. "You're two minutes late," she barked and walked back into the room.

"I'm so sorry. There must have been a mix-up as nobody told me the time we were meeting." Carrie did her best to remain polite, reminding herself she had to work closely with this woman.

"Take a seat," said Rachel.

The room was beautiful, with high ceilings and huge windows along the back wall, which looked out onto a small courtyard with a water feature in the middle. It reminded Carrie how little she had explored the hotel. Rachel cleared her throat, reminding Carrie why she was there. In the middle of the room was a table with chairs around it. Rachel sat on one side and gestured for Carrie to sit opposite her.

"I thought you might like a little treat." Carrie placed the tray on the table and put a plate down in front of Rachel, whose nose instantly scrunched up.

"I don't eat sugar," she said, pushing the plate away. Carrie suppressed an urge to roll her eyes. She'd met people like Rachel before.

"No bother, I'll have to eat yours, too." Carrie took both plates.

She bit into the pastry, and cream oozed out. A groan escaped Carrie's lips, and Rachel shot her a glare across the table. "Perhaps you'd like to put that down and concentrate?" Rachel suggested.

"I'm happy to multitask." Carrie smiled back.

"Fine, but if you think about acting like this around our clients, you'll be collecting your pay and walking out the staff door. Do you understand?"

"I understand perfectly."

The meeting took just over an hour, and Carrie left the room in a foul mood. Rachel could have condensed the meeting into just ten minutes or, better yet, an email. There were just three weddings in the months Carrie would be there, including the high-profile one. She would meet with each couple to discuss their wedding cake and any other sweet treats they wanted. It all sounded straightforward, which Carrie had made the mistake of saying out loud. Rachel had threatened to bring the hotel manager in and fire her on the spot if she didn't show more enthusiasm and care for *Hotel Mayfair's* clients. Carrie kept quiet after that. Her first meeting with the high-profile couple was tomorrow, and she wanted to make a good impression on them.

A shadow fell over Carrie as she walked back to the kitchen. It was Lucas. He had stepped out of another meeting room.

"You look very chef-like," he commented, glancing down at her flour-caked leggings.

"I didn't have time to change," she explained.

"It's a good look on you." His eyes twinkled as he smiled at her.

"Thanks." She couldn't help but mirror his smile.

"How was your meeting with Rachel?" he asked.

Carrie glanced behind her, checking Rachel wasn't following her. She thought about lying to Lucas and telling him it had gone well, but she decided it might be better if the truth came from her.

"Honestly, it didn't go well."

"I'm sorry. Rachel isn't the easiest to work with."

"Is there an online diary for meetings? I only found out about my meeting with her ten minutes before."

"I'll sort you a work phone. Rachel can contact you on it and share her diary with you."

"Thank you." Carrie smiled at him.

"Do you have a notebook? I'll give you my number, then you can send me yours." His question caught her off guard. She stumbled, and the plates tumbled from the tray, crashing onto the floor below. As the sound of china shattering filled her ears, Carrie realised he wasn't asking for her number for personal reasons. Her cheeks flamed, and she bent down to clear up the mess she'd made. A tiny sliver of the plate had wedged itself in the corner. Carrie reached for it at the same time Lucas moved towards it. Their hands brushed each other, and Carrie watched a blush spread across Lucas's face.

"Sorry," he mumbled as she pulled her hand back.

Carrie kept her gaze on the tray in her hands. "Please, don't apologise. Your presence seems to turn me into a clumsy mess! I've usually got a really steady hand." Carrie's eyes widened.

Lucas cleared his throat and stood up. "Anyway, I ought to be getting on. I'll add my number to your work phone."

"Of course. Have a lovely day." Carrie focused on the pieces of china on her tray, ensuring she didn't drop any.

"You too. I'll get someone to come and give this hallway a quick hoover in case we missed any." He gave her a quick smile and started walking off. Carrie hung back, not wanting to bump into him again.

"Carrie." He turned around, and Carrie's heart hammered in her chest. "You have flour on your face." With a wink, he turned and walked away.

Carrie frantically rubbed at her face before resting her head against the wall, waiting for her heart to slow. She couldn't have a crush on the hotel manager.

"You look stressed," Camille commented as Carrie walked back into the kitchen. The lunch rush was over, and there was a momentary lull in the kitchen before everyone launched into dinner preparations.

"I've just had a very last-minute meeting with the events planner."

Camille raised her eyebrows. "I've only had the misfortune of meeting Rachel a handful of times, but I can understand why you might look stressed. Have you had lunch?"

"No. But I ate two cream-filled choux buns to annoy Rachel." Carrie groaned as the memory came back to her. She'd become too used to working for Lachlan, knowing he would always have her back. It was different here. Here, she was just another member of staff who they could replace.

"Why don't I see what leftovers there are, and we can grab a quick lunch before you start baking?"

Carrie glanced at her watch. Afternoon tea service would begin in an hour's time, but she had everything prepped. She'd earmarked the rest of the day to bake and get ahead of herself for tomorrow, but she could always stay late and make up for the lost time.

"That sounds perfect. I've only got half an hour."

Camille filled two bowls with leftover pasta salad and lead Carrie up the staff stairway. "It's worth the climb, I promise," she said, out of breath from the three flights they'd already climbed. Two more flights of stairs later, Camille pushed open a fire escape door. Beyond was a small rooftop with asphalt covering the floor. Deckchairs stood in a circle in the middle, and a pallet in the centre was being used as a table. The view was stunning. They weren't quite at the top of the hotel, and they were around the back, but still, they could see the towering buildings of London surrounding them. It was imposing and oppressive, and it made Carrie's heart soar.

"Take a seat," Camille instructed and handed her a bowl.

"This is amazing," Carrie said, sitting so she

could look out at the city.

"My favourite time to come up here is sunrise. Watching London wake up is beautiful."

They sat in silence for a few minutes, both eating their lunch.

"How're you finding it here?" Camille asked.

"I love having a challenge and being back in London. Although I do feel a little homesick."

"What made you leave Scotland to come here?"

"I'd been seeing someone for a couple of months. It was only short, but it reminded me how nice it was to share my life with somebody. Then he ended it, and it left me feeling empty. I'm not saying I thought he was my soulmate because I'm sure he wasn't. It was just nice having someone on my team. When he ended things, I felt so isolated." An involuntary sigh escape Carrie as she finished.

"I'm glad you came here." Camille shot her a reassuring smile. "I've noticed the way you look at Lucas as you walk past each other."

"Look at Lucas? I've only been here three days and seen him a handful of times."

"I've seen that look on enough faces to know what it means. You fancy the pants off of him!"

Carrie couldn't help but giggle. "He's a very good-looking man, but he's my boss. He also lives in London, and although I'm enjoying my time here, my home is very much back in Scotland. I ought to get back for the afternoon tea service."

"Okay, sorry, little miss defensive," teased

Camille.

"Pop by at the end of service, and I might have a pastry for you." Carrie blew her a kiss and left before she could ask her anything more about Lucas.

"Are you busy tonight?" Camille called over just as Carrie reached the door.

"No. Why?"

"A few of us are going out for dinner. Do you want to come?"

"I'd love to."

"Good, meet us in reception at seven. I'll see you soon for my pastry."

Carrie jogged back down the stairs to the kitchen to prepare the afternoon tea service. She was already wondering what to wear for her first evening out in London with her new colleagues.

The afternoon tea service went without a hitch. Lily had helped to load the cake stands with all the yummy treats as Carrie put the final touches to the choux buns. Carrie brushed down her leggings and straightened her chef's jacket to take the last cake stand out. She'd not been into the dining room yet and wanted to see it filled with happy customers. Following Camille, Carrie walked into the room and stopped as she took in her surroundings. The room was stunning. On the opposite wall was a huge marble fireplace with an ornate gilded mirror hanging above it, reflecting the enormous vase of blooming lilies on the mantel. Between the white walls and the white marble floors, light bounced around the room. Tables draped with pastel linens were scattered around, each distanced to give the party some privacy. Carrie's cake stands were placed on the tables. She glanced at the customers, all with huge smiles on their faces as they feasted on their afternoon teas. Carrie took a deep breath and inhaled the sweetness of the cakes mixed with the floral smell. It was truly an experience for all the senses.

"It's that table over there." Camille nudged her, reminding Carrie she was in the room for a reason.

With a final glance at the room, Carrie returned to the kitchen, where Lily took a couple of leftover sandwiches and waved goodbye.

"Are you not staying to clean up?" Carrie asked.

"I'm not very good at it," replied Lily.

"You'll never be any good unless you try."

"I don't want to be good at it. Bye."

Carrie tried to look annoyed, but a smile burst out on her face. She loved how brutally honest Lily could be. With a wave, Lily left, and Carrie turned to look at the mess she had to tackle. If she did it quickly, she could get some baking in and get ahead of herself for tomorrow.

As she wiped down surfaces, Carrie heard footsteps approaching. The kitchen was quiet at this time of day, a lull before preparation for dinner service started.

"Your pastry is in the fridge," Carrie called, expecting Camille.

"Excuse me?" Lucas's reply came, making Carrie jump.

"Sorry, I thought you were someone else." Carrie put her cloth down and turned to face Lucas.

"I wanted to drop this off." He handed her a phone. Carrie wiped her hands on her apron and took it from him, careful not to brush her fingers against his.

"Thank you," she whispered, unable to meet his eyes.

"I'm sorry about earlier. I had to rush off." He rubbed across his chin, drawing Carrie's attention to his rough stubble.

"Would you like a cup of tea and a pastry?" she asked. He looked as though he needed a sit-down, and Carrie wanted the chance to impress him. It would be nice if he would walk away from a conversation with her, thinking she was capable.

His entire body sagged, and she watched his thoughts play out across his face. "I'd love to," he eventually replied.

"Take a seat." Carrie motioned to the stool as she flicked the kettle on.

"This is a nice treat to sit down and not be working," he commented, looking around at her workspace.

"Why are you so understaffed?" Carrie was genuinely interested, but she was also trying to learn as much as possible to help Lachlan with his hotel once it opened.

"The owner put everyone on zero-hour contracts, so many people left to find stability elsewhere. I don't blame them."

"That's rough." Carrie held up the sugar in a silent question.

He shook his head. "We have just the core staff left and now we're getting in lots of temps."

"Is that why they hired me?" She slid his cup towards him with a bottle of milk so he could pour his own.

"You were hired because I fired the previous pastry chef."

Carrie gulped, a thousand thoughts spinning around in her head. "Was she not good enough?" She asked, regretting offering him a choux bun.

"She was good, not as good as you. Your shortbread was amazing. I'm passionate about creating a supportive environment and the previous pastry chef wouldn't work with Lily. The hotel owner asked me to try to work through it, but I couldn't."

"Well, I'm glad you fired her. Not just because I got the job, but also because Lily deserves to be trained. She has a real passion for baking." Carrie went to take the pastries out of the fridge and popped them on a plate, putting it down in between her and Lucas as she took the other stool.

"Speaking of Lily, is she not here helping you?" Lucas asked, blowing on his tea before taking a sip.

"She helped with service, but then announced she was useless with cleaning up, so she plated herself up a late lunch and left." Carrie chuckled, remembering her bluntness.

"I'm sorry. I'll have a word with her."

"No, please don't worry. I've never had an assistant before, so any help is appreciated. She enjoys baking, and I don't want to dampen her passion by asking her to clean up. We'll build up to it."

"You're too kind." He sent her a smile, causing Carrie to look away before a blush spread across her face.

"Don't forget your choux bun. It's filled, so be careful when you bite into it."

She watched as he picked the pastry up and lifted it to his lips. Her eyes focused on the way his lips parted as he bit into the choux pastry. Cream squelched out, and a blob fell on his chin.

"I warned you!" Carrie giggled and pulled a piece of kitchen towel off the roll. Without thinking, she leaned forward and wiped the cream from his chin. Her fingers lingered on his face and his hand came up to cup hers. Carrie could feel her heart thumping in her chest as his fingers intertwined with hers.

A pan fell to the floor somewhere in the kitchen. The crashing noise threw them apart, and Carrie cleared her throat.

"Sorry," she whispered, balling up the piece of

kitchen towel and throwing it into the closest bin.

"It's my fault. You tried to warn me." Lucas smiled as if nothing had happened. "These are delicious, by the way. My mum used to make the most amazing chocolate éclairs."

"I love éclairs. I make some with a cream, raspberry, and whisky filling and white chocolate piped over the top. Next week, I'll make some and you can take one home with you to give to your mum."

"They sound delicious. My mum would love them if she was still alive." His eyes dropped to the choux bun still in his hand, and Carrie felt her heart plummet into her stomach. Of all people, she should know better than to assume his mother was around.

"I'm sorry. When did you lose her?"

"It's been almost ten years since we lost our parents."

"We?"

"My sister. I'd just turned eighteen, she was nine, so I became her legal guardian."

Carrie reached forward and took his hand in hers, squeezing it. His eyes had clouded over and the twinkle had faded from them.

"I lost my parents when I was around the same age as your sister. But I was lucky enough to have my grandparents. They brought me up. The hole they leave never closes, does it?"

Lucas glanced up at her. He squeezed her hand and gave her a timid smile.

"Sorry, I don't usually sit down to tea and

pastries with staff and dump my emotional trauma on them." He sniffed and dropped her hand, leaving it feeling cold and empty. "I ought to go. I have a free hour, and I need to drop my sister off at her evening class."

"It was nice talking to you, Lucas. I'm always here with tea and treats."

"I might take you up on that. Next time we'll stick to happier topics. I'd love to hear how you got into patisserie."

"I look forward to it." She waved him off and watched as he walked away, with half a choux bun still gripped in his hand.

Carrie stuffed the rest of her choux bun in her mouth and pulled out her personal phone to text Eve. She tapped away at the screen, trying to avoid dropping a blob of cream on it.

S.O.S I've got a crush on my manager xxx

She hit send and washed up the plates and mugs they'd used. Her phone beeped with a reply as she dried them up and put them back in the cupboard.

Not sure I'm the best to advise. I'm marrying my manager... xxx

Carrie chuckled. Eve made an excellent point. She didn't know what she wanted from Lucas, but there was nothing to stop her from having some fun while she was in London. She'd come here for an adventure and a challenge.

Going out tonight with some new work friends. Will call you tomorrow xxx

Carrie hit send, and for a few minutes, she allowed her mind to wander. She wondered what Eve was up to right now. It was late afternoon, so she would be overseeing the prep for dinner service while trying to calm Lachlan down over some unforeseen incident. Her mind then wandered to her grandmother at the McLeod's castle. This time in the afternoon, she'd be sitting with a cup of tea and chatting with her colleagues, Alfred and Graham, before she cooked dinner for them. When there were no guests at the castle, there was little to do, and yet her grandmother always found something to keep her busy.

There was no more time to indulge in her thoughts. Carrie needed to decorate a few desserts for the restaurant, and then she wanted to make up some dough for the morning. There was a dedicated team for the restaurant's desserts. However, the menu was basic and the most exciting offerings were apple pies and chocolate fudge cake. Carrie had tasted a selection. They were lovely, but it wasn't very in keeping with the hotel's reputation for its indulgent afternoon teas. Carrie sought the pastry team's approval to revamp the menu. They'd agreed, and together they'd chosen to create a menu of decadent and pretty tarts. Carrie had baked individual tart shells, and she was about to fill them under the watchful eyes of the dessert team. After some debate, they'd kept the apple pies but modernised them in a tart. Carrie had filled the shells with caramelised cinnamon-infused apples, and the top was a pattern of sliced caramelised apples. It looked pretty, but it was in keeping with the traditional pie. Then Carrie moved on to a lemon meringue tart and a pear and dark chocolate one. The three options were simple, but with a little extra time put into the presentation, they looked lovely and were something the hotel could be proud to serve. It gave Carrie a sense of excitement to know she was spreading her passion for creating tasty but beautiful food. She'd only been there for a few days and she was already shaking things up.

CHAPTER SEVEN

With a final slick of lipstick, Carrie glanced in the mirror at her appearance. She'd spent the last hour getting ready for her night out with Camille and other staff members. Once the sun had set, it was chilly out, so she opted for a pair of leather trousers, a slouchy white jumper, and some heeled ankle boots. Her hair had dried into its natural ringlets and tumbled down her back. It was a treat not to have her hair caked in flour. Carrie had finished the look with dark-smoky eye makeup. She took a quick picture of herself in a mirror and sent it to Eve for a second opinion. A reply came back instantly, telling her she looked amazing and to have a lovely evening. Carrie smiled, excited to have her first group night out in London. Lately, her idea of a *wild* night was sitting in her silk pyjamas by a roaring fire and trying new cocktails she and Eve were trialling in the restaurant. Although she enjoyed her nights at home, tonight was about letting her hair down. A night out at home meant either a trip to the local pub or travelling and paying for a night at a hotel somewhere, then having to get home with a horrible hangover. The beauty of London was that everything was on her doorstep, and Carrie could stumble home after a few drinks too many.

At seven on the dot, Carrie walked out of the lift and into the reception area. Immediately, she spotted Camille waiting for her on a sofa. She wore a black maxi dress and biker boots, and she'd curled her dark hair in loose waves.

"You look gorgeous. Your hair!" Camille exclaimed as she spotted Carrie.

"What about you? I feel underdressed." Carrie glanced down at her own outfit, worried she'd underestimated how much everyone would dress up.

"Ladies, you both look beautiful." Lucas appeared, and Carrie felt her heart flutter as she took in his appearance. He'd neatly styled his hair, so it didn't flop over his forehead, and he was wearing tight-fitted blue jeans and a black polo jumper. His gaze lingered on her for just a moment longer than the others.

"You don't look too bad yourself," teased Camille. Lucas rolled his eyes, but Carrie noticed the slight blush that coloured his cheeks.

"Who else are we waiting for?" asked Carrie. She needed to keep the conversation flowing to stop her eyes from wandering back to Lucas's face.

"Jamal is just changing, then he'll be out. We're meeting everyone else at the restaurant." Camille explained.

Carrie was forming an excuse in her head to run back to her room when Jamal appeared. "Are we ready?" he asked. Carrie instantly forgot about her inner turmoil as she took in his outfit. He wore a pair of hot pink smart trousers with a black shirt unbuttoned to just above his belly button.

"Jamal, you look amazing!" Carrie threaded her arm through his as they walked out of the hotel.

"Thank you, darling. So do you. Although I think Lucas wins the best dressed for tonight."

"What have I told you about flirting with me at work?" Lucas chastised him, but the smirk on his face gave him away.

"Jamal's got good taste," Carrie blurted out. She clapped a hand over her mouth as the others turned to look at her.

"If you're all sucking up for a bonus, it's not working!" Lucas chuckled. He was careful not to meet Carrie's eye.

"You're no fun." Jamal pouted.

The restaurant was a short walk, and Jamal filled the silence with stories from his day, which had them all in stitches. A waiter showed them to their table, where others were already seated. Carrie recognised some of them as members of the waiting staff Camille had introduced her to on her first day. She waved at everyone and took an empty seat beside Camille.

"Here, Lucas, this spot's free." Camille pointed to the other side of Carrie. Carrie wanted to slide off her chair and hide underneath the table.

"Thanks." He smiled as he took the seat next to her and rolled up the sleeves of his jumper. Carrie couldn't help but glance down at his tanned arms. "If I sit next to Li, she'll spend the entire meal moaning about how understaffed the housekeeping team is. It doesn't seem to help when I point out the entire hotel is understaffed."

"No talking about work tonight!" Camille leaned across and swatted Lucas on the arm.

"Okay, sorry." He held his hands up.

"I'm afraid the food might not be up to your normal standard," Lucas commented, glancing at Carrie.

"Yes, we saw you being wined and dined at a Michelin-star restaurant," Camille chipped in.

"Oh, yes, I remember. Lily knocked on the window. I was having dinner with Lachlan." Carrie shrugged her shoulders.

"*The* Lachlan McLeod!" Camille squealed. Carrie often forgot that Lachlan was a celebrity on the food scene. To her, he was like an annoying brother.

"It's just Lachlan." Carrie rolled her eyes. Even Eve didn't swoon over Lachlan this much, and she was marrying the man.

"Is his food good?" Lucas asked. His brow had furrowed, and he was playing with the edge of his menu.

"It's out of this world," Carrie replied.

"I've never been much of a foodie. Probably because I'm busy running from one place to another. I usually just grab anything I can and eat it on the go."

"Can you cook?"

Lucas opened his mouth to reply, but he was interrupted by the waiter coming over to take their drinks order. Carrie ordered a cocktail for herself, and Lucas ordered a beer.

"In answer to your question, I can cook pasta, or I can put something in the oven. If I'm feeling adventurous, I can just about rustle up a roast dinner, if the meat comes in one of those tin trays and tells me how long it needs to go in for."

Carrie sipped her cocktail as she considered his answer.

"Did you not want to learn?"

"I did and I still do. It's just there's never enough hours in the day. After a long day at work, I just need something quick for dinner. I don't have the energy left to try something new just for it to turn out awfully and have to come up with a backup plan."

"I can understand that. My grandmother has worked as a cook for my entire life, so I was brought up to feel confident in the kitchen and allowed to experiment from a young age."

"Are your dinners as good as your desserts?"

"Not quite as good, but they're passable."

"You'll have to cook for me sometime." He

winked at her over the top of his empty beer bottle. Carrie gulped.

"Just tell me when and where."

Before their flirting could escalate any further, they were pulled into other conversations around the table. The warmth that had flooded Carrie's body slowly ebbed away as she turned her back on Lucas and focused on Camille.

As dinner came, Carrie felt her leg bump against something under the table.

"Sorry," Lucas whispered.

"No bother." Carrie smiled. She reached out for her strawberry mojito and finished the dregs at the bottom of the glass. "Could I have another?" she asked the waiter, who had just put Lucas's meal in front of him.

With the rum setting alight to her insides and giving her a boost in confidence, Carrie reached under the table and rested her hand on Lucas's thigh. She saw his posture stiffen beside her. He cleared his throat and glanced over at her. Carrie turned in her seat to look at him. She held his gaze and flexed her fingers. A shiver ran through her body as their eyes fixed on each other. The sounds of the restaurant melted away, and Carrie could feel herself falling into a bubble with just her and Lucas. Nothing around her mattered. His eyes locked on hers, and she couldn't tear herself away.

"Your mojito," the waiter said. He leaned in between her and Lucas to put the drink down, completely oblivious to the moment he'd just interrupted. Instinctively, Carrie pulled her hand from Lucas's leg.

"Thank you," Carrie said, still feeling as though she were in a daze.

As the waiter walked away, she chanced a look in Lucas's direction, but he had turned his back towards her. She felt the sickening hit of rejection and reached for her drink, squishing the paper straw between her lips.

"Slow down. We're going to a bar next," warned Camille, noting how quickly the cocktail was disappearing.

"Oops!" Carrie giggled, feeling the rum wash over her, dulling the humiliation.

The bill came, and they each paid for their food and drinks. Carrie winced as she realised just how many fancy cocktails she'd ordered. She'd have to pace herself at the bar they were going to.

"Are we ready?" Jamal asked, taking on the role of organising everybody.

"I've got to go," Lucas said, glancing down at his watch.

"Come for one drink?" Jamal asked.

"Sorry, guys. I'm already running late. Remember, you're all working tomorrow." His eyes lingered on Carrie for a millisecond longer than everyone else before he smiled and walked out of the bar.

Carrie moved with everybody as they made their way to a bar. Her mind was still firmly on Lucas and how he made her feel. Carrie had never lost herself in someone's eyes before. She'd thought it was something romance authors made up to hook the reader into thinking love was something magical.

"You okay?" whispered Camille. She slipped her arm through Carrie's and held her back as everyone walked ahead of them.

"I've made a fool of myself." Carrie sighed.

"What did you do?"

"I flirted with Lucas."

"I knew it! You look like love-sick teenagers whenever you bump into each other at work."

"Camille! I do not." They'd reached the bar, but they waited as everyone trailed in.

"What happened?" Camille asked once she was sure everyone was inside and nobody would overhear their conversation.

"We've had a couple of moments, so I took it a step further tonight. Oh, Camille. I only touched his leg, but it was clear he wasn't interested. He seems like such a lovely and caring man and I can't deny that I'm attracted to him. I thought he'd been flirting with me earlier in the evening." Carrie groaned and held her head in her hands. The fresh air had sobered her up, and the humiliation had come crashing over her.

"I'm sure you'll both have forgotten about it by the morning."

"I doubt it. Did you see the way he ran off?"

"I'm sure that wasn't you, Carrie. Lucas is always rushing off somewhere. He probably had to pick his si—" Jamal came skipping out of the bar, interrupting Camille.

"Happy hour ends in ten minutes. Come on, get in there and order your drinks!" He wrapped an arm around each of their shoulders and guided them into the bar.

CHAPTER EIGHT

Carrie switched on the shower and cringed when she turned to see her reflection in the mirror. She had last night's makeup smeared across her face. Her head was pounding, and her eyes felt as though someone had poured sand into them. Carrie watched her makeup wash down the drain. She rested her forehead against the cool glass of the shower door as memories from last night struck her.

"Oh god," she groaned, remembering Lucas's rejection.

Carrie got ready for work, doing her best to move her head as little as possible. She'd taken some painkillers, but they hadn't started working yet. If she didn't pick up her feet, she'd be late, and her entire schedule would fall behind. With her half-dried hair pulled back into a low bun, she grabbed her earphones and made her way to the kitchen. She clicked on the kettle in her workstation to make a coffee, not wanting to risk the staff room in case Lucas was there.

With a coffee in hand, she dialled Eve's number and began making the dough for miniature tarts. Eve picked up on the second ring as Carrie turned the dough onto a floured surface.

"Morning!" Eve's joyful tone filled Carrie's ears. It was like nails down a chalkboard as she reached for her phone to turn the volume down.

"Shh, some of us have a hangover," she whispered.

"Sounds like you had fun last night," Eve teased.

"Eve, I need the ground to open up and swallow me." Carrie kept her voice low. She doubted anyone could hear her over the pans clattering and the hobs sizzling, but she didn't want to risk it.

"What happened?"

Carrie recounted the events of the previous evening, cringing as she relived it. All the while, she continued to mix the ingredients. She was making lemon and elderflower tarts for her meeting this afternoon with the high-profile wedding clients. Despite Rachel's dislike towards her sweet treats, Carrie couldn't imagine meeting the couple without bringing a sample of her baking.

"Carrie, I'm sorry. At least you can blame your actions on the alcohol."

"I should never have left Scotland."

"Just remember, you'll never have to see this

Lucas again once your time in London is up."

"But what if I want to see him again?" The question came out as a whisper, but her earphones picked it up, and Eve heard.

"What is it about him?" asked Eve.

Carrie lowered her voice. "Obviously, there's the physical attraction. But beyond that, he's caring, hardworking, and I just feel this silly connection with him. Perhaps I'm being stupid and he's just being a good manager. I don't know, Eve. There's just this feeling I have around him. I could see a future with him, cooking meals, and sitting down to eat with a glass of wine. Both of us smiling and looking forward to spending the evening together. I'm just being silly and fantasising. I'll be home soon, and this will all be a distant memory."

"I'm sorry, Carrie. Maybe we can put on some speed dating nights at the castle? We'll find you your person."

"Eve, I love you, and I appreciate the thought, but speed dating at the castle? Lachlan would never agree."

"Carrie, you seem to be under the impression Lachlan makes all the decisions."

"Fair point. I miss you, Eve." Carrie could imagine standing opposite her in the castle's kitchen, both working on their own dishes as the world around them woke.

"I miss you, too. I'm only a phone call away."

"I ought to go. I need to get ahead of myself. There's a meeting with the high-profile couple this afternoon."

They said their goodbyes, and Carrie pushed the tart shells into the oven and set a timer. Each time she thought of home, the pull strengthened. Maybe she wasn't as eager for an adventure as she'd thought she was. Truthfully, she no longer knew what she wanted. It was just easier to be lost amongst a sea of people in London.

The morning whizzed past as Carrie crafted beautiful, mouthwateringly delicious treats for the afternoon tea service. It already felt a little repetitive to bake the same treats each day. Carrie was tempted to ask Lucas whether they could change the menu, but she was reluctant to speak to him after last night's rejection. Lily hadn't shown up for work, so Carrie had to work twice as hard to get everything prepared for service. Her new work phone beeped as she sent the last cake stand out with a waitress. She groaned and reached for it. It was a text from Lucas asking her to meet him in the Tulip meeting room in half an hour. She glanced at the time and saw she wouldn't have time to change between meeting him and her clients. She pulled the miniature elderflower and lemon tarts she'd made earlier from the fridge and sprinkled some candied lemon peel on them. Then she raced up to her room to get changed into something with less flour covering it. Her eyes looked tired, and her skin was sallow from last night's drinking, but there was no time to do anything about it. She redid her hair in another bun and raced to the kitchen to pick up the tray.

Lucas was sitting alone in the meeting room. He looked up from a pile of paperwork as Carrie walked in.

"Sorry, I've got a meeting with the high-profile wedding clients after this, so I had to make myself presentable." Carrie smiled as she sat down at the table. She really ought to find out the couples' names. She couldn't keep referring to them as 'the high-profile couple'.

"That's okay. I'll be sitting in on the meeting. I'm just going through applications for various roles while I wait, so there was no rush." He gave her a strained smile.

Carrie tapped her fingers against the tabletop, waiting for him to say something more, but he didn't. "I'm sorry about last night," she said, wanting to get the awkward conversation over with.

"No, Carrie, I'm sorry. I've probably been giving you mixed signals. You're beautiful and very talented, but I'm not looking for a relationship." He paused, his mouth opened and closed, but nothing came out. He cleared his throat and rubbed his hand over his face. "Also, I'm your manager." His eyes were firmly focused on the pile of papers in front of him.

"Are you okay?" she asked as his hands shook.

"I probably shouldn't tell you this, but if we have an inspection right now, we're so understaffed that we'll lose our five-star rating."

"That's awful." Carrie wanted to help, but she knew it was beyond her abilities.

"I just can't add anything more to my mental load." He sighed.

"I understand. Would you like a lemon and elderflower tart?" Carrie asked. She couldn't solve his problems, but she could offer him a delicious dessert.

"Yes, please. Anyway, I doubt your boyfriend would be very happy about you flirting with me."

"Boyfriend?" Carrie asked.

"The man we saw you having dinner with? I assumed that was why you were here in London." He took a fork and broke off a piece of tart, popping it into his mouth.

"Lachlan?" Carrie screeched, almost spitting out the bite she'd just taken.

"Is that his name?"

"Lucas, Lachlan is like a brother to me. My grandmother has worked for his family for her entire adult life. We grew up like brother and sister, and I trained at his restaurant in London. His fiancée is also one of my closest friends."

Lucas lifted his head to look at her. "I'm sorry. I just assumed."

"It's okay." Carrie shrugged her shoulders and picked at the tart in front of her. There was a heavy feeling in her chest. They'd only known each other for a short while, but did he really think she was the type of person to flirt with him when she already had a boyfriend?

"What's it like in Scotland?" he asked. His voice was just above a whisper.

"Where I live is very quiet. I live at Lachlan's new restaurant, which is in a castle. He's hoping to open a hotel there."

"Don't tell Lily. She'll be wanting to visit you."

"She's always wel—" Carrie was interrupted as the door swung open, banging against the wall with a loud thump. Rachel stormed in. Her eyes were burning with rage, and her hair was sticking out in all directions.

"That's it. I quit!" she screamed.

Carrie sat in silence, blinking furiously at the sight in front of her. Rachel's silk blouse had a giant white stain down the front of it, and there was a cut on her right cheek.

"Rachel, what's going on?" asked Lucas. His eyes were wide as he froze in motion, his hand halfway to his mouth.

"I've had it! Do you know what I've just spent the last hour doing?" she paused, but Carrie and Lucas stayed silent. "I've been painting the ceiling in the ballroom because apparently we no longer have any maintenance staff here during the day."

"Do we not?" asked Lucas.

"I think you're missing Rachel's point," whispered Carrie.

"Yes, you are. I've fallen from a ladder painting your stupid ballroom. I could earn twice the amount elsewhere, yet I've stayed at *Hotel Mayfair* out of some silly, misguided loyalty. But I've had enough. I'm on a zero-hour contract, so I don't need to give you any notice. Goodbye, and good luck,

Carrie. I hope you're happy now the last of the hotel's budget has been spent housing you in a prestigious suite." With a swish of her hair, Rachel stormed out of the room, leaving Lucas and Carrie sat in stunned silence.

"What does she mean, the last of the budget?" Carrie kept playing Rachel's words over and over in her head.

"I did some digging to find out why the stingy owners had opted to house you in one of our suites. We don't have any live-in staff, so we don't have any live-in quarters. At first, I assumed it was because we make a higher profit from our cheaper rooms. The hotel's reputation is slowly dwindling amongst those with money, so our suites aren't selling out. However, after going through an email chain, I found an email from the owners. They know who trained you, and they know you have connections to the McLeod family. I think they were trying to schmooze you."

Carrie opened and closed her mouth as she allowed the information to sink in.

"I can move out of the room," she whispered.

"Carrie, you deserve that suite. These weddings are the only thing keeping this hotel afloat. Besides, as I said, we make more profit from the cheaper rooms at the moment."

"How long until the meeting?" asked Carrie. The words echoed around the room as Lucas glanced up at her, panic flooding his tired eyes.

"Five minutes." He gulped.

"How well do you know the brief?"

"I've sat through all the meetings, so I know roughly what they want."

"Good. It looks like you're going to be the hotel manager and events organiser for the foreseeable future. As long as we speak confidently, they'll never know that Rachel just quit, okay? We're going to make these weddings a success and make sure *Hotel Mayfair* keeps its reputation."

Lucas nodded. His eyes had glazed over, and a layer of sweat glistened on his forehead. Carrie sighed and walked into the little kitchenette to hide their empty plates and make pots of tea and coffee for their clients. She'd worked at the McLeod's castle long enough to know how to deal with troublesome guests.

There was a knock at the door just as Carrie set the tray on the table. She shot Lucas a quick look, hoping it conveyed her reassurance, before turning to the door as it swung open. In walked Camille, followed by a very glamorous couple.

"Camille, thank you." Lucas stood and immediately slipped into work mode. Carrie felt her tightly wound shoulders loosen. "Milo, Sasha, how lovely to see you both!" He walked over, shook Milo's hand, and kissed Sasha on the cheek. Carrie held back, not wanting to overstep with these clients. "Please, take a seat." Lucas gestured over to the table, which Carrie was standing beside.

Milo was wearing a designer suit and a Louis Vuitton tie with the logo printed across it. He'd combed back his dark hair with what looked like half a pot of gel. Meanwhile, his huge dark sunglasses covered half of his face, leaving just his pout visible. Sasha, meanwhile, was wearing a white trouser suit, with a Louis Vuitton bag over her arm, in the same style as Milo's tie. Her blonde hair tumbled down her back in soft curls, and her makeup looked flawless from where Carrie was standing. Her frame towered above Lucas in her skyscraper heels. She followed Milo to the table, her hips swaying with every step. Despite them being high profile, Carrie didn't recognise them.

"Can I get either of you a drink?" asked Carrie, stepping forward to greet them.

"Milo, Sasha, please let me introduce you to Carrie, our new pastry chef. Carrie was trained by a patisserie master at a Michelin-star restaurant."

Carrie winced, but quickly rearranged her features, trying to hide her reaction to Lucas's description. "Lovely to meet you." She reached out and shook both their hands.

"We'll both have a coffee, please. No sugar or milk." Sasha smiled and took a seat.

"Of course. Please, help yourself to a miniature lemon and elderflower tart, they were made fresh this morning." Carrie busied herself with pouring the drinks and handing them out. She made herself and Lucas a coffee, suspecting he needed the caffeine as much as she did. Lucas was making small talk as Carrie sat down. She reached across and took one of his notepads so she could make her own notes.

This meeting was about Milo and Sasha meeting her and letting her know what they wanted. Carrie took a deep breath and took charge of the conversation. "Would you mind giving me a quick overview of the wedding? I'm sure you're sick of repeating yourself, but it would really help to hear it from you." Carrie smiled sweetly at them, hoping they wouldn't protest.

"Of course. I'm sure you've heard lots about it, but you're right. It's best if it comes from us." Sasha launched into a long spiel about how they were going for the 1920s meets a modern glamour theme. Carrie nodded along, trying to disguise her confusion.

"So the wedding ceremony is 1920s glamour, but the evening reception is modern?" Carrie thought she'd finally understood the theme.

"That's an excellent idea! Lucas, write that down and let Rachel know. Actually, where is Rachel?" Sasha's eyes searched the room as if Rachel was hiding somewhere.

"I'm afraid Rachel has decided her future isn't with *Hotel Mayfair*." Silence shrouded the room as the couple processed Lucas's explanation.

"Who's taking over?" asked Sasha. She spoke slowly, enunciating each word.

"I am." Lucas didn't miss a beat with his reply.

"We'll be working closely with the entire team to deliver your perfect day," Carrie chipped in.

"Do you know how many magazine deals

we have? This wedding will be global." Sasha was hyperventilating. Carrie reached forward and took the woman's hand in hers.

"Sasha, I promise you, your wedding will be nothing less than perfect." Carrie crossed her fingers under the table. She hoped she could deliver on her promise.

"Okay. I'm going to need both of your numbers, and you must both be available to me at all times." Sasha stared at them. A small crease had appeared on her forehead.

"Of course. Lucas can send them over in an email once this meeting is finished. You can let me know when you're available for cake tasting, and I'll liaise with our head chef to see if we can combine his tasting with mine. I'm sure your schedules are very busy."

"Perfect. Well, it sounds as though you've both got everything under control." Milo nodded. He looked as though he would rather be anywhere but in the room, discussing wedding plans. "This tart is delicious, by the way." He reached for another.

"Okay. Lucas, I'll see you on Friday for the meeting with the florist." Sasha glanced over at Lucas.

"Isn't that on Thursday?" Lucas asked. Carrie glanced over to see he had Rachel's calendar open on his laptop.

"Just testing you." Sasha drummed her long fingernails on the tabletop.

"I'll see if I can make the meeting, too. It will

be helpful if I can see some samples of the flowers, so I know what shades the cake needs to be."

"Perfect. I'll be in touch." With that, Sasha stood, and Milo followed. "Goodbye." She gave them a wave and walked out of the room with Milo following her, shouting a quick goodbye to them.

"I think we got through that relatively unscathed." Carrie breathed a sigh of relief.

"Yes, but Carrie, I don't know the first thing about planning a wedding. What am I going to do?"

"We need to find a replacement for Rachel."

"What if we can't?" Lucas reached for the pot of coffee and poured himself another, heaping in two spoonfuls of sugar.

"Then we're planning a high-profile wedding. Think how good it will look on your CV." Carrie tried to crack a joke, but Lucas's face remained solemn.

"I need a new job," he moaned, suppressing a yawn.

"Late night?" Carrie teased. She instantly regretted it.

"Something like that." He rubbed a hand over his face before finishing his cup of coffee.

"Well, if it makes you feel any better, I'm running on painkillers and caffeine after drinking far too much."

"I am really sorry about last night, Carrie. I've probably been a little over-friendly with you."

"Over-friendly is fine," she whispered, staring down at her nails.

"It's not. I'm your manager, and as lovely as

you are, I have too many other commitments for a relationship."

Carrie blushed. "You think I'm lovely?" she asked.

"Of course I do... anyway, you're focusing on the wrong part of that sentence. I'm your manager, and even if I wasn't, I'm not looking for anyone." He stood up and straightened his suit jacket. "I need to go. I'll send you all the details of the weddings we have booked. You're welcome to use Rachel's office. There should be a work laptop in there. Take it and study the information on it." He gave her a nod and walked out, leaving her staring after him.

Carrie groaned and rested her head on the table. The painkillers were wearing off, and her head was thumping. She had wanted a challenge in coming to London, but this was proving to be more than she bargained on. She might have experience with awkward guests, but she'd never planned a wedding before. With a final groan into the empty room, Carrie tidied up the plates and stacked them on the tray before she went in search of Rachel's office and laptop. Tomorrow was her first day off, so she would spend the day studying notes on the weddings.

The afternoon tea service whizzed past without a hitch. Petite strawberry cheesecakes, pecan pies, petit fours, and chocolate mouses adorned the top tier of the cake stands. Each miniature-sized bite was intricately decorated. The middle tier held the scones. Two types. One plain and one with dried fruit, with glass dishes with clotted cream, butter, strawberry jam, blackberry jam, and apricot jam scattered around. The bottom layer was where the neatly cut, crustless finger sandwiches were. Camille ran cake stands out while waiters collected pots of tea for patrons to enjoy alongside their sweet treats. It was an indulgence of all the senses. Carrie had assembled each afternoon tea in a daze. There was still no sign of Lily, and Carrie was beginning to worry. She'd assumed Lily would have the same days off as her. Carrie pulled off her apron. She had finished for the day, and with no afternoon tea service tomorrow, she had nothing to bake for the following day. The hotel had reduced their afternoon tea service to give Carrie time to prepare for the weddings, and to allow her some time off.

"You all finished?" Camille asked.

"Yeah. It's been a long day, and I have a day of research ahead of me tomorrow."

"I heard Rachel left."

"Yes, she rather dramatically quit just before you showed Sasha and Milo into the meeting room."

"No! What are you going to do?" Camille reached forward and gave Carrie a quick hug.

"Lucas and I are going to be the wedding planners until he finds a replacement."

"Those meetings will be filled with sexual tension," teased Camille.

"Camille!" Carrie hid her face behind her hands.

"Did you speak to him about last night?"

"Yes. First, he thought I already had a boyfriend, and then he said it was inappropriate because he's my manager. He also said he had too many commitments to have a girlfriend. It just felt like a generic brush-off."

"I'm sorry, Carrie. Lucas means a little too well sometimes. He needs to learn to think of himself."

Carrie wanted to ask Camille more, but she decided against it. Hearing about what a good person Lucas was wouldn't help dampen her attraction to him. "Anyway, I now have far too much to do to worry about flirting with anyone."

"How are you going to get up to speed with the weddings?"

"I've got Rachel's work laptop in my room. Unless she wiped it as a parting gift, I'll be spending all of tomorrow holed up studying every crumb of information stored on it."

"You'll be in your room all day?" asked Camille.

"Yeah, why?"

"I'll bring lunch up to you on my break. You can talk everything through with me. It might help to have someone to go through it with you."

"Camille, you are a star!" Carrie threw her arms around the woman. "I'll see you tomorrow. I'm going to pop out for a coffee."

Carrie walked out of the kitchen and shook her

hair out of its bun. She hoped it wasn't caked in icing sugar. It was raining outside, so she pulled on a branded coat from the staff room and went to the staff exit at the back of the hotel.

"Carrie?" someone called after her.

Carrie turned around to see Lily standing there waving at her.

"Hi, Lily. Are you okay? I was worried about you when you didn't turn up for work today."

"I hurt my hand last night. Didn't Lucas tell you?" Lily held up her bandaged hand.

"No, he didn't. What happened?"

"I tried to make myself dinner, and I burnt myself." Lily shrugged as if it was nothing.

"Oh, Lily. That must be so painful." Carrie wanted to pull the girl into a hug, but she knew Lily didn't always like physical displays of affection.

"It's blistered." She shrugged.

"Do you want to come for a coffee with me?" Carrie asked. After the day she'd had, she could do with some company.

"Let me check with Lucas," Lily said, walking off before Carrie could respond.

Carrie sat on the bench by the door and waited for Lily to return. As she waited, she pulled out her phone and sent a quick text to Eve, telling her about Rachel quitting. Lily still wasn't back by the time she sent the message, so Carrie went through the pictures she'd taken in London and chose a few to attach to an email to Alice. She'd add her message later. Carrie chose a picture of the pastel, floral petit fours she'd made, a picture of her bedroom, one of her workspace, and she snapped a quick selfie to attach so Alice could see she was okay.

"Okay, let's go." Lily bounded back into the room, a huge smile across her face.

"Come on. Where shall we go?"

"Starbucks. But let's go through the arcade." Lily threaded her arm through Carrie's, and they walked into the rain.

The arcade Lily referred to was Burlington Arcade. It was undercover, and there was a fancy security guard at the entrance. With Fortnum and Mason behind them, they walked through the arcade. Their eyes swivelled from one side to the other, taking in the expensive shops. The sound of rain pelting the windows in the arched ceiling above echoed through the space. It was beautiful and opulent. Carrie's mind wandered to how many people had walked in the same footsteps as her over the last two hundred years. This building was steeped in history and people's memories. It was the kind of place she'd love to sit and look at. To watch as families walked past and to imagine the people that walked in those same footsteps all those years ago when the arcade opened.

They came out the other side and weaved their way through the crowds of people to the Starbucks across the road. As they passed Savile Row, Carrie glanced down and felt a bubble of excitement in her stomach. She was in the heart of London with her new friend and with a challenge in front of her.

This was everything she had wanted. Yet there was a niggling feeling in the depth of her soul that longed for home. There was simply no pleasing her.

"Come on!" Lily pulled on her arm as Carrie slowed to glance down the road. Her attention was pulled back to the present, and Carrie picked up her feet, almost running to the coffee shop.

They shook themselves off as the warmth of the coffee shop engulfed them. Carrie pulled off her wet coat and encouraged Lily to do the same. She was relieved to see Lily had kept her injured hand in her pocket, so the bandage had stayed dry.

"What would you like?" Carrie asked, leading Lily to a table near the window.

"A double chocolatey chip Frappuccino, please," asked Lily.

Carrie just nodded. It sounded like an awful amount of sugar. "I'll be right back."

Lily's Frappuccino was a mountain of chocolate and whipped cream, making Carrie's flat white pale in comparison.

"What were you cooking when you did that?" asked Carrie. She'd just taken the first sip of her coffee and felt her body relax back into the worn leather chair. Her headache had finally eased, and it was nice to be away from the stresses of the hotel.

"I was making myself dinner." Lily took a sip of her drink and winced.

"Brain freeze?" Carrie chuckled. "Was nobody else around to make you dinner?" Carrie knew it wasn't her place to pry, but she'd seen how Lily was in the kitchen and in the short time she'd known her, she knew Lily could be forgetful of the temperature of things.

"My friend dropped me at home after my swimming class, but my brother was late getting home." Lily loaded up her finger with cream and ate it.

"Lily!" Carrie chuckled.

CHAPTER NINE

Despite having the day off, Carrie woke as the sun was rising above London. She made herself a coffee from the pod machine in her room and turned a chair to face the window to watch the city come to life. Other than a few sickly looking pigeons, there was very little nature on the streets outside. Over the last year working at Lachlan's castle, Carrie had grown used to taking her morning coffee break by the river and watching the fish swim. In the summer, insects crawled across the grass, and bees and butterflies flitted across the sky in the early morning haze. She felt split in two. She yearned for Scotland. The remoteness of the castle and the stillness surrounding it were like a tonic for her soul. The other half was enjoying her time in London with the city whirling around her and a list of things to do so long it towered above her.

Carrie's phone buzzed, and she ran back to her

bedroom to grab it from the bedside table. Eve was Face Timing her.

"Hello!" Carrie greeted her as she waited for the camera to connect.

"Morning! I have someone here who wanted to say hello," Eve said, turning the camera around.

"Gran!" Carrie let out a squeak of delight as her grandmother appeared. Alice was squinting at the screen.

"Carrie? I think I can make you out," Alice said. Eve was chuckling in the background.

"How are you, Gran?" Carrie settled back into her chair and picked her coffee up in her free hand.

They chatted a while, catching up on the week since Carrie had left. Alice and Eve were busy making preparations for Alexander and Isla's wedding. Carrie told them about Rachel quitting, and they promised to be at the end of the phone if she needed any advice.

After saying goodbye, Carrie put the phone down and drained the dregs of coffee in her mug. She winced as she realised it had gone cold. Outside, the street was buzzing with people going about their morning. Carrie pushed all thoughts of the castle from her mind and focused on the task at hand. She showered, threw on some loungewear, and pulled out a brownie she'd stashed in a Tupperware box last night and brought back with her. Carrie needed all the sugar she could get her hands on today. With a last glance at the bustling city below, she pulled Rachel's old work laptop onto her lap and powered it up.

The morning whizzed by, and before Carrie knew it, Camille was knocking at her door with their lunch.

"I can take a long lunch break since Lucas isn't in today, and there are very few lunches booked in," announced Camille. She'd slipped past Carrie with a silver tray in her hand with a dome covering the food.

An emptiness flooded Carrie and weaved its way around her chest like prickly vines at the news Lucas wasn't in today. She had spent the morning imagining him wandering around the hotel, tending to various tasks. As the monotony of Rachel's emails overwhelmed her, Carrie's mind had wandered. She'd imagined going down to the kitchen and bumping into Lucas.

"Stop thinking about him!" Camille frowned at her as she put the tray of food down on the table

"I'm not! I'm just thinking about what food you have under that dome."

"No, you weren't. Your eyes had glazed over, and you had a dreamy smile on your face.

Carrie shrugged her shoulders but didn't argue. She lifted the dome to see what Camille had brought up.

"I persuaded the chef to cook a couple of hamburgers for us," Camille explained as Carrie lifted the dome to reveal two towering burgers. They were filled with salad, gherkins, sauces, and bacon.

"Camille, these look amazing. I need this.

Thank you." Carrie took a handful of fries and shoved them into her mouth. Hunger had crept up on her and the smell of food made her stomach rumble. Carrie glanced at the clock. It was much later than she had realised.

"How're you getting on?" asked Camille, wiping sauce from the corner of her mouth.

"There is so much information. I found some notebooks and compiled the information for each wedding in its own notepad. Sasha and Milo's wedding is the most complicated, and they have high-profile guests and magazines in attendance. We have to pull it off, or everyone's reputation is at risk!"

"Do you think you and Lucas can do it?"

"I think so. The difficult stuff is outsourced, like florists, celebrants, and live bands. We coordinate everything and ensure the hotel is dressed for the day. It'll be a lot of work. Especially because we don't know what we're doing. We'll have to triple-check everything."

"I have confidence in you." Camille smiled.

"Thank you." Carrie popped the last bite of the burger in her mouth. "Did you grow up in London?" she asked once she'd finished chewing. Camille had a distinct accent, but Carrie couldn't put her finger on where she'd heard it.

"Almost. I grew up in Essex, but I spent the last five years living up north."

"I thought I recognised your accent! What were you doing up north?"

"Everyone recognises the accent." Camille grimaced. "I moved up north with my ex-boyfriend." Camille's eyes darkened and her shoulders slumped.

"I'm assuming you didn't part on good terms?"

"No. He spent five years isolating me and chipping away at my confidence."

"Camille, I'm so sorry."

"I'm slowly taking back control. After I left, I moved back in with my parents and got this job. I'm saving up to go travelling." She shrugged her shoulders as if it were nothing.

"I may have only just met you, Camille, but I'm so proud of you. You'll have to visit me in Scotland when you start your travels."

"I'd love to."

"We're opening a hotel there soon, so we'll probably be run off our feet if you need a job for a few weeks. I'm sure I could pull some strings with Lachlan and Eve."

"Thank you, Carrie. What about you? Any horrible ex-boyfriends hiding in your past?" Camille effortlessly shifted the attention back to Carrie.

"No horrible ones, I'm afraid. Usually, me living in Scotland is a problem, so relationships end quite quickly."

"Is there not anyone local?"

Carrie thought about the few boys she'd gone to school with. She'd attended the local village school with just a handful of other children. There were so few pupils that the age groups were mixed, so there were enough children in each class. Being close to the McLeod family meant Lachlan, who thought it was his job to protect Carrie from any male attention, had scared many of the boys away. The McLeod brothers had gone to school in London. During their holidays at the castle, Lachlan would threaten any boy that looked her way with the McLeod ancestral sword. She appreciated him thinking of her, but it meant she was a rather late bloomer in the romance department.

"Are you off on the same day next week?" asked Camille.

"Yes, unless I'm snowed under with wedding preparations." It was looking very likely that she would be.

"You deserve some time off. Why don't I book the day off and we can meet at Borough Market? I think we could both do with some downtime."
Carrie thought about it. Even if she had wedding preparations to take care of, she could catch up with it in the evening. "That sounds wonderful." She smiled at the thought of spending a couple of hours wandering around a foodie's heaven with her new friend.

"Perfect. Why don't I meet you there at around midday? I'll text you where to meet me once I'm there."

"It's a plan." Carrie grinned, hoping the week would fly by so she could indulge in all the food.

Camille left with a tray piled with empty

plates and Carrie went back to her research. She could feel her eyes growing heavy and her attention to detail was faltering. The emptiness that had filled her upon learning Lucas wasn't in the hotel today was still lying heavy on her chest. She glanced over at her work phone before reaching for it. It had come pre-loaded with lots of numbers, so she scrolled through the address book until she found Lucas. It was his day off. She really shouldn't contact him. He'd made it clear he wasn't looking for a relationship. She could just send him an update. He didn't have to reply until he was back at work.

Deciding to take the risk, Carrie worded a polite, if somewhat formal, text to Lucas, telling him she'd gone through most of the correspondence on Rachel's computer and had a good idea of what the clients wanted. She hit send and made herself another cup of coffee so she didn't keep checking the phone. Carrie picked a pod, a caramel latte, and popped it into the machine, hearing the hiss as it slotted in. The hot coffee spurted out of the machine and Carrie was reminded of when her coffee overflowed in front of Lucas. She'd spent her entire time at *Hotel Mayfair*, making a fool of herself in front of him. She had to get these weddings right to prove to him that she was capable. Even if there was no hope of anything more than friendship between them, she couldn't bear the thought of him not knowing the real her.

The machine clicked off at the same time Carrie's phone beeped with a notification. She held her breath as she picked up the phone. It was a text from Lucas.

Thank you so much for going through Rachel's correspondence on your day off. I owe you a drink. Lucas.

It was formal. But he said he owed her a drink. Carrie frowned. She was reading into this far too much. Texting Lucas had been a terrible idea. She pushed her work phone away from her and turned her attention to the window as she drank her coffee. It was still light outside and probably would be for another hour. Deciding she needed a break from her room, Carrie threw on some jeans, a jumper, and a coat and made her way to Covent Garden.

The square was busy with people just finishing work and tourists stopping by to have dinner or browse the luxurious shops. Carrie watched all the couples milling around, hand in hand. She strolled over to The Punch and Judy pub and ordered some food and a beer. Deciding to sit outside, she chose a table and watched the people around her. As she watched a young couple that looked to be on their first date, her mind wandered to Lucas again. Would he wrap his coat around her if she had shivered as the woman had? Would Lucas be sitting opposite her with a beer, a glass of wine, or maybe a soft drink? Carrie's thoughts were interrupted by the arrival of her food.

CHAPTER TEN

Carrie suppressed a yawn and stretched her arms above her head. The last couple of days had been busy with wedding preparations and an influx of afternoon tea bookings. She'd had conference calls with the other wedding clients to discuss their demands. The first wedding was in two weeks, and she and Lucas had an endless list of things to do.

"Can you stop that?" Lucas snapped at her, staring pointedly at her fingers drumming on the table.

"Sorry," mumbled Carrie.

They were in the ballroom, waiting for Sasha, Milo, and the florist. Carrie had stayed up late last night, going over every detail about their wedding. She hoped it would show during the meeting. She'd also Googled Sasha and Milo to find out just how high profile they were. It turned out they were on a reality television show a couple of years ago.

"No, I'm sorry. I'm just stressed. It seems every wedding planner with an ounce of experience has been snapped up."

"It's wedding season." Carrie shrugged.

"Yes, thank you, Carrie." He let out a heavy sigh.

Carrie stilled her fingers and turned to look at Lucas. The shadows under his eyes had darkened, and his face looked drawn. No matter what happened with these weddings, Carrie knew she had the castle, Lachlan, and Eve to return to. Lucas's entire life was wrapped up in this hotel. If they didn't pull this off, he could lose everything he'd worked so hard for.

"Would you like another coffee?" asked Carrie.

"I shouldn't. I'm running on the stuff at the moment." He rested his elbows on the table and leaned his forehead against his hand.

"What about something to eat? Take a couple of cake samples. I'll just cut the others in half, so it looks like I brought more."

Lucas didn't argue. He took a bite of cake, his eyes closing as he bit into the soft sponge and velvety buttercream icing. "This is amazing," he mumbled around the mouthful. "You're amazing, Carrie."

Carrie gulped and looked away.

"Glad you like it." She cleared her throat. A soft tap at the door saved Carrie from any further embarrassment. Lucas jumped up and opened the door, welcoming Sasha, Milo, and the florist.

"Good afternoon." Carrie smiled and greeted them, introducing herself to the florist.

The meeting whizzed by as Carrie did her best to absorb all the information. By the time they walked out of the ballroom, Carrie's hand was numb from all the notes she'd furiously scribbled down. Sasha wanted the impossible, and somehow the florist was making it happen. The hotel would be a feast for the senses, with exotic flowers covering every surface. They had agreed on a colour scheme for the cake. After tasting the cake samples, they had chosen the orange blossom sponge with vanilla cream icing. After some persuading, Carrie had convinced them to opt for edible flowers to decorate the six-tier cake rather than the Swarovski crystals Sasha wanted.

"Thank you for helping me persuade them to go for the edible flowers. For a minute, I thought we'd have to pick out crystals from each slice of cake before guests could eat them."

"I can just imagine you doing that." Lucas's smile lit up his eyes and the frown lines on his forehead disappeared.

"Don't even joke. Knowing Sasha, she'll change her mind, and it'll be all hands on deck!"

"Just don't let Lily near it. She'll keep some crystals for her collection." Lucas chuckled.

Carrie's stomach rumbled, reminding her she hadn't had time for lunch between the afternoon tea service and preparing for their meeting.

"Come on. Let's see if the chef will make us

a late lunch." Lucas glanced at his watch. "Actually, make that an early dinner. Do you know where Lily is?"

"We did afternoon tea service, and then I left her looking for Jamal with a plate of freshly baked shortbread."

"Perfect. She'll be doing poor Jamal's makeup before they're even halfway through the plate of shortbread."

Carrie smiled and followed Lucas out of the room and down the hallway. It was heartwarming to see how Lily had befriended everyone at the hotel. She treated everyone like her best friend from the moment she met them. And her passion for food, especially anything with sugar in it, picked Carrie up on the days she struggled to motivate herself.

"Let's get the lift. My legs feel like I'm training to do a marathon with the constant back and forth." Lucas pressed the button to call the lift.

"Have staffing levels improved?" asked Carrie. She was still making mental notes on the hotel's set-up to take back to Lachlan.

"Not enough to make my job easier." Lucas leaned against the wall and rubbed his eyes. Carrie had to clasp her hands firmly by her sides as the urge to reach forward and take his hand in hers overcame her. He looked as though he needed someone to force him to take a break. She looked down at the floor and pushed away those thoughts. It wasn't her place to get involved in his life.

"You might feel stressed and are hardly

sleeping, but it's admirable how much you care about this hotel and your staff."

"Thank you." He glanced down at her, and their eyes met. Carrie felt an electric shock pulse through her body.

The lift doors pinged open. "After you," said Lucas, holding his arm to gesture to her to walk ahead of him. Carrie smiled her thank you and walked to the back of the lift, propping herself up against the wall.

"What was your favourite cake sample?" Carrie asked, trying to keep the conversation light as the lift doors closed.

"Chocolate."

"Out of all those lovely flavours, and you're choosing the most basic?"

"I am basic." He shrugged his shoulders. The lift was for staff use only, and it was small. As Lucas's eyes settled on her, the space felt like it was shrinking around them, forcing them closer.

"Are you the type of person who likes an oily takeaway pizza and a side of soggy fries?" Carrie tried to ignore her ragged breathing, which felt too loud for the enclosed space.

"After a late shift, you cannot beat it. There's a takeaway shop on the corner of the road as I walk out of the station. It beats cooking after a long day at work."

"I've always enjoyed cooking. When I trained at Lachlan's restaurant, I spent all day in the kitchen learning how to cook beautiful delicate pastries.

Then I'd get home and cook dinner. Lachlan would have fired me on the spot if he caught me eating an oily pizza."

Lucas opened his mouth to reply, but the lift lurched, throwing him across it and into Carrie's arms. Their eyes met, and Carrie felt his hands rest on her sides, steadying them. He didn't step back. Their bodies pressed against each other, with Carrie's back firmly against the wall of the lift. Her lips parted, and she stared up at him. His eyes bore into hers as he slowly lowered his head, his lips brushing against hers.

"Please call for assistance. Press the button 'Assistance 'on the keypad," an automated voice echoed around the lift. Lucas jumped back and shook his head. His eyes were wide and glazed over. Carrie slowed her breathing and reached to press the button, since Lucas seemed frozen to the spot.

"Are there any members of the maintenance team left?" asked Carrie once she'd pressed the button. She was choosing to ignore the moment they'd shared. The confined space and the indefinite time trapped together would not be conducive to an awkward conversation.

"Marvin should be on shift for another half an hour if he hasn't gone home early." Lucas kept his eyes firmly on the floor.

"Oh no," groaned Carrie.

"The lift should be hooked up to a central service system. Pushing the assistance button should call a lift engineer, but I've no idea how long it will take." Lucas pulled out his phone and cursed under his breath. "I've got no signal."

Carrie pulled hers out, but she also had no signal. Her stomach rumbled again, reminding her she'd only eaten cake samples since breakfast.

"Sorry, we were going to get food. It's my fault for suggesting we take the lift."

"Well, we're here now. Nothing we can do about it." Carrie slid down the wall until she was sitting on the floor with her knees pulled up against her chest. Lucas followed her lead and sat down opposite her.

"I'm sorry about that." His eyes flickered off of her and onto his hands, which were clasped firmly in his lap.

"It's no bother, honestly." Carrie looked down at her hands, wishing they weren't having this conversation... again.

"I am sorry," he whispered.

"Is this an' *it's not you, it's me* 'spiel?" Carrie quipped, refusing to let her disappointment show.

"I suppose it is. Sorry."

"Stop apologising!"

"I don't know what else to say."

"Then say nothing, and definitely do not kiss me again. We have to work together, so I think we should just do our best to keep our relationship professional." Carrie puffed out her chest as she finished the sentence with just a slight wobble to her voice.

Lucas nodded in response and returned his

attention back to his phone. An awkward silence filled the lift, neither wanting to be the first to break it. Lucas seemed to understand that Carrie didn't wish to speak further, so he tapped away on his phone. Given the lack of signal, Carrie assumed he must be making notes or drafting messages to send later. There'd been no update from the maintenance team, so they didn't know how much longer they would be trapped.

The ghost of his apologies echoed around the lift. Carrie sat with a scowl across her face, staring down at the burgundy carpet. She had to stop being so open to any man that showed an interest in her. After the rejection from her parents at such a young age, Carrie had fought not to put walls up and push people away. Perhaps she'd fought too hard and now she was too willing to show her heart. A voice floated through the intercom, interrupting her musings.

"We're here and working as quickly as possible to free you," said the voice. There were high pitch squeaks and noises of metal grinding against metal. Carrie refused to look at Lucas. After a loud thump, the doors prized open, and a man peered in at them.

"There we go!" he announced, beaming in at them.

Carrie thanked him before scurrying off, leaving Lucas to arrange the repair. In need of fresh air, she walked to Lachlan's restaurant to pull some strings to get herself a takeaway. After the events of the afternoon, the last thing she felt like was sitting in the restaurant with the noisy buzz of conversation around her.

CHAPTER ELEVEN

Over the next few days, Carrie did everything in her power to avoid Lucas. She'd even hidden in the cold storage for five minutes when she heard him walking alongside the chef, discussing the upcoming wedding menu. Her teeth were chattering by the time she walked out. Camille knew there was something wrong, so on Saturday evening, once their work was finished, the two women went out for dinner and cocktails. With some liquid courage inside of her, Carrie told Camille about their almost kiss in the lift. Camille's jaw had dropped, and she'd immediately ordered another round of drinks. Sunday's afternoon tea service had been completed with a pounding headache and a churning stomach.

By the time Carrie woke on Monday morning, the sun was already shining. She'd left the bedroom curtains open last night. From her bed, she could see the beautiful blue sky, with just the odd fluffy white cloud floating by. She smiled and stretched out on the bed. It was her day off, and she had a trip to Borough Market planned with Camille. She checked her phone to see a text from Camille telling her to meet her by the underground station next to the market at midday. Carrie immediately messaged her back, saying she couldn't wait. It would be busy at midday, but the delicious food would make up for the crowds.

Once showered, Carrie opted for a pair of blue Mom jeans and a thin white jumper. She pulled on a baseball cap over her unruly hair and a pair of comfortable trainers. With her phone and a tote bag in hand, she decided to head towards London Bridge. She'd be early, but she could stop and get a coffee on her way. Carrie marched through the hotel reception area, doing her best not to make eye contact with anyone in case Lucas was around.

It was a lovely day, so she opted to walk to Charing Cross and get the train across the river to London Bridge. The streets were busy as Carrie weaved her way through to Green Park. Tourists and workers were walking in all directions, some determinedly marching towards their destination, others just milling around and soaking up London's atmosphere. The bright spring day attracted lots of visitors to the park. Carrie watched a small fluffy dog prance across the green grass, a spring in its step as it sniffed at the long blades of grass.

At the other side of Green Park, Carrie crossed

over and continued her journey through St. James's Park. She walked along the edge of the lake, avoiding the small children whose weary parents had brought them out to say good morning to the ducks. There was a sense of anticipation in the air; everyone was starting the day with little idea as to how it would turn out. Leaving the park, Carrie passed Trafalgar Square and wandered into Charing Cross's concourse. She had a bounce in her step as she brought her ticket and boarded a train to London Bridge.

The train pulled out of the station. Carrie rested her head on the cool window and watched as they crossed over the Thames and through Waterloo. As they approached London Bridge, Carrie pulled her phone out and snapped a quick picture of The Shard to send to Alice. Her grandmother had only been to London once to visit Carrie at Lachlan's restaurant. Lachlan had travelled down with her and treated her to dinner at his restaurant. The buzz of the city had overwhelmed Alice. Although she'd kept a smile on her face for Carrie's sake, they all knew Alice was itching to get back to the castle. Her grandmother enjoyed the familiarity of her home and her job.

The train alighted at London Bridge, and Carrie stepped onto the platform. She stumbled along, straining her neck to look up at The Shard. She tripped over someone's suitcase and stumbled into a group of tourists.

"Sorry," she apologised. They smiled at her and steadied her, but Carrie didn't recognise the language they spoke. She smiled back and waved, eager to keep walking.

Carrie made her way to where she was meeting Camille, but she was still an hour early. Knowing it was close by; Carrie found the Monmouth Coffee Company and joined the queue for a coffee. She had lots of time to spare, so she didn't mind waiting.

With a coffee in hand, Carrie found an empty bench and settled down to enjoy it. She could spend the next half an hour people-watching while she waited for Camille. At five to twelve, Carrie made her way to their agreed meeting point. She'd enjoyed watching everyone, creating stories in her head about who they were and what they were up to.

Carrie felt her stomach somersault as she approached the tube station. She recognised the person standing there, but it wasn't Camille.

"Lucas, what are you doing here?" asked Carrie, walking up to him. He visibly jumped and snapped his head around to look at her.

"Carrie?" he asked, his brow knitted together.

"Yes, the one and only. What are you doing here?"

"I'm meeting Camille. What are you doing here?"

"I'm meeting Camille."

"She's set us up," whispered Lucas.

"No, she wouldn't. Maybe she's just running late. Perhaps Camille thought it would be a nice team-bonding trip? I'm sure she'll be along soon with Lily and Jamal."

"Nobody else is coming, Carrie."

Refusing to accept her fate, Carrie pulled out her phone. There was a message from Camille flashing on the screen. It simply read 'have fun'.

"We've been set up," confirmed Carrie.

"I told you." Lucas smiled at her.

Carrie sucked in a deep breath." I'm sorry for avoiding you," she said, deciding to confront the uneasy atmosphere between them.

"No, Carrie, it's my fault. I should have sought you out and righted things between us. I just feel this pull towards you, so I've been avoiding you."

"I feel it, too," Carrie whispered, she was scared their bubble would burst if she spoke too loudly.

"But we can be professional, can't we? Now Rachel's left, we'll be working together preparing for the weddings."

"Lucas, what if I'm not asking for a future together? Neither of us can deny there's a growing attraction. I'm in London for the next couple of months and we're both single. At least I hope we are?" Carrie held her breath and clasped her hands in tight fists by her sides as she opened herself up to rejection. Her evening out with Camille had got her thinking about how quick she was to let people into her life and into her heart. It was time she approached life differently. Why couldn't she enjoy a fling with Lucas?

"I'm definitely single," promised Lucas.

"We're two single adults in London. There's

nothing stopping us from having some fun together?" Carrie stepped closer to him, ignoring the bustling street surrounding them. Her nerves fizzed every time she was near him. She couldn't keep ignoring him and the way he made her feel.

"Miss Mackenzie, are you suggesting a spring fling?" He reached out and wrapped his arms around her waist, pulling her to him.

"I am. What do you think?" her voice was a whisper as his lips hovered close to hers. He didn't answer. Instead, he brought his lips down to meet hers.

"I like this." He tugged at her cap as they stepped apart. Carrie groaned, remembering how little effort she'd put into her appearance, thinking she was only meeting Camille. "You look beautiful." He smiled at her and leaned forward to kiss the tip of her nose. "Shall we have a wander round and get some lunch? I owe you dinner after getting us trapped in a lift."

Carrie nodded, and he reached out to take her hand in his. His fingers intertwined with hers, and Carrie felt a warmth wrap around her as they walked hand-in-hand into the kitchen area of the market. Stalls of delicious food surrounded them with a mixture of scents in the air, making Carrie's stomach rumble. The sound of tills ringing, people chatting, pans sizzling, and coffee machines whirring filled her ears, but it all seemed far away. With Lucas by her side, she felt as though they were ensconced inside their own little world.

"What shall we eat?" asked Lucas. Instead of looking around at the stalls, he was staring at her.

"We need to walk around first. There are so many options, I don't want to regret my choice."

Lucas chuckled and squeezed her hand, walking her towards the outer edge of the stalls so they could start at the entrance. The smells were overwhelmingly delicious as they sauntered from stall to stall, trying to decide what to eat.

"What about a burger?" Lucas suggested. They'd been looking at the stalls for almost half an hour now.

"But what if I miss out on something delicious because I've chosen the burger?"

"Then I'll bring you back next week and you can try something new."

"Really?" Carrie's eyes glimmered as she turned to look at him to see whether he was being serious.

"Of course." He smiled and bent down to press a soft kiss against her lips. The food around them was quickly forgotten as Carrie wrapped her arms around Lucas's neck. His hands went to her waist as he pulled her closer and deepened the kiss.

"Do you mind?" Somebody barged into them, causing Carrie to wobble. Lucas steadied her but stepped back to create some space between them.

"I think we ought to queue for a burger," he said.

Carrie hadn't needed to worry about missing out on the flavours. The burgers were delicious.

With greasy fingers, she screwed up the empty packaging and threw it in the bin. She glanced at Lucas and saw he had fixed his eyes firmly on her.

"Good?" he asked, smirking at her.

"It was amazing," Carrie confirmed, glancing down to see Lucas still had half a burger left. "Did I inhale that?" she asked.

"It was nice to see you enjoying it. After all, you put a lot of thought into it," he teased.

"Oh, stop teasing me. Why don't you tell me something about yourself?"

"Is that a good idea?" He put down his food and wiped the grease from his hands.

"What do you mean?"

"Well, if this is just a fling, is getting to know each other a good idea?"

"I don't know, Lucas. It might only be a fling, but I'd still like to know something about the person I'm having a fling with." Carrie shrugged her shoulders, trying to mask her feelings. When he uttered the words *just a fling*, her stomach dropped. She felt as though someone had punched her in the gut. Although it was just a fling and she knew they could be nothing more, she still really liked him and wanted to spend time in his company. Perhaps he didn't feel the same. Maybe she could have been anyone. It was just someone's hand to hold while he ate lunch.

"I just don't want either of us to get hurt." His tone softened, and he reached out to squeeze her hand. "What do you want to know?"

Carrie squeezed his hand back. "Did you always want to be a hotel manager?" she asked. It was the first question that popped into her head.

He took another bite of his burger and chewed for a moment before he answered. "Not always," he admitted. "When I was younger, I dreamed of being a pilot. I wanted to travel the world and fly aeroplanes. I'd even applied for a course and had been accepted. Then when our parents died, and I became my sister's guardian, I realised quite quickly that I needed to get a job. My parents' life insurance helped, but we couldn't live on it indefinitely. I'd worked as a waiter in our local Italian restaurant while studying for my A levels, so I started applying for jobs in the hospitality sector. I started as a kitchen porter, then moved up to a waiter. Eventually, I found myself in admin roles, still in hospitality. Then the job at *Hotel Mayfair* became available and the owner at the time took a chance on me. I think the real reason they took a chance on me was because they were struggling financially and I was cheap. The hotel was successful, but as the budget tightened, attention to detail was dropped. Then two years ago the new owners bought it and we've been struggling ever since."

"Do you think about leaving?" Carrie wanted to pry more into the young boy whose parents died and who took over the care of his sister, but she knew that didn't align with a fling.

"Every day. I can't, though, not unless I have another job lined up. *Hotel Mayfair* needs me, and that gives me job security." He'd finished his food now and was fiddling with the empty packaging.

"Well, you're defying the odds and keeping *Hotel Mayfair* afloat. Your hard work will pay off. You might even find yourself headhunted." Carrie smiled as a slight blush tinged his cheeks at the compliment.

"What about you, Carrie? Did you always want to be a patisserie master?"

"No, but I suppose the signs were there from a young age. I was always begging my grandmother to bake with me. She's worked at the McLeod's castle my entire life. The family visited a few times a year, and less so as Lachlan and Alexander grew older. When the castle was empty, Gran and I would use the kitchen to bake in on a Sunday afternoon. I used to love to decorate the shortbread with piped buttercream and sprinkles. Even before my parents passed away, I spent most of my time with my grandparents. I worked hard at school but never seemed to get very far with my grades. Then, after I turned eighteen, I had a bit of a wobble. Scotland was suffocating me. I felt as though I didn't know who I was. Life was meaningless. Lachlan would come back to the castle for weekend visits while he was at culinary school and we'd cook together. He recognised a passion in me and when I lost my way, he offered to help me. That's how I eventually found myself at his restaurant, being trained by a master of patisserie. Since then, I've worked at The McLeod's castle and then Lachlan's as a pastry chef, until I felt as though I was suffocating again. Now I'm in London for an adventure before I go back to Scotland to settle down and find my path. I've had everything handed to me, so I felt as though I needed to get away and prove myself."

"You seem to have everything worked out."

"I'm not so sure about that. My heart feels as though it's torn in two. Half of me is still in Scotland, while the other half is enjoying every second of being here. I don't know what will make me happy, and I'm terrified of making the wrong decision."

"You know what I think, Carrie?"

"What do you think?" Carrie reached under the table with her foot and rubbed it against Lucas's leg. He raised his eyebrows at her and rubbed his thumb across her knuckles.

"I think you're overthinking everything. It sounds like you have found your passion for baking by accident. What's stopping you from finding your future by accident?"

"You make it sound so simple."

"Carrie, life is simple. You just have to follow its flow. I thought I'd be a pilot, travelling the world by now, but then life happened. I'd be lying if I said I don't feel sad that I never got to experience that, but I also really enjoy my life. When the hotel was flourishing, I loved my job. I work with some amazing people, and the family I have left is very supportive, and they always put a smile on my face. I've learned that there's no point in planning life because it never turns out how you expect it to."

"You're very wise," Carrie commented, letting his words sink in.

"I know. Now, I'm sorry to cut this afternoon short, but I need to be getting home." He checked his watch and frowned.

"Are you okay?"

"Yes, sorry, I just need to get going or else I'm going to miss an appointment." He sounded distracted.

"Come on, let's walk to the tube."

Carrie threaded her arm through Lucas's as they pushed their way through the crowds of people to the tube. Her insides fluttered as he made her laugh.

"I'll see you at work tomorrow?" she asked as they came to a stop by the ticket barriers.

"Of course, but I think it might be a good idea if we don't let anyone know about us." He pressed his forehead against hers, keeping the closeness between them.

"I agree." It would be hard to pass him and not reach out to touch him, but she knew he was right.

"I'll see you tomorrow." He kissed her quickly before disappearing behind the ticket barriers.

Carrie pressed a finger to her lips, still feeling the ghost of his. She felt as though she were in her own little world as everything around her was fuzzy, and her feet felt like she was walking on clouds. Deciding against the crowds and stuffiness of the tube, she went in search of an iced coffee and embarked on the long walk back to the hotel.

Once back in her room, Carrie ran herself a bath and poured in some of the fancy bubble bath from the room's toiletries. A lavender scent filled the room as white frothy bubbles rose in the tub. The overhead spotlights were set to dim lighting, and Carrie stepped into the bath, allowing the warm water to wash over her body. Her legs and feet ached from the day's walking. She closed her eyes for a moment and inhaled the scent as memories from her day flooded her mind. The soft pressure of Lucas's lips against hers and the weight of his hand in hers. Carrie opened her eyes and realised she had a soppy smile across her face. She reached out for her phone, putting it on loudspeaker to call Eve.

It was early evening, and the kitchen would be prepping for dinner service, but she needed to speak to someone. Camille had texted her, but Carrie had ignored it. If they weren't telling anyone about their fling, Carrie couldn't speak to Camille about today.

"Hello?" Eve's voice echoed around the bathroom.

"Eve, it's Carrie. Are you busy?" Carrie sank into the bath so just her chin was above the water.

"I'm never too busy for you. Give me two seconds." Eve's voice faded, but Carrie could hear her giving instructions to someone to take over from her. "Right, you have my full attention. I'm going up to the flat so nobody can eavesdrop on our conversation."

"I've been on a date," blurted out Carrie.

"With your dishy manager?"

"Yes."

"How did that happen?"

"I was set up. My friend Camille arranged for us to meet at Borough Market today for a walk around. But when I got there, Lucas was waiting for me. She'd told him we were having a staff trip out. We were both set up by her."

"She sounds like my kind of woman," Eve joked.

"Hey, no siding with her!"

"So, what happened next?"

"We had a lovely lunch, and he kissed me."

"That sounds lovely, so why do you sound as though him kissing you was the worst thing that could have happened?"

Carrie exhaled. Somehow, Eve could read her thoughts and feelings without her ever having to express them. "His life is in London, Eve. I'm loving my time here, but there's a part of me that's counting down the days until I come home. We spoke about how different our lives are and the distance between us and realised there would never be a future for us. So, we've decided on a spring fling."

"A spring fling, hey?" Eve suppressed a giggle.

"Don't tease me, Eve." Carrie ran her hand through the water, watching the ripples as they crashed over the bubbles.

"Sorry. I think it sounds like a good idea, Carrie. I just don't want you to get hurt. You fell for Rhys really quickly, remember?" Eve's tone was soft as she brought up Carrie's most recent heartbreak.

"I know, but I thought we had a future." Carrie sniffed, not wanting to admit how quickly she'd allowed herself to fall for him.

"I don't want to dampen your spirit, Carrie. Lucas sounds lovely, and I hope you have lots of fun together. We're always looking for a new hotel manager if he falls head over heels in love with you."

"Eve, what happened to the not teasing me?" Carrie had to stop her mind from running away with itself as she thought about Lucas returning to Scotland with her to run Lachlan and Eve's new castle hotel. He'd made it very clear that his life was here in London. She pushed the thought from her mind and refocused on Eve's voice.

"—misses you."

"Sorry, Eve, I didn't catch all of that."

"I was just saying that Alice misses you. We had a meeting with Isla last night to discuss their wedding plans. It wasn't the same without you there."

"I'll be home soon," Carrie promised.

"Not too soon. You've got a spring fling to indulge in first."

Carrie asked Eve questions about the restaurant and laughed as Eve recounted a story about some awkward customers. With her mind scrambled, Carrie yearned for the comfort and familiarity of the rolling hills of home and the smell of her grandmother's cooking. Eventually, Eve had to go so she could start the evening service.

Once off the phone, Carrie lay in the bath until the water went cold. She pulled on her dressing gown and ordered room service before setting Netflix up on her laptop, ready to relax for the evening and push all thoughts of Lucas Raven from her mind.

CHAPTER TWELVE

Carrie woke to a knock on her bedroom door. She wrapped the hotel dressing gown around herself and went to look through the spyhole to see who it was. Her stomach flipped as she spotted Camille on the other side of the door, almost bouncing up and down in excitement.

"What do you want?" Carrie asked, opening the door. She was still annoyed at Camille for setting them up.

"Charming, and after I arranged a lovely date for you yesterday." Camille stepped into the room.

"Good morning, Camille, please do come in," Carrie sarcastically quipped.

"Hold on. You are alone, right? I'm not about to walk in on a half-naked Lucas, am I?"

"You're fine. I came home alone."

"Are you mad at me?" Camille's excitement dipped as she wandered into the living room and sat down.

"No. Yes. I don't know. I actually had a lovely time."

"I knew it! You two are perfect for each other." Camille clapped her hands together.

"Camille, don't. There's no future for me and Lucas. His life is here in London, and my life is in Scotland. My job here is temporary. I'll be going home once my contract's up."

"Oh, Carrie." Camille stood and pulled Carrie into her arms. Carrie allowed her head to rest against her friend's shoulder.

After her chat with Eve yesterday, Carrie had assured herself she could be detached and enjoy her new fling, but in the cold light of the morning, she wasn't so sure. But if she admitted it to Lucas, she knew he'd end things immediately. She couldn't risk that. Instead, she had to silence those thoughts and focus on the joy he brought into her life.

"I'm running late for my shift. Do you want to meet me on my lunch break?" Camille rubbed Carrie's arm.

"I'm fine, thank you, though." Carrie wished she didn't sound like she was trying to convince herself.

"Well, I'm here if you ever need to talk. Be careful, Carrie. Lucas is lovely, but he's not worth you losing your spark over." With those parting words, Camille left Carrie alone, worrying about the day ahead.

Carrie didn't know how she hadn't given away her and Lucas's fling the moment she laid eyes on him. She walked into the staff room to make herself a coffee, and Lucas was there talking to the chef. They were going over the menu for the day. As she walked through the door, his head snapped up, and his eyes sought hers. Carrie fought the urge to find an excuse to drag him into the cold storage and steal a kiss.

"Ah, Carrie, I need a word with you once I'm finished here. Would you mind hanging around?" Lucas asked, not quite meeting her eyes.

"Sure. I'll just get myself a coffee and breakfast while you finish your meeting." Carrie gave a quick smile to the chef and turned her attention away from them.

Someone had left a few bottles of sugar syrups on the side, so Carrie added a shot of vanilla to her coffee and grabbed a banana from the fruit basket. She had lots of baking to do after her day off. Carrie remembered to switch the machine off before her coffee overflowed. She peeled her banana and popped a piece in her mouth as she stirred milk into her coffee. Lucas's soft voice floated across the room as he flicked through pages of paper, and the chef furrowed his brow. Carrie fought the urge to listen in to the conversation. It was none of her business.

Lucas's meeting continued as Carrie finished her banana and drained the dregs of her coffee. She

143

glanced at the clock, thinking of everything she had to do. As much as she wanted a moment alone with Lucas, she couldn't keep putting off starting work.

"I think that's us finished. I'll catch up with you tomorrow once you've had a moment to think." Lucas stood up and shook the chef's hand before turning his attention to Carrie. "Shall we?" he asked, gesturing towards the door. Carrie nodded and followed him, not knowing where he was taking her.

"Where are we going?" Carrie whispered, following Lucas through the maze of corridors in the staff area.

"To my office." He shot her a smirk over his shoulder.

Lucas opened the door to his office and clasped her hand, pulling her in behind him. He closed the door and pushed her up against it, cupping her face with his hand. Carrie's eyes flickered closed as his lips came crashing down against hers. Her hands snaked around his neck, and her fingers intertwined in his hair.

The phone in Lucas's office let out a high pitch ring, and he stepped back. "I should probably answer that," he whispered, his forehead leaning against hers. Carrie took a deep, ragged breath, still leaning against the door to steady herself. Her lips tingled from his. She took in his appearance with his hair tousled from her wandering hands.

"I should get back to work," she said.

Neither of them moved as the phone continued to ring in the background. "You really ought to get that," Carrie whispered.

"I should." His head dipped, and he brushed his lips against hers. Carrie's heart pounded in her chest as his lips trailed kisses along her jaw and down her neck. Her hands found their way back into his hair as she threaded her fingers through it. The loud shrill of the telephone silenced, and they filled the room with their laboured breathing. Carrie's hands felt their way down to the top button of Lucas's shirt, and her fingers fumbled to undo it.

As she reached the third button, Lucas's mobile rang. He stopped peppering kisses along her collarbone and held a finger to her lips.

"I really do need to get this. It's a conference call with the owners." His eyes lingered on her and he made no move to answer the phone.

"I should get back to the kitchen. I'm going to be behind as it is." Carrie straightened her T-shirt. She pulled the hair tie from her half-fallen-out bun and redid it. Her eyes caught the sight of Lucas doing up the buttons on his shirt. She gulped as he covered up the bare skin that her fingers had been touching mere moments ago. "I'll see you around," she said, reaching for the door handle.

"We have a meeting this afternoon with this weekend's couple." Lucas reminded her.

Carrie cursed under her breath. She'd completely forgotten. Their wedding was this weekend, and the bride had been emailing Carrie for the last few days with instructions for the cake. She wouldn't be able to think straight with Lucas sitting in the same room as her.

"I'll see you later." She gave him an awkward wave and left, her fingers crossed, hoping she didn't bump into anyone with her flushed cheeks and swollen lips.

Carrie pulled open the door to the staff stairway and delighted in the cool air hitting her. The door slammed behind her with a loud bang, which echoed through the stairway, making her jump. She leaned back against the wall and took a few deep breaths as the air washed over her. Somehow, she needed to get control over her body and her emotions before she stepped into the kitchen. A glance at her phone told her she was running late.

She was forty-five minutes late by the time Carrie walked into her workspace to find Lily already there and measuring out ingredients.

"You're late," Lily said very matter-of-factly.

"Sorry, Lily. I had a quick meeting about this weekend's wedding." Carrie put on her apron and glanced over at the scone mixture Lily was making. She had the tendency to be a little heavy-handed with the ingredients, so she hoped they'd turn out okay.

"The gold cake!" Lily exclaimed, remembering the conversation they'd had in the coffee shop about the upcoming wedding.

"Yes, that's the one." Carrie smiled as she remembered how excited Lily was at the idea of a gold cake. She had over-enthusiastically sipped her drink and ended up with a big blob of cream on the tip of her nose.

Carrie retrieved some miniature pie cases from the freezer and put them to the side as she whipped up a strawberry mousse to fill them. She'd over-ordered gold leaf for the wedding cake and so she planned to sprinkle some on the miniature delights. Carrie had learned to always have enough tart shells for Lily to steal a handful of them.

"I've got to go to the hospital tomorrow," announced Lily. She was rolling out the scone dough on the workbench and using a cookie cutter to cut each one out. Sometimes Lily struggled with pushing the cutter through the dough, but today she was managing it.

"What for?" Carrie asked. She fetched Lily a ramekin and cracked an egg into it for her to brush over the tops of the scones before they went into the oven.

"My heart." Lily's answer was short.

"What do you mean by your heart?"

"It's poorly."

"Lily, put that pastry brush down and look at me for a moment."

"What did I do wrong?" Lily asked. Her face had fallen. She put the brush back into the ramekin with the beaten egg and turned to face Carrie, a frown across her face.

"You've not done anything wrong, Lily. I just want to know a little more about your hospital appointment." Carrie reached out and squeezed Lily's shoulder. Lily tensed for a second before she relaxed and smiled shyly up at Carrie.

"I go lots. Just ask Maria."

"Who's Maria?" asked Carrie. She tried to flick back through all her conversations with Lily to see whether she could recall the name, but she couldn't.

"My friend. She comes with me to the hospital."

Carrie nodded. "And this hospital visit? You said it's about your heart?"

"Yes."

"What's wrong with your heart, Lily?"

"It's broken." Lily shrugged, her eyes wandering back to the tray of scones waiting for their egg wash.

"But you're okay to be working? What about all the sugar you eat?"

"I've had it since I was a baby. Don't tell Lucas about the desserts." Lily's eyes filled with panic.

"I won't tell anyone, Lily. I love having you working with me, so I wouldn't risk you losing your job. But I need you to cut back on the desserts, okay? If you've got a bad heart, we need to fill you with healthy food, not sugar."

Lily pouted, but she nodded in agreement.

"Okay, now get those scones in the oven and set a timer. Then you can help me pipe the strawberry mousse into these tart shells." Carrie turned her attention back to the desserts she was making, but she made a mental note to ask Camille about Lily's heart problems. She needed to know how much she could push Lily.

The final afternoon tea went out with Camille as the oven timer went off. Carrie glanced at the clock. She'd be cutting it fine to cool and ice the cake before her meeting. She pulled the small cake tins out of the oven. The sweet scent of desiccated coconut permeated the air. Carrie used a knife to loosen the edges of the cakes. While they cooled in their tins, she mixed up a gold buttercream, before turning them out onto cooling racks. She had an hour until the meeting, so she put the cakes in the fridge and ran up to her room to get changed.

With a shower cap protecting her curls, Carrie washed the flour off of herself. She then changed into a smart cream trouser suit with a double-breasted jacket. Her curls fell around her face, and she ran some product through them, defining them. A quick dab of concealer and some lip gloss, and Carrie made her way back to the kitchen. She had twenty minutes to ice the cake and get to the meeting room.

The cake was a miniature version of the wedding cake. She'd baked the larger tiers before afternoon tea service and had frozen them for the weekend. Carrie made a miniature mock-up of the cake with the leftover batter. *Hotel Mayfair* was in a precarious position with no events planner, so she wanted to do everything within her skill set to put the couples at ease. Carrie covered the two-tier replica in gold buttercream and smoothed it out before stacking the smaller tier on top. She sprinkled a small amount of the gold leaf over it and grabbed a couple of edible flowers from the walk-in. It wasn't as extravagant as the sketches Carrie had sent to the bride, but it was a little peek at what was to come, and since it was the same cake batter, she'd know whether they were happy with the taste.

Carrie pulled off the fresh apron and checked her suit for any splodges of gold buttercream, but somehow, she'd kept herself clean. With the cake transferred to a pretty tray and a dome covering it, she held it in one hand as she pushed open the door and made her way to the meeting room. She'd texted Lucas to say she was bringing sweet treats and to prepare drinks. His reply made her blush and stuff her phone into her pocket before anyone caught a glimpse of her screen.

"Ah, here's Carrie," Lucas announced as Carrie pushed open the meeting room door with her hip. He jumped up and held it open for her.

"Hello, so sorry I'm late." She put on her most professional smile and walked over to the table, setting the tray down in the middle. Carrie did her best to keep her eyes from wandering to Lucas. The very last thing she needed was to lose herself in his proximity when they had such an important meeting ahead of them.

"It's our fault for being early. Lovely to meet you in person, Carrie. I'm sure you're sick of my constant emails. I'm Veronica and this is my fiancée, Leon." She stood up and shook Carrie's hand, her fiancée following her lead and doing the same.

"Lovely to meet you, Veronica and Leon." Carrie took in the woman's appearance with her abundance of gold rings, bracelets, and necklaces. Her stipulation for a gold cake was making sense. "I have a little surprise." With a flourish, Carrie lifted the dome to reveal the miniature wedding cake. There were gasps all around, with Veronica instantly pulling out her phone and snapping pictures of it.

While the couple were distracted admiring the cake, Lucas reached under the table and squeezed Carrie's hand. He let go quickly as Veronica asked if they could cut it.

The small kitchenette was stocked with plates and cutlery, so Carrie went to retrieve them.

"Would you like to do the honour?" she asked, handing them a knife.

There were squeals of delight as Veronica cut into the cake and discovered the white chocolate-flavoured gold buttercream in the centre. Everyone declared the cake to be delicious, and Carrie let out a soft sigh of relief, knowing whatever else happened, the cake would taste good.

The meeting whizzed by, and it seemed everything was set for the wedding. Lucas had worked tirelessly to ensure everything was in place and all preparations were underway. The couple seemed none-the-wiser that this would be Lucas's first wedding as a stand-in events planner. Carrie said her goodbyes and told them she couldn't wait to present them with their wedding cake on Saturday. Lucas gestured for them to follow him back to the hotel's reception area to show them the best spots for photographs. As they went their separate ways, Lucas glanced longingly back at her.

"Where have you been?" Camille shouted after her as she walked into the kitchen.

"Hello to you, too!" Carrie chuckled, rolling her eyes.

"You didn't answer my question." Camille raised her eyebrows.

"I've just had a meeting with Saturday's couple. I made them a mock-up wedding cake." Carrie gestured to the empty tray. They had eaten every crumb of the cake during the meeting.

"Was Lucas there?" Camille teased.

"Of course he was." Carrie turned and walked towards her workstation to put the tray in the dishwasher and to avoid Camille's questions.

"Are you seeing him again?" she asked, watching Carrie aimlessly move things around.

"We haven't arranged anything. Actually, I was hoping to bump into you. I wanted to ask you something. Lily mentioned today that she has a hospital appointment tomorrow for her heart. Do you know anything about it? If she's unwell, I need to know so I can reduce her work."

"I think it's just a regular checkup. From what I understand, it's something she's had since birth. Her support worker, Maria, usually takes her to the appointments, so I don't think it can be anything too serious. Lucas wouldn't allow her to be working with you if he thought it would compromise her health."

Carrie nodded, wondering whether Lucas's opinion might change if he knew how many sweet treats Lily stole from the kitchen.

"Why don't you just talk to Lucas about it?" Camille asked, undoing a Tupperware box with macaron shells inside. She took one out and popped it into her mouth.

"We don't get much talking done when we're together," Carrie quipped. Camille inhaled the macaron shell and started coughing, causing Carrie to giggle.

"That was nasty!" Camille gasped, reaching for the glass of water Carrie had poured for her.

"Then stop prying! Anyway, I'm going to run upstairs and get changed before I do some baking for tomorrow. Between you, Lily, and Jamal, my stock needs replenishing!"

"Say hello to lover boy for me!" Camille called after her. Carrie flipped her the finger as she walked away.

CHAPTER THIRTEEN

Days passed in a blur of confectionary sugar, gold buttercream, and edible flowers. By Saturday morning, the three-tier wedding cake towered above Carrie. She had to stand on a stool to add the flowers to the top of the cake. The last week had been stressful. Carrie had helped Lucas as much as she could. Each time they completed a task, five more would appear. They'd hardly found a moment alone. However, that hadn't stopped them from texting. Carrie would fall asleep with her phone clasped in her hands, waiting for Lucas's reply. They'd been messaging into the early hours. Carrie was tired, but it was worth it for the smile playing on her lips.

"That looks amazing!" Camille exclaimed. She'd walked into Carrie's station carrying a tray of champagne flutes. Camille was overseeing the food service and had spent the last week reading up on the etiquette for fine dining service. Carrie had almost lost her temper yesterday when Camille asked her to observe a trial service to see whether the waitresses were synchronised. Lily had kept side-eyeing them, knowing they were playing on Carrie's last nerve.

"Isn't it lovely?" Carrie said. She stepped back to look at the masterpiece. It was her first wedding cake at *Hotel Mayfair*, so she had much to prove.

"Oh my gosh, that's amazing!" Jamal poked his head around the corner and gasped as his eyes settled on the shimmering gold cake.

"Thank you." Carrie smiled. She shuffled her feet as people wandered over after hearing Jamal's reaction. Everyone praised her and commented on how wonderful the cake looked.

"Shouldn't you be getting changed?" asked Camille, shooting Carrie a quick wink.

"I should. I didn't realise that was the time. Where's Lily?" Lily had returned to work on Thursday morning with a huge smile on her face. She was excited to be involved in the preparations. Carrie had tried asking her about her hospital appointment, but Lily was too excited to focus on her questions. All Carrie discovered was that the appointment had been 'good'.

"You go get changed, and I'll get Jamal to look for her while I arrange to transport the cake to the ballroom. We'll meet you there in half an hour?"

Camille suggested.

"Sounds perfect, thank you." Carrie waved goodbye to everyone and left them to admire her masterpiece. Without bumping into anyone, she made it up to her bedroom and let out a sigh of relief as the door closed behind her, and she was alone. She wanted to enjoy the moment but knew she didn't have enough time.

Half an hour later, Carrie waited for the lift to take her to the ballroom. She'd changed into her uniform for the day and had pulled her hair back into a somewhat presentable low bun. When they'd received the email with Veronica's requests for a new staff uniform, Lucas went shopping. Which was why Carrie's gold pumps pinched her toes. They were a smidge too small, but nobody had time to exchange them.

The lift pinged, and the door opened. A little squeal escaped Carrie as she saw Lucas standing alone inside the lift. He hadn't escaped the prescribed uniform. He wore his own black trousers, a white tucked-in shirt, and a gold tie. His hair was shorter and neater. He must have squeezed in a haircut yesterday evening.

"Hello, you." He smiled at her, looking up from the phone in his hand.

"Fancy seeing you here," Carrie replied, stepping inside the lift.

"Is this a good idea? Last time we were in a lift together, I tried to kiss you, and then the lift broke down."

"Well, why don't we change course, and I kiss you this time?" She looked up at him through her lashes and stepped closer.

"We have three floors to go, so you best be quick." He wrapped his arms around her and pulled her to him. Carrie let out a small squeak as her hands landed on his chest.

With little time to waste, she reached up on her tiptoes and pressed her lips to his. Time slowed and sped up all at the same time. Too soon, the lift pinged to signal its arrival. Carrie stepped back, and Lucas cleared his throat, moving his weight from one foot to the other.

"How's the cake looking? I've been hearing whispers about how amazing it is all morning." Lucas did his best to keep a professional tone as the door opened to a corridor with staff milling around.

"Why don't you come and take a look at it?" Carrie's eyes twinkled with mischief as she looked at him, her back towards the lift doors so nobody could see her flushed appearance.

"Come on then, lead the way." His eyes met hers, and they shared a look, wishing their moment together could have lasted longer.

Side by side, they walked down the corridor. Carrie noticed Lucas had stepped away, leaving some space between them. She was grateful for it, or else the temptation to reach out and touch him might be too much. There were people everywhere, from serving staff, sous chefs, and doormen, all doing what they could to help. Carrie even spotted a few of the housekeepers doing some last-minute polishing. There were also people she didn't recognise, brought in to help with the day. Three women frantically ran back and forth with boxes of flowers, arranging them into show-stopping displays in the ballroom. The wedding ceremony would take place in the ballroom. Then the guests would have canapés in the courtyard while they transformed the ballroom into the reception area for the wedding breakfast and the evening entertainment. They needed all the help they could get for the transformation, so today, Carrie was not just a pastry chef but also a runner.

"Let's see this cake, then." Lucas stepped aside to allow her to walk ahead of him into the ballroom. Carrie shot him a smile and held her breath, crossing her fingers by her sides, hoping the cake had made it there in one piece.

She gasped as she looked ahead to see the cake in the small kitchenette off of the ballroom. Carrie made a mental note to ensure she was around when they carried the cake into the ballroom. She needed to be there for any last-minute touch-ups.

"You're so talented," whispered Lucas. His breath tickled her neck as he leaned in to whisper. People rushed around them, but nobody took any notice. A glass shattered in the ballroom and it brought them both back to their senses. Lucas cleared his throat and straightened up.

"I ought to see if the kitchen needs any help," Carrie choked out.

"Yes, good idea. I need to visit the bride and

groom to check everything is running smoothly. I'll be working until tomorrow morning, so perhaps we can find a moment together once the guests have left." His hand brushed against hers as he walked past her.

"See you later." Carrie smiled. Her hand tingled from where his fingers had brushed against hers.

The kitchen was buzzing as Carrie walked in. They were still open to guests and the public, so there was double the amount of work, with only half the necessary staff. It was a big ask, but Carrie knew the team had the motivation to succeed.

"How can I help?" shouted Carrie over the deafening noise of plates clattering and oven fans whirring.

"Can you pipe cream cheese onto the blinis for the canapés?" the chef called across the kitchen.

"Yes, Chef," she replied. Trays of blinis covered a workbench on the far side of the kitchen, waiting for their toppings. Carrie spooned the cream cheese into the piping bag and piped the mixture into a small dome in the middle of each blini. Once finished, she added a pre-cut slice of salmon and squeezed a drop of lemon over them all. Each one looked perfect and delicious.

"Thanks, Carrie. Perhaps you could see if the dessert team needs any help with the restaurant side?" Chef suggested.

Carrie's work phone buzzed from her trouser pocket as she scooped a perfectly round ball of ice cream onto a plate beside a steaming apple tart. She hadn't eaten today, and the smell of caramelised sugar and cinnamon was intoxicating.

"Service!" she called, putting the plate onto the serving hatch. With a lull in orders, she pulled her phone out to see who was messaging her. Her eyes widened as she spotted the time. Lucas had texted to say the ceremony was over, and the guests had just left the ballroom, so they were about to transform the room.

"I'm needed in the ballroom. You've all got this. See you later!" Carrie smiled up at the overwhelmed dessert team.

"Thanks for your help, Carrie. Here, take this." Yevette, the dessert team head, handed her a plate with a fresh apple tart on it.

"Yvette, I could kiss you!" Carrie squealed, taking the plate and using the fork to break off a piece. She shoved it into her mouth as she walked away.

Carrie took the lift to savour a few seconds of peace and to eat her apple tart. It was steaming hot and burnt the roof of her mouth, but she didn't let that stop her.

"There you are! I was just coming to find you." Camille was waiting on the opposite side of the lift doors as they opened. "There's been an incident with the cake."

"What do you mean, an incident?" Carrie lowered the spoonful of tart back to the plate.

"One of the flowers was wonky and Lily tried to correct it. Only she lost her balance and caught the edge of the cake." Camille was wringing her hands and refused to meet Carrie's eye.

"Let's see the damage. Could you take this?" Carrie handed Camille the plate with her half-eaten tart on it. "I left some emergency buttercream and flowers in the kitchenette next to the ballroom. Would you get them? I'll go have a look."

"How are you this calm?"

Carrie chuckled at the question and went in search of the damaged cake. She didn't want to let on to Camille just how nervous she felt. Her entire reputation was pinned on this one cake. If it went wrong and word got out, she could lose her contract at *Hotel Mayfair*. She pushed aside those thoughts, not wanting to think about having to leave Lucas earlier than planned.

As Carrie pushed open the door to the ballroom, she could hear raised voices.

"What's going on?" she asked, looking at the scene in front of her. Lily was sitting on a chair with tears running down her face as a waitress stood shouting at her.

"She's ruined your cake," the woman spat out.

"Nobody has ruined anything. How dare you raise your voice at Lily?" Carrie's tone was carefully controlled, so she didn't lose her temper.

"*She* shouldn't be working here!" screeched the woman.

Carrie felt anger tear through her. She clasped her fists at her sides as her cheeks filled with heat.

"I'll go," Lily whispered.

"Don't you dare go anywhere!" Carrie put a hand on her shoulder to stop her from getting up and leaving. "The only person going anywhere is you." She turned her attention back to the waitress.

"What's going on?" Camille asked as she walked in holding the emergency cake repair kit.

"I'm afraid you're going to be down a waitress."

"You're not my manager. You can't fire me," argued the waitress.

"What's happened?" asked Camille.

Carrie explained the scene she'd walked in on and how the woman had spoken to Lily.

"I'll take you to Lucas. Carrie, would you mind stepping in as an extra waitress for me?"

"Of course."

Carrie put an arm around Lily's shoulders as they watched Camille escort the waitress out of the ballroom.

"I'm sorry, Carrie." Lily sniffed.

"Accidents happen." Carrie shrugged. "But you're not getting out of helping me fix it. Come on, let's see what we can do."

Carrie was relieved to find there was just a small patch of buttercream that had been taken off.

She added more and smoothed it out before putting a flower over the fix. It looked as though nothing had happened.

"There we go. Just like new!" Carrie took some pictures on her phone to send to Eve and Alice when she had a moment. Lily also took a picture to show her friends.

"Well done, you two. It looks fantastic!" Camille exclaimed. "Lily, Maria is in reception waiting for you. Thank you for all your help today."

"Yes, thank you, Lily. I'll see you next week."

"I can't wait to show Maria pictures of the cake. We're having a sleepover. Bye, Carrie." Lily left with a wave.

"Is she okay?" asked Camille as they watched Lily leave.

"She seemed to be. What happened to the waitress?"

"Lucas was fuming. He fired her on the spot and is intending to complain to the agency he hired her from."

"Good. I felt awful when I walked in. Lily was crying. She said she shouldn't be working here."

"I don't think she'll be saying anything like that again after the way Lucas just spoke to her. We'll make it up to Lily next week. Perhaps we could have afternoon tea with her during our break?"

"That sounds perfect."

"How's the cake?" Camille glanced towards it.

"You'd never know anything happened. All wedding cakes have a few knocks! I was well-prepared to fix it." Carrie shrugged.

"Accidents happen. Come on, there's so much to be done. I left Jamal organising a team to stack the chairs so we can put the tables out. We've cleared the dance floor, and the band should be here in fifteen minutes to set up. Are you ready to practise synchronised service?"

Carrie rolled her eyes. "You've got this all planned out."

"My parents used to host a lot of parties." Her tone suggested there was an entire story behind that brief statement, but there wasn't time to unpack it. "Right. You grab tablecloths and put them on once they've set up each table. There's a steamer in the cleaning closet next to the ballroom if they've got creased on their journey up from laundry."

The clock chimed midnight as the last few stragglers gathered their belongings and headed into the night. Carrie caught Lucas's eye across the room, and he smiled at her. They'd been so busy that she'd hardly caught a glance of him all evening. The day had been a tremendous success but at the expense of everyone's feet. Carrie didn't even want to think about how they had to do all this again for the other weddings.

"Goodnight. Thank you for coming." Carrie waved off the last guests and closed the ballroom doors behind them. The bride and groom had departed an hour ago, but the guests had opted to mill around and chat for a little longer before leaving, despite the many subtle hints from Lucas that the beds upstairs were sumptuous with cloud-like pillows.

"Finally," Lucas whispered. He popped into the kitchenette and came out with an armful of bin bags. "Everyone take a bag. Please try to keep recyclables in one bag and general rubbish in another. Just because we're tired doesn't mean our standards should drop."

Everyone returned a sarcastic 'yes, boss' and set to work clearing up. Carrie's eyes kept drifting to Lucas. He'd promised her some time together once the wedding was over, but they were both so exhausted she didn't know how they would keep their eyes open.

They left the room debris free and decided to tidy away the chairs and tables the following morning. Lucas sent everyone home for the night and promised them a hearty breakfast when they returned.

"Chef is going to have your guts when you tell him he's cooking a hearty breakfast for the staff," Carrie whispered as they watched everyone leave.

"I know. I'll have to cook it myself."

"Can you cook a breakfast?" Carrie raised her eyebrows.

"I can cook enough to burn some bacon and overdo some eggs."

"I'll help you."

"I'm sorry, Carrie. I promised you some time once everyone had gone, but I didn't expect to be this late or for us to be this exhausted." He suppressed a yawn.

"Don't worry about it. I'm just relieved we pulled it off."

"I've been wanting to talk to you all evening, but I've not had the chance. Thank you for standing up for Lily the way you did. I called her while you were serving dinner and she's okay. She told me you told off the waitress."

"It was horrible, Lucas. The way she spoke to Lily."

"Well, thank you for standing up for her."

"She's very welcome. I'd be lost without her. Are you going home now?"

Lucas glanced down at his watch and groaned. "No, by the time I get home, I'll only have an hour in bed before I need to get up and head back to work. We're fully booked with guests from the wedding, so I'll probably just catch a couple of hours in my office."

"You can't do that! Not after you've been running around today. Why don't you come back to my room? The bed's huge. I probably won't even notice you there."

"I've not made a very good impression on you if you think you can invite me into your bed and not even notice I'm there." Lucas teasingly raised his eyebrows at her.

"You know what I mean." Carrie swatted his

arm.

"I might take you up on your offer. I'll grab my overnight bag from my office and meet you in your room." He dipped his head and pressed his lips to her forehead.

"Do you know my room number?"

"Of course. I memorised it the second I saw you tiptoe through the reception in the early hours of the morning with your clunky boots and fiery hair." He winked at her before spinning on his heel and leaving her staring after him.

Carrie let herself into her bedroom and found her pyjamas, leaving them in the bathroom to change into. She unclipped her hair from its bun and let it tumble down her back. Her scalp ached from how tight her hair had been all day, so she gave it a quick massage. A knock on the door interrupted her, and Carrie went to let Lucas in.

"Ah, yes. Your upgraded room," he commented, looking around the space.

"Now can you see why I thought there'd been a mix-up?" she asked.

"I can, but I can also see why the owners gave you this suite. You're very talented Carrie Mackenzie." He dropped his bag in the hallway and strode over to her, cupping her face in his hands and bringing his lips to hers.

Their kiss was interrupted as a huge yawn rippled through Carrie. "Sorry." She blushed.

"No, don't be sorry. It's been a long day. Carrie, as much as I want to wrap you in my arms and take you to bed, I don't want our first time together to be like this. I want to take you out for dinner and woo you. Us stumbling into bed for a fumble while we're half asleep is not what I have in mind."

"I agree. So, is that an offer to take me out for dinner?"

"We both have Monday off. I'm not sure I can make dinner, but what about lunch?"

"Sounds perfect. I'm just going to change." Carrie awkwardly pointed towards the bathroom and excused herself. With the door closed behind her, creating a barrier between them, she slumped against it and let out a breath.

CHAPTER FOURTEEN

Carrie woke to the sound of a shrill alarm piercing the air. She rolled over to turn her phone off but collided with another body.

"Morning," Lucas said, reaching to turn the alarm off.

"Good morning," Carrie whispered.

"Did you sleep well?" he asked, pulling himself into a seated position.

"Fine. Did you?" Carrie rubbed her eyes.

"I don't think I've slept that well in a long time." He leaned down and kissed her. "Why did I agree to cook breakfast for everyone?" Lucas sighed, breaking off the kiss.

"Because you're a good person." Carrie smiled.

"As much as I would love to stay in bed with

you today, I should really get up and start breakfast prep." Lucas raised his arms above his head to stretch and Carrie couldn't tear her eyes away from the way his T-shirt pulled taut. She jumped out of bed, grabbing her dressing gown to throw on.

"Good idea. Would you like to use the shower first?" she offered.

"Yes, please. I'll only be a few minutes." He shot her a smile before disappearing into the bathroom with his overnight bag in hand.

Carrie shook her head and went to the window to look out. He was completely oblivious to the storm he'd stirred up inside her. The noise of the shower switching on resounded throughout the room. Carrie tried to block it out, but her mind wandered to Lucas in the shower. She cleared her throat and stepped away from the window, forcing her legs over to the coffee machine. There was a drawer filled with coffee pods, which Carrie pulled open and picked out a pod. She grabbed an espresso cup from the side and placed it under the machine's nozzle. The hiss of the machine made Carrie jump. Her entire body was on edge, her nerves fizzling, waiting for something that was not coming.

The coffee was scalding hot and not what she would usually have opted for, but Carrie threw the cup back and swallowed the espresso shot in one gulp.

"Rough morning?" quipped Lucas.

Carrie whirled around to see him leaning against the doorframe, dressed in smart navy trousers and a grey Ralph Lauren jumper. His hair was wet and beads of water ran down his forehead.

"Do you want a towel for your hair?" Carrie asked, trying her best to hide how flustered she felt.

"No, it'll be dry by the time I get downstairs. I'm going to go drop my bag in my office, then I'll get started in the kitchen. Shall I meet you down there?"

"Sounds good." Carrie forced herself to smile.

"Okay, see you soon." He returned her smile and left her standing, staring after him with the empty coffee cup in her hand.

"What was that about?" mumbled Carrie as the door clicked shut behind him. She shook her head and went straight to the shower, hoping the monotonous task of washing her hair would stop the barrage of doubts running through her head.

It didn't work. As Carrie furiously scrubbed at her scalp, she kept replaying his goodbye over and over. He'd kept the distance between them, not even crossing the room to give her a kiss goodbye. She let the water pour over her head as the realisation settled in the pit of her stomach like a tonne of lead; he'd wanted to get as far away from her as possible.

"It's just a fling," Carrie shouted as she turned the water off. It was ridiculous how much she was overthinking his actions. They weren't in a relationship and he'd spent the night with her because his only other option was his office floor.

Once dressed in a pair of leggings and a pale blue jumper over a black t-shirt, Carrie grabbed her phone and texted Eve to tell her the first wedding went well. She decided against telling her that Lucas had spent the night in her bed. It would only lead to questions Carrie didn't want to answer right now. A glance at the time told Carrie everyone would arrive shortly, ready to start their shift. She ought to see whether Lucas needed any help. Their awkward night together wasn't the staff's fault and everyone deserved a nice breakfast after yesterday's hard work. Her hair was still wet, so she twisted it into a neat bun at the nape of her neck. She didn't bother with any makeup since she'd be in the kitchen all day.

Carrie's nose screwed up as she walked into the little staff kitchen. Smoke filled her nostrils and her eyes stung as she stepped closer to see Lucas tipping the contents of a pan into the bin. She'd gone straight to the hotel's main kitchen, but the chef immediately informed her under no circumstances would he ever allow Lucas to cook in there. Instead, the chef had sent him to the staff's tiny kitchen.

"What are you doing?" Carrie asked. She opened a window before the smoke alarms went off and the hotel's sprinkler system activated.

"Cooking breakfast." He huffed and slammed the pan down on the worktop.

"Do you need some help?" she asked as her instinct kicked in and she buzzed around the kitchen, gathering ingredients before Lucas could accept her offer.

"I only fried some bacon," he said, looking at the pile of charred-beyond-recognition bacon in the bin.

"What are you trying to make?" asked Carrie, looking at the pots and pans Lucas had got out and left on the side, the stack of plates to the left, and a mountain of napkins.

"Bacon sandwiches. I had wanted to do a full English, but I lowered my expectations when Chef banished me to this kitchen."

"Be grateful Chef banished you. He'd have thrown you out if he'd seen how much smoke you've created from just attempting to fry bacon."

"I'm sorry," he whispered, standing back as Carrie stacked packets of bacon by the hob.

"Did you not have to learn how to cook when you lost your parents?" she asked. "Here, you can start buttering the bread." She handed him the butter and a knife.

"At first, neighbours and friends dropped dinners off for us. Then my sister's support worker started cooking for us and on her days off we get a takeaway or one of those meals you throw in the oven. I can boil pasta."

The door to the kitchen swung open and Camille walked in. "I heard you'd been banished to the galley kitchen. Now I can see why." Camille laughed as the smoke lingered in the room.

"I've had to take over." Carrie pointed to the hob in front of her where she had two pans frying bacon.

"Lucas, why don't you get teas and coffee for everyone in the staffroom? I'll take over here. I'm sure Carrie could do with some help, not a liability."

Lucas looked relieved at the offer to swap with Camille. "I'll see you two in a bit. Shall I send some people down to bring up plates of sandwiches?"

"Yes, please," Carrie said, filling a plate with cooked bacon. Camille immediately jumped in and started filling sandwiches with it. "Take these with you."

"So?" asked Camille the second Lucas was out of earshot.

"So what?" Carrie replied, focusing on the new packet of bacon she was opening.

"It didn't escape my notice that you hung back with Lucas as we all left last night. What happened?"

A thousand thoughts traipsed through Carrie's mind at once. They'd agreed to keep their fling a secret from everybody at the hotel, but Carrie couldn't bear it any longer. Camille had already guessed something was going on, and she needed to talk to someone about it and about how she was feeling. As much as she loved talking to Eve, she needed someone who could stand in front of her and tell her to stop being so silly.

"Nothing happened, but Lucas came back to my room and slept in my bed last night."

"He slept in your bed and you expect me to

believe nothing happened?"

"Nothing happened, Camille." Carrie let out a forlorn sigh as she turned each rasher.

"Wait, really? Nothing? Not even a cheeky little fumble?" Camille stopped buttering bread and turned all her full attention on Carrie.

"Not even a cheeky little fumble," Carrie confirmed.

"What was he thinking? You're gorgeous, and he was in bed with you."

"He didn't even kiss me goodbye this morning. Well, he kissed me in bed, but then he just showered and left."

"You think he regretted staying with you?" Camille asked.

"He couldn't get out of my room quick enough. Maybe he had second thoughts in the shower?" Carrie shrugged.

"I hate to break up this little tête-à-tête, but I've been sent for more sandwiches." Jamal was standing at the doorway, peering in.

"Of course. The bacon is done. Camille just needs to make up the sandwiches." Carrie tipped out the bacon onto a plate and started the next batch.

"For the record, if he regrets spending the night with you, then he's an absolute idiot who is not worthy of your time." Jamal turned on his heel and walked away with two plates of sandwiches.

"He's right," Camille chimed in.

Once the sandwiches had been made, Carrie and Camille took a plate for themselves and headed up to the staffroom to join everyone.

"Ah, here they are. Thank you to both Carrie and Camille for our breakfast." Lucas beamed at them as they walked through the door. "I'll get you both a drink in a minute, but before that, I'd like to thank everyone." Lucas launched into a speech, thanking everybody for their hard work yesterday.

Carrie smiled around at everyone as they trailed past her and thanked her for breakfast. Camille had wandered off to speak to her team, leaving Carrie alone by the coffee machine.

"What would you like?" Lucas asked, moving away from the crowd to where she was.

"A cappuccino, please. Don't forget, you have to manually stop the machine," she joked, trying to ease the tension between them.

"Coming up. I'm sorry about this morning," he murmured, inching closer so nobody could overhear their conversation.

"It's fine," she lied.

"No, it's not fine. I just panicked and ran. When I woke up to see you lying beside me, I can't even begin to describe how happy it made me. I wanted nothing more than to wrap my arms around you and pull you close, watching as your eyes flickered open for the first time today. I had this overwhelming urge to be the first thing you saw when you woke up. Then my alarm went off, waking you, and I panicked. It took all my resolve to break our kiss and get in that shower. Then my thoughts got the better of me. I really like you, Carrie. This is just supposed to be a fling. I got scared by how much I want to wake up next to you every day."

Carrie gulped as she took a moment to process everything Lucas had said. He seemed to understand, and he turned his attention to her coffee as he poured in sugar and stirred it. Carrie's thoughts had scattered, and she had very little hope of putting them back together again before he expected some sort of reply.

"I don't know what to say, Lucas," she admitted.

"You don't have to say anything, Carrie. I just wanted you to know that my behaviour this morning was my fault. It had nothing to do with you."

"So, is this you ending things between us?" Carrie took the coffee from his outstretched hand and forced herself to take a sip. It was the very last thing she felt like, but she needed a distraction.

"No, I don't want to end this. Do you?" Lucas's brow furrowed.

"I don't want to end this either. You're right, I have to go home, but we still have time. Let's have some fun together and worry about me leaving nearer the time."

"So, can I still take you out tomorrow?" he asked, a huge grin on his face.

"I'd love that," she replied, mirroring his smile.

CHAPTER FIFTEEN

"What shall I wear?" Carrie asked, staring at the sparse selection of clothes in her wardrobe.

"What are you doing today?" Eve replied, her voice floating through the phone, which was propped up on a pile of pillows in the middle of the bed. She was squinting over FaceTime to see Carrie's petite figure against the vast wardrobe.

"I don't know," replied Carrie, pulling out three different jumpers, inspecting them and then putting them all back.

"Carrie, just relax. If he were taking you anywhere you needed to be smartly dressed, he would have told you. Just go for some jeans, a nice t-shirt, and some comfortable shoes in case he's planning to make you walk far."

"Okay, jeans and a nice t-shirt," repeated Carrie. She pulled out a pair of blue fitted jeans and a soft grey t-shirt with long sleeves and a square neck.

"That looks perfect," Eve called. There was a huge clatter in the background and she turned to look at it.

"Do you need to go?" asked Carrie, placing the clothes on the bed and picking her phone up so she could see Eve.

"I'm sorry, Carrie. Lachlan is interviewing hotel managers today, which means I'm having to pick up his work, too."

"That's fine. How're interviews going?"

"Terribly. The only people applying are locals and they just don't have the necessary experience. We had one applicant whose previous experience was in farming." Another clatter in the background had Eve running to the other side of the kitchen.

"I'll let you go. Speak soon."

"Text me to let me know how your date goes! Love you." Eve put the phone down before Carrie could reply. She wanted to protest that it wasn't a date, but even she wasn't sure she could say it very convincingly. Could it be considered a date if they were just having a fling?

Lucas texted Carrie to say he was just leaving and would be at the hotel in half an hour. Carrie felt as though she had an entire aviary of birds flying around in her stomach. She pulled on her clothes and added a pair of small silver hoops to her ears and slipped on a matching ring Eve had gifted her at Christmas. Since it was her day off, she was enjoying being able to have her hair down and so she smoothed her fingers through her curls in an attempt to tame them. It did very little to help.

After applying some basic make-up, Carrie pulled on some trainers and grabbed her phone and cardholder, slipping them into her pocket. Lucas should be there any moment, so she went down to reception to wait for him.

The reception area was quiet since it was past check-out time. Their long-weekend guests had all departed and there was a slight lull before the midweek guests checked in. Carrie settled herself on one of the sofas and pulled her phone out of her pocket to check her emails. Lachlan had forwarded her the CVs for some students so she could think about having some help in the kitchen when she returned. Once the hotel was open, they hoped to be much busier. As Carrie scrolled through them, she thought about how she would soon have to leave Lily behind. She wasn't the most efficient help, but she always put a smile on her face and made her excited to start work in the morning. Lily's enthusiasm was contagious, and she was always happy to sample anything Carrie baked.

Her phone vibrated in her hand, making her jump. Carrie opened the text from Lucas to say he was around the corner but didn't want to come in. She texted him back saying not to worry, she'd be with him in a couple of minutes. He had a valid point. If the staff saw Lucas picking her up on their day off, they would gossip.

It was a beautiful sunny day as Carrie crossed the road to meet Lucas by the entrance of Green Park tube station. As she neared, she spotted him standing there in jeans, a jumper, and sunglasses. Her heart fluttered before breaking into a thunderous pounding rhythm, causing Carrie to lose her breath momentarily. She sucked in a deep breath of the London air and was hit by the smell of exhaust fumes. For a brief moment, a longing for her home and the fresh air filled her. But she forced herself to keep moving and focus on Lucas. He'd spotted her walking towards him and a big smile spread across his face as he raised his hand to give her a quick wave.

"Good morning," he said, stepping forward to greet her.

"Morning," she replied. Her feet stilled as she waited to see what he would do next. Lucas reached for her hand and pulled her towards him, capturing her lips with his as she stumbled against him.

"Very good morning," he murmured against her lips as he pulled back.

"Indeed. So, what do you have planned for today?" she asked. She stepped back but kept her fingers threaded through his.

"It's a surprise. Come on." He walked towards the tube station, pulling her along beside him.

"You're really not going to tell me?" she asked, almost having to jog to keep up with his long strides.

"Nope. Come on, keep up."

He kept their destination a secret from her as they hopped from one train to another. Eventually disembarking at Liverpool Street Station. The hot, stuffy air hit them as they walked along the platform amongst the crowds of commuters and tourists.

"Where now?" asked Carrie. She followed him up the stairs to the exit.

"This way," he said as they walked out onto the busy street above.

Carrie followed Lucas down a side street until he stopped outside a building. Glancing upwards, she saw the name of the place and let out a squeal of excitement. He'd taken her to *Junkyard Golf.* It was somewhere she'd wanted to go for ages, but hadn't had the chance last time she was in London.

"What do you think?" he asked.

"This is great!"

"You sure? We can do something more serious if you'd like. Sightseeing? Brunch? The museums?" He rubbed his fingers over her knuckles.

"Lucas, we've spent the last few weeks doing nothing but being serious. I want to do something fun and forget our responsibilities for an hour. Come on!" She pulled his hand and led them through the door.

They checked in. Lucas had booked the *'Dirk'* course, which was 90s themed.

"You're a little early, so why don't you grab a drink at the bar?" The woman checking them in suggested.

Hand in hand, they wandered over to the bar and stared at the cocktail menu.

"Is it too early?" Carrie wondered out loud.

"It's five o'clock somewhere!" commented the barman.

"Come on. We agreed we wouldn't be serious today. Let's ignore the time and have a cocktail. Besides, I'm so bad at mini golf you might need a drink before you have to watch me."

"Okay, I'll have a bubblegum sunset." The idea of vodka, Cherry Sourz, bubblegum, and sweets all in one drink had swayed Carrie.

Lucas squinted at the menu. "Could I get a Bourbon Bakewell?" he asked, settling on the bourbon, Disaronno, Campari and Maraschino cherry concoction.

Music thumped around the room as the barman handed them their lavish drinks. They looked as though they would glow in the dark if given the opportunity.

"Cheers," said Carrie. She held up her glass. Lucas smiled and clinked his glass against hers.

"How is it?" he asked as he watched her take a sip.

The overwhelming taste of sickly sweetness and alcohol assaulted Carrie's tastebuds, but she went back for another sip. "It's amazing!" she called over the music. Shania Twain's That Don't Impress Me Much played, and with the alcohol buzzing through her veins, Carrie felt her nerves tingle with happiness. Only in her wildest dreams would she have imagined being in London on a date with Lucas.

"You can go onto the course now," the barman

called over to them.

They thanked him and took their drinks over. Spice Girls blared out over the speakers as they picked up their clubs and balls. Lucas took a scoresheet and a little pencil so he could record their progress. There were a few people playing ahead of them, but nobody was behind, so they could take their time.

"Do you want to go first?" Lucas asked, setting his drink on a ledge and pulling out the scorecard, filling their names in.

Carrie took a sip of her drink before placing it next to Lucas's. She took her ball and club and walked up to the start. Whilst she hadn't played much mini golf in her life, she had hit many shots on the McLeod's estate under the watchful eye of the McLeod brothers who were quick to teach her how to hone her aim, and how to control the speed at which she hit the ball. Focusing on the ball, Carrie did her best not to allow her surroundings to put her off. It was a fun date, but she couldn't quell her competitiveness. With the tiny club in her hand, Carrie lined the shot up and expertly hit the ball. She held her breath as she watched the neon ball navigate the course and roll to a stop just inches from the hole.

"Woah!" Lucas called from behind her.

"Beginner's luck." She shrugged it off, not sure whether she could recreate the shot again.

"Let's hope the same goes for me." Lucas chuckled as he took her spot at the start of the course.

Carrie bit her lip to stop herself from chuckling. Lucas was standing head-on to the course and swinging the club as if he were playing croquet.

"Wait!" shouted Carrie as he lined up the club to swing it and hit the ball.

"What?" Lucas whipped his head around to look at her.

"Are you being serious?"

"What do you mean?"

"You're actually going to take a shot like that?"

"Like what?" He looked down at the club, still clasped in his hands.

"Do you know how to hold the club?"

"Like this?"

A sly smile spread across Carrie's face as she walked over to him. "Turn like this." She stood beside him, demonstrating how he should be standing.

"Okay, now what?" he asked.

Carrie walked behind him and wrapped her arms around his waist, her chest pressed flush against his back.

"Like this." She reached for his hands and wrapped them around the club, showing him how to gently swing the club.

"Can you show me one more time? But I think you need to get a little closer."

Carrie couldn't see his face, but she knew if

she could, his eyes would be sparkling with mischief and his lips would be curled into a wicked smile.

"You're on your own now." Carrie stepped back and grabbed her drink, needing something to keep her hands busy as she yearned for the feeling of his body pressed against hers.

"Where shall we go for lunch?" Carrie asked Lucas as she handed their golf clubs and balls to the woman at reception. "Thank you." She smiled at the woman before turning back to Lucas.

"I thought we could head back towards the hotel and eat somewhere nearby. I'll have to head home shortly after we eat, so I'd rather leave you closer to the hotel."

"Okay." Carrie's smile froze as she hid her disappointment. She'd hoped today with Lucas would never end.

"Is there anywhere you'd like to go for lunch?" Lucas asked as they were sitting on the tube. He'd pulled her hand into his and intertwined their fingers. The alcohol had caught up with Carrie, so she rested her head on his shoulder. As they sped through the tunnels, Carrie caught their reflection in the opposite windows. Her mind wandered as she saw the couple reflected in the window. She had to pull her thoughts back and remind herself that they were just a fling. Nothing more.

"I don't mind." She shrugged, still wrapped up

in her thoughts and not paying much attention to what Lucas was saying.

"Oh. I was hoping you might have a suggestion."

"Sorry." She lifted her head from his shoulder. The movement felt as though she'd pulled away from him. The reminder that they were just a fling was like a wall between them. Becoming higher each time Carrie remembered. And yet, her feelings still grew, determined to find a way over the wall, no matter how hard she tried to halt them. Carrie racked her brains for somewhere new and exciting to eat, but her thoughts were too scrambled from Lucas's proximity. "What about Pizza Pilgrims?" she said, unable to think of anywhere else.

"Pizza sounds amazing." He let go of her hand and wrapped his arm around her shoulders, encouraging her to lean in and rest her head on his shoulder. Carrie closed her eyes as her head rested on Lucas and inhaled his scent.

"Come on, sleepyhead. We're here," he announced, shaking her awake as the train pulled into the station. He reached out a hand for her to take.

Lucas kept Carrie's hand in his as they exited the station and walked through the crowds of Regent's Street. Carrie led Lucas to the restaurant and took him to the table she'd sat by herself at on her first full day in London. Lucas excused himself to find the bathroom, and Carrie sat back in her seat and let out a sigh of contentment. A soft breeze blew through her hair, brushing it against the back of her neck, tickling her. As she waited for Lucas to return, Carrie mused over how her life had changed in the few weeks since she'd last sat at this table. Back then, she'd thought Lucas was just a grumpy employee who she'd made a terrible impression on. But now, here she was, worried her feelings towards him were growing. She kept trying to catch them, to rein them in, but they were growing too fast for her. Carrie knew that if she wasn't careful, she'd run head-on into heartbreak, but his charming smile made it all seem worth it.

"Do you know what you're having?" asked Lucas, slipping into the seat opposite her.

"I'm just going to have a Margherita with extra olives." The sickly sweet cocktail was doing somersaults in Carrie's stomach, so she opted for a plain pizza.

"Olives? On a pizza?" asked Lucas, his eyebrows raised.

"It's delicious!"

"Sounds disgusting."

"You can try some." Carrie scooted forward in her chair to lean across the table, closing the gap between them.

"What if I don't want to?" He looked at her from over his menu.

"Then I'm getting up and leaving you to have lunch on your own. I can't be seen with anyone who isn't willing to try new foods." She shrugged her shoulders, leant back in her chair, and examined her nails as if walking away would be easy.

"Fine, I'll try some." He smiled, but Carrie hadn't missed the flash of panic in his eyes as she threatened to leave.

The waiter came, and they ordered their lunch. Lucas ordered a plain Margherita with no extra toppings. Carrie asked for water, and Lucas ordered a beer. The waiter scribbled their order on a piece of paper and took their menus away. Lucas reached across the table and took her hand in his.

"I'm going to miss you," he whispered, staring down at their intertwined hands.

"Don't, Lucas. I don't want to think about it." Carrie felt a crushing panic rise in her chest and threaten to burst. If she explored her feelings, the fear would explode and it would consume her.

"I wish I could come with you, Carrie. If life were different, I'd follow you across the globe. I'm addicted to you and your passion for life. In the short time I've known you, I'm sure my heart has grown. You make me excited to get out of bed each day because I know there's a chance I'll see your beautiful smile." His eyes were set on their hands.

"Come with me, Lucas. You're so put-together; always weighing up the risks with everything. For once, don't do that. Lachlan needs a manager for the hotel he's opening and I think you'd be perfect for it. One word from me and I know he'd give you the job." Carrie was on the edge of her seat, gripping Lucas's hand in both of hers. She was willing his eyes to look up at her, but they were resolutely focused on their hands.

"Carrie, I would love nothing more than to come with you, and if life was different, I would. But it's not just me I have to think about. My sister's life is here in London. I could never drag her to Scotland with me." He let out a pained sigh.

Carrie's hand loosened, and he pulled his hand back. It was an impossible situation. Despite not knowing him for long, Carrie knew he wasn't capable of making such a selfish decision to uproot his sister, and she respected him for that. But it meant that there was always going to be an end to whatever was between them.

"Would you rather get this to takeaway?" Carrie choked out. She felt as though her throat were closing in on itself.

"Carrie, I don't want to lose a second with you, but if you'd rather go back to the hotel now, I understand." His eyes finally flickered up to meet hers.

"I don't want to lose a second with you either," she whispered, unable to tear her eyes from his gaze.

"What about long-distance until your sister has her own life?" Carrie suggested. She refused to give up so easily. There had to be a way.

"She'll always need me, Carrie."

The waiter interrupted them and placed their drinks and food down on the table in front of them. It took all of Carrie's energy to smile and mumble a thank you.

"Let's drop the subject for now and just enjoy the rest of today." Carrie glanced down at her pizza as the smell of cheese drifted up towards her.

"Come on, cut me a slice with an olive on." Lucas winked at her, opening his mouth for her to feed him.

Carrie ignored the way her stomach fluttered and fed him a piece of her pizza. Her eyes lingered on his mouth as he licked his lips and closed them.

"I hate to admit this, but you're right. Olives taste amazing on pizza." He conceded, distracting Carrie from the way his lips moved.

"Told you so."

The carefree atmosphere returned as they left the serious topics behind and enjoyed their lunch together. Carrie glanced down at her plate to discover she'd finished her pizza. She'd scarcely noticed each bite. As she tried to recall the taste, she realised she couldn't. Her mind had been focused on Lucas. On what he was saying, the way the edges of his eyes creased as he smiled, and the way his foot crept up her leg underneath the table.

"I'm just going to make a call," he announced once their empty plates had been taken.

Carrie nodded and watched as he wandered off, his phone pressed to his ear. He paced around the little courtyard, his hands waving in the air, gesticulating whatever he was saying on the phone. He was too far away for Carrie to read his lips to decipher the conversation.

"I've just freed up the afternoon," he

announced, pulling her up from her chair and into his arms. "I've also just paid the bill so we can leave now and head straight back to the hotel," he whispered in her ear, his lips grazing the top of her neck.

They walked back, holding hands. Lucas pulled Carrie to a stop as they neared the hotel. He cupped the back of her head with his hand and bent down to kiss her. Carrie's fingers ached to pull at the edge of his jumper and tug it over his head so she could trail her fingers down his chest. Lucas pulled back, resting his head against her forehead as they both fought to control their breathing.

"Go in on your own. I'm going to use the staff entrance," he whispered, his voice breathless.

Carrie nodded her reply, unable to speak. He kissed her forehead and strode off in the opposite direction. She shook her head and focused on getting into the hotel and up to her room, with no one noticing her swollen lips or dazed expression.

It was a miracle, but Carrie avoided everyone on the way to her room. It was peak check-in time, so everyone was busy tending to the guests' needs.

Once in her room, Carrie closed the door and leaned against it. Her fingers flew to her lips and traced them. She held her breath as she heard footsteps coming down the hallway. As a knock sounded on her door, she let out the breath she'd been holding.

"Hello, you." She smiled, opening the door a crack to let Lucas slip in.

"Sorry, I got held up by—"

Carrie silenced him by reaching up on her tiptoes and pressing her lips to his. His arms snaked around her waist, and he walked her backwards until she was against the door. This time, Carrie didn't hold back. Her fingers went to the hem of his jumper and tugged at it. She broke the kiss to pull it over his head.

"If I'm losing clothes, so are you." He pulled her into his arms, throwing her over his shoulder and carrying her to the bedroom. She landed with a squeal on the bed as he walked over to the windows to close the curtains. In the dim lighting of the room, Carrie let her eyes travel down his bare back. The muscles in his shoulders tensed as he reached up to close the curtains in one swift movement. She took a shallow breath, watching him turn around to face her again.

"You're wearing far too many clothes," he said, walking over to her in just a couple of strides.

CHAPTER SIXTEEN

Carrie stretched out an arm, expecting to feel Lucas beside her, but her fingers slid across a cold, empty space. She rolled over and looked at the crumpled side, before casting her eyes around the dark room, looking for any sign that Lucas had been there. His aftershave lingered in the air, but that was all. She reached out and checked the time on her phone. It was almost half-four in the morning. Carrie threw an arm over her eyes and tried to push away the memories of yesterday. The way Lucas trailed kisses from her neck down to her chest. She shook her head and forced herself to get up. If she stayed in bed, she'd only replay their time together over and over. Carrie showered, not bothering to wash her hair. It would take too long to dry, and she wanted to get into the kitchen as soon as possible. Nothing helped her sift through her thoughts like baking. Her stomach rumbled, reminding her she'd missed dinner. She didn't know what time Lucas had left. He hadn't left her a note or texted her to let her know he was home safely. It was just a fling. She shouldn't have expected him to stay the night.

The kitchen was awash with preparations for the day, but Carrie slipped past everybody and went straight to her area. Her fingers itched to create a masterpiece and challenge her abilities. She slipped her earbuds in and scrolled through the playlists on her phone, shying away from any 90s music that might remind her of her date with Lucas. Opting for a playlist filled with tunes from musicals, Carrie pulled out the ingredients for choux pastry. She'd seen some beautiful creations while scrolling through Pinterest and wanted to see if she could recreate them. As the pan warmed up over the heat, Carrie mixed with her wooden spoon. With each scrape around the pan, she pushed away another memory of Lucas's hands roaming across her body. If she were at home, Eve would have prised the information from her by now over steaming hot cups of coffee and leftover croissants. But without her friend there, Carrie had reverted to the quiet introvert she had been before Eve had whirled into the McLeod's castle.

"Oh, shut up, Carrie. Stop throwing yourself a pity party for one," she grumbled to herself, taking the pan off the heat.

Carrie focused on piping the choux onto the baking tray. Her concentration meant there was little room in her mind to think of anything else which suited her. Usually, afternoon tea consisted of miniature desserts. However, Carrie was piping full-sized éclairs. If they were small, she wouldn't have the space to decorate them how she wanted.

She put the tray in the oven and went over to the kettle to make herself a coffee. While the kettle boiled, Carrie pulled out her phone to see if Lucas had messaged her. There was nothing on either her personal or her work phone. "It's just a fling, Carrie," she mumbled to herself.

The coffee was bitter, but it was caffeinated, so Carrie forced herself to drain the cup. Her nose crinkled, but she gulped it down. She dumped her empty mug in the sink to wash up later, and the timer went off for the éclairs. Carrie put them to the side to cool as she turned her attention to mixing three different buttercreams. She mixed a cream-coloured vanilla-flavoured one, a pale purple blackberry-flavoured one, and a pink buttercream with a hint of rose water. She hadn't mixed the flavours before, but she hoped the tart blackberry would cut through the sweetness of the vanilla and rose. Carrie would pipe a plain cream in the centre of the éclairs before serving them.

With the piping bags prepared and lined up, Carrie set out the éclair shells in front of her. She took a deep breath and pushed every thought of Lucas from her mind. She had to concentrate to make these perfect and couldn't risk her hands shaking as his feather-light touch filled her mind.

It took Carrie over an hour to pipe thirty éclairs, but as she stepped back, she puffed out her chest. They looked spectacular. Each one had piped purple flowers, cream-coloured stars, and she'd filled the gaps with a beautiful swirl of pink. They were an explosion of pastel-coloured, floral, buttercream. Carrie pulled her phone out and snapped a picture of them for the hotel's social media and to send to Eve.

She attached the picture to a message; *Not bad for a morning's work xxx*

Carrie put the éclairs into the industrial-sized fridge in her work area, ready to get them out for the afternoon tea service. She'd made a couple of extras and had eaten one for her breakfast. The sweetness had been a little much, so she'd swirled some blackberry jam into the cream piped into the centre, and it had been perfect.

"You're early," said a voice from behind her.

Carrie whirled around to face Lucas. He was dressed in his usual work uniform of a white shirt and navy trousers. The rough stubble that had been on his chin yesterday was gone and his hair was neatly styled away from his face.

"You left," she whispered, not wanting anyone to overhear her conversation.

"I'm sorry. I had to go home before I started my shift. You looked so peaceful. I didn't want to wake you." He glanced around before he reached forward and pushed a strand of hair behind her ear.

Carrie had put it into a tight bun, but a few strands had come loose.

"You could have texted me." She shrugged, moving her face away from his fingers.

"Ah, yes. I think I might have left my phone in your room."

"I need to go up and redo my hair. Do you want to come with me to look for it?"

"I don't think that's a good idea." His eyes darkened, and Carrie watched his throat bob as he swallowed.

"Okay." Carrie looked down at her feet. The rejection slid through her like ice through her veins.

"No, Carrie. I want to, but if I come with you, neither of us will be leaving your room before dinnertime."

"Oh," she squeaked.

Lucas stepped forward again, closing the distance between them. He stretched his fingers out and trailed them down the side of her face. "I'm really sorry I left without saying goodbye. I knew I had very little time to get home and then back to work in time to start my shift." His thumb brushed her lips and Carrie felt her heart rate quicken.

"Carrie?" Lily's voice called.

They sprung apart, and Carrie stepped back until she hit the worktop. She took a deep breath, waiting for Lily to appear. For once, she was grateful for the woman's love of shouting across rooms for her.

"Lily!" Carrie beamed, hoping her smile

wouldn't give her away.

"You'll never guess what I did yesterday!" Lily bounced into the workspace, pushing past Lucas, who was standing staring at Carrie, his eyes not leaving her.

"What did you do yesterday?" Carrie suppressed a giggle as she thought about how Lily would never guess what she got up to yesterday.

"I had a sleepover!" Lily announced, clapping her hands together.

Carrie felt her forced smile slip into something more natural. It was impossible to fake emotions around Lily. Her enthusiasm was contagious.

"I bet that was so much fun!" Carrie didn't tell Lily that she'd also had a sleepover. Her eye caught Lucas's over the top of Lily's head, and she knew he was thinking the same thing. "I made something for you, Lily. There's extra if you'd like one, too, Lucas."

Carrie pulled the tray of éclairs from the fridge and she was met with gasps from both Lily and Lucas.

"Look at them!" Lily cried, diving straight in to swipe one from the tray.

"Carrie, these are beautiful," Lucas whispered, looking between her and the éclairs.

"Thank you." She smiled, hoping her face didn't give away the butterflies fluttering in her stomach from the look he'd given her.

He reached out to take one, purposely brushing his fingers against hers. Carrie's hands trembled, and she gripped the tray harder so she didn't drop it.

"These are amazing!" Lily shouted, her mouth full of the éclair.

Carrie chuckled. The moment between her and Lucas had been broken. He took a bite of his and moaned at the taste.

"She's right, this is amazing. Are they going out with today's afternoon tea?" asked Lucas. She could see his entire demeanour had changed. He was in work mode now.

"They are," Carrie confirmed.

"Have you met Lucy?"

Carrie shook her head. She didn't know who Lucy was.

"She's our social media manager. Only works two days a week, but she's in today. I'm going to get her to come down and take a few photographs of these for the hotel's social media. Don't worry about anything. She'll stage it all and take the pictures." Lucas finished the last bite of his éclair and went to pull out his phone before realising he didn't have it on him.

"I'm going to make myself a coffee," Carrie announced. She pulled her room key from her pocket and slid it into Lucas's hand as she walked past him. They didn't have to worry about Lily spotting anything, as she was still engrossed in her éclair.

"I'll return it to you as soon as I can," he whispered.

"Do you want anything from the staff room, Lily?" Carrie asked.

Lily shook her head to say no and Carrie walked off in the direction of the staff room, away from Lucas.

As promised, Lucas returned her room key as soon as he could. He found her in the staffroom eating a sandwich before the afternoon tea rush.

"I've just seen Lily," he commented, sitting down opposite her. The staffroom wasn't busy, but there were enough people in there for news to spread fast if he sat beside her.

"Ah, yes. She's very determined." Carrie had left Lily with a fresh batch of shortbread and piping bags filled with pastel-coloured buttercream. She'd begged Carrie to teach her how to recreate the piping on the éclairs. So far, she'd piped a flower, but her finish was clumsy and it smudged whenever she moved the nozzle. But Lily was determined and so she'd opted to spend her lunch break practising. Carrie had tried to explain to Lily that piping took years to master, but she was stubborn and refused to give up. Knowing she wouldn't persuade Lily otherwise, Carrie had left her to practise. Jamal was at the workstation across and she'd asked him to poke his head around the corner now and then to check she wasn't eating all the biscuits.

"You have such patience with her. Thank

you." Lucas smiled warmly at her.

"Someone once had patience with me and look where I am." She took a bite of her egg and cress sandwich.

"I wish you were staying, Carrie. I'd love someone with your patience and passion to help launch an initiative at the hotel to help young people find their passion in hospitality and the kitchens."

"I'm sorry, Lucas." It was a painful reminder that their time together was limited.

"Please, don't apologise. I just know you could do wonders."

"I have had a chat with Lachlan about starting our own initiative at his castle restaurant. We could even extend it to the hotel side once it's up and running. I'd like to inspire as many people as possible and give others the chance that was given to me."

"Perhaps we'll visit you in Scotland one day." Lucas's smile was still plastered on his face, but it no longer reached his eyes.

"I'd like that," Carrie whispered, putting down her sandwich. Her stomach churned at the thought of having to say goodbye to *Hotel Mayfair*. Leaving Lucas would be painful, but she'd also be leaving behind all of her new friends. She cleared her throat, pushing the thoughts from her mind. Her time in London wasn't up yet. There was no point in upsetting herself now.

Lucas cleared his throat and straightened up. Without realising, he'd started leaning across the coffee table between them. "I ought to leave you to your break. Thanks for this." He slid her key card across the table after checking nobody was nearby to see.

"See you around?" She hadn't meant it to come out as a question.

"Keep your phone handy." He winked at her and left, leaving her to her sandwich.

Carrie chewed the sandwich, not tasting it as she slipped her keycard into her pocket. Leaving Scotland had been easy because she always knew she'd be coming back. But leaving *Hotel Mayfair* would be entirely different. Camille had promised to visit her at the castle when she went travelling, but what about everyone else? Jamal was intent on breaking into the London theatrical scene. His work here as a sous chef was just to fund his lifestyle while he waited for his big break. Carrie's throat closed up as she realised she might never see Lily or Lucas again.

"Carrie! Afternoon tea service starts in ten minutes!" Camille burst through the door, her hair flying in all directions.

"Oh, no!" Carrie had lost track of the time while she was talking to Lucas. She dropped her half-eaten sandwich in the bin and followed Camille back to the kitchens.

Lily had pulled out the cake stands and was spreading them out across the worktop. "Lily, you're a star!" Carrie beamed at her as she grabbed her apron and started pulling cakes and Tupperware boxes from the fridge.

"Look what I did!" Lily announced, pointing to the iced biscuits.

"Lily, they're amazing!" Carrie didn't have the time to stop and look at them, but she didn't want to disappoint Lily. While they weren't as delicate as the piping Carrie had done earlier that day, they were still amazing. "Why don't we do afternoon tea service, then we'll go round and give your biscuits to our favourite members of staff?" Carrie suggested. She couldn't serve them to the guests as she hadn't been watching Lily ice them and she knew she had the tendency to stick her finger in the buttercream to try it.

With Camille's help, they stacked the twenty-four cake stands for the people booked in for afternoon tea, and a few extras who had dropped by on the off chance they had space. Lucy had been around earlier and had set up a beautiful cake stand filled with Carrie's perfect creations. Carrie had watched in awe as Lucy pulled edible flowers and gold leaf to transform the display into something truly magical. The pictures had gone live on the hotel's social media and had led to an influx of bookings. Carrie had also asked Lucy to send her the pictures so she could recreate her set-up.

As promised, after service, Carrie and Lily dropped her biscuits off to various staff members. Everyone received theirs with a big smile on their faces and marvelled at Lily's masterpiece.

"I'm going to take one to Lucas. Are you

coming?" Lily asked as they returned to the kitchen to distribute the final few biscuits.

"Sorry, Lily, but I need to borrow Carrie." Camille jumped in to save her. She'd joined Carrie and Lily as they trailed around the hotel, giving the biscuits to their favourite staff members.

"Okay. See you tomorrow." Lily waved goodbye and took two biscuits with her.

"I have a break. Shall we get out of here? It's lovely outside." Camille untied her apron and put it down on Carrie's workspace.

"Let's take the leftover biscuits, get a coffee from the staffroom, and walk over to Green Park," Carrie suggested.

It was another sunny day, and it felt as though everyone in London had decided to visit Green Park that afternoon. They'd been lucky so far with the April weather, with just a handful of grey and rainy days. May was in a few days, and Carrie hoped the rain would hold off for a little longer. She still had so much she wanted to do in London. They ambled over to a spot underneath a tree with fewer people milling around.

"I'm going to miss this," Carrie commented, watching people wandering by.

"Carrie, stop being so dramatic. Your time with us isn't up yet. You're moping as though you're going home next week. If you don't stop it, you'll ruin your time here." Camille's tone was stern as she pulled the Tupperware box out of her canvas tote bag. She opened the lid and handed Carrie a biscuit.

"You're right. I'm being silly." Carrie nibbled at the edge of the biscuit as she considered what Camille had said. She was acting as though her time in London was up, but she still had time to explore, challenge herself, and, of course, make memories with Lucas.

"You're being really silly." Camille agreed.

"Sorry." Carrie apologised. She took a sip of the cappuccino she'd made and poured into one of the hotel's branded travel mugs to bring with her.

"Is this to do with Lucas?" Camille asked. Her shrewd expression told Carrie she already knew the answer to her question. Carrie nodded and took another bite of her biscuit as an excuse not to reply.

"Carrie, you've got so much ahead of you. Your talent is beyond anything I've ever seen, and your passion is contagious. I saw Lily practising her piping when you went to get lunch. There was such determination on her face. She looks up to you and wants to create desserts that you're proud of. Don't let some silly man extinguish your spark."

"Thank you, Camille." Carrie allowed herself to relax, slumping against the tree behind her. Camille was right. She needed to focus on herself and her experiences in London. She'd already learned so much that would make her a better patisserie chef. Each day she was coming up with new business ideas for Lachlan's castle restaurant and hotel. Yet, all of her energy was going on Lucas. He was a small part of her time in London, but he was casting a shadow over everything. Carrie popped the rest of the biscuit in her mouth and resolved to keep Lucas at arm's length. Her time with him should enhance her time in London, but at the moment, it was doing the opposite.

"I needed this." Carrie hummed, draining her coffee.

"The coffee or my pep talk?" teased Camille.

"Both," Carrie admitted.

"Just give me a shout whenever you need one of them! I've booked my first flight to go travelling." Camille's eyes shone as Carrie shot up and focused all of her attention on the woman.

"Camille!" she squealed. "That's huge news. When do you leave?"

"Just after you. I'll tell Lucas in the next couple of days to give him a heads up before I officially hand in my notice."

Carrie spent the next hour questioning Camille about her travel plans and trying to pinpoint when she might visit her in Scotland. She was excited for her. They even discussed the possibility of Carrie flying out to meet her somewhere next year.

Returning to the hotel, Carrie was determined to enjoy her time with Lucas and not to allow her feelings to get carried away. If he started consuming all her thoughts and time, she would have to stop whatever was between them.

CHAPTER SEVENTEEN

"Hello?" Carrie answered her phone. She tucked her legs underneath herself as she settled into her spot at Green Park. It was the first day of June and the blazing sun was beating down upon her. She'd shifted underneath the shade of a tree as her phone screen lit up with Eve's number.

"Carrie!" Eve's voice squealed down the phone. "It's so good to hear from you."

"I know. I'm sorry I've been so silent. We had two weddings on consecutive weekends and it's been so busy." The last month had flown by. Lucy's pictures on social media led to an influx of customers coming to the hotel for afternoon tea. Then they'd had a last-minute wedding to arrange after the couple's original venue cancelled on them. They'd been reluctant to agree to do the wedding, but the bride had been desperate and everywhere else was fully booked. With the limited staff, everyone was juggling multiple roles to keep their new customers happy. Meanwhile, Lucas was fretting about the reputation the hotel was building for itself. He kept pulling at his hair and asking her what they would do when she left. Carrie had promised to use her contacts to ask around to see whether she could find a replacement patisserie chef, but so far nothing had come of it.

"How did the weddings go?" asked Eve. A chair scraped along the floor and echoed down the phone. Carrie could imagine Eve pulling out a stool in her private kitchen and looking out over the walled garden below. Carrie pushed away the beginnings of homesickness and pulled her legs up to her chest.

"They went amazingly. Did you see the pictures I posted on Instagram of the wedding cakes?" Lucy had insisted Carrie create her own business page to showcase her masterpieces. Reluctantly, Carrie had agreed, and Lucy had immediately given her a lesson in 'how to use online spaces to market yourself'.

"I did. They looked amazing. Lachlan's been watching your Instagram followers soar, and I think he's feeling a bit jealous. Yesterday, a new camera and a tripod arrived for him, so I think he's turning it into a bit of a competition."

Carrie chuckled at the thought. She could just

imagine Lachlan challenging her to see who could gain the most followers in a month.

"I've learned lots about online marketing and I'd like to implement some of it when I'm home."

"We'd love that, Carrie. Actually, I want to talk to you about the castle, but it can wait for the moment. First, I want to hear all about that handsome hotel manager that you can't keep your hands off."

Carrie blushed and was grateful there was nobody around to see the pink hue across her cheeks.

"We've hardly seen each other the last couple of weeks," Carrie said. She'd been trying to find time with Lucas for a while now, but something always came up. They'd been especially busy lately. They'd stolen kisses when she'd walked past his office and he'd hauled her inside. But, usually, there was always someone else around. Lucas was either working in the evening or had to rush home to his sister, so there was little hope of another *sleepover*. Carrie ached to feel his touch again. She shook her head. Her conversation with Eve wasn't the time for her mind to wander back to her time spent with Lucas.

"But you want to see him?" asked Eve, breaking through her thoughts.

"I do. I've got just over a month until my contract ends and I'd like to spend as much time as possible with him. Right now we're constantly texting and it's only making me want to see him more. I can't leave my phone for more than a few seconds without wondering if I've missed a reply from him."

"Carrie, is this a good idea?"

"Probably not. I walk around every corridor, hoping I'll bump into him. When I lay in bed and I know he's working a night shift, I listen for footsteps, hoping he's found a way to sneak up to my room. I've been going to sleep late just so I can stay up texting him. Eve, I'm already in too deep. I might as well enjoy my month with him. Either way, I'm going to be heartbroken when I come home."

"I'll be ready with the ice cream and wine."

"Anyway, enough about me. How're you? How's the castle and your search for a hotel manager?"

"It's awful. We still haven't found anyone appropriate. As much as we want to take a chance on someone and offer them an opportunity, neither of us has ever run a hotel before, so we need someone with experience."

"It sounds awful. I've been taking lots of notes on everything I've learned here."

"You're a star, Carrie. I don't know what we'd do without you. There's something Lachlan and I want to talk to you about. He's given me the go-ahead to tell you now so you can think about it before you come home."

Carrie held her breath as she waited for Eve to continue. Her stomach churned as a million different scenarios played out in her head.

"Eve, come on. Just tell me!" Carrie snapped,

unable to stand the silence on the other end of the phone.

"Well, you know Lachlan wants to transfer some shares in the castle to me once we're married?" Eve paused briefly. "We've been talking, and we'd also like to offer you some shares."

Carrie felt as though the ground had been pulled from beneath her. It was the last thing she'd been expecting. Her mouth was dry and her tongue was stuck to the roof of her mouth as she tried to find her voice.

"Eve, I can't afford to buy in," she whispered. The reality was settling around her, and Carrie felt her shoulders sink. She'd love nothing more than to be a shareholder in the castle. To have a say in how they ran the restaurant and the hotel. But she could never afford to buy in, even with her savings. They were meagre compared to how much the castle was worth.

"We don't want any money, Carrie. It would be a gift. We can both see how passionate you are about the business venture and we'd like to offer you the chance to make decisions. Lachlan told me all about the scheme you want to implement, and I love it. We'd all be equal business partners. You don't have to answer me now, Carrie. Just think about it."

Carrie felt the world spinning around her as Eve's words sunk in.

"Eve, are you and Lachlan sure about this?" she asked, afraid to allow herself to dream.

"Carrie, we both love you, and we know how

much you love the business we're creating. It's hard work creating a destination restaurant with a boutique hotel attached to it. You have so many fantastic ideas and are ready to dive in and help us. From a business point of view, we don't want to lose you, Carrie."

"Aren't you worried I'll suddenly take off again?" Carrie's voice wavered as she voiced her concerns. Eve and Lachlan had so much faith in her. What if they had too much faith in her?

"We're not worried, Carrie. Anyway, as I said, we don't need an answer now. Just think about it."

The conversation ended soon after, and Carrie watched people milling around the park. Her head was in a daze. Becoming a shareholder in the castle would mean the world to her. She could experiment with her baking and forge ahead with the various schemes she'd been planning in her head. But could she trust herself to settle? A niggling worry inside Carrie reminded her of her parents and how they could never settle. Was she more like them than she realised?

Carrie glanced at the time on her phone. She needed to get back to the hotel. Although it was her day off, she had to redesign Sasha and Milo's wedding cake. Sasha had called in the early hours of the morning, to let Carrie know she'd just seen the most perfect wedding cake on Pinterest, and asked Carrie if she could recreate it. Obviously, Carrie couldn't say no, so she'd been awake since three this morning, jotting down notes for her show-stopper cake. Sasha wanted the cake adorned with fresh flowers, gold macarons with buttercream flowers piped between the delicate shells, and a marbled red and gold icing beneath it all. Carrie had held her breath and counted to ten on the other end of the phone. Contractually, she was not allowed to say no to Sasha and Milo, despite her new cake design requiring hours more work. Sasha didn't just want a handful of macarons, she wanted the entire bottom tier covered in them. She'd also seen the hotel's Instagram pictures of Carrie's elaborate éclairs and decided her guests needed them. Carrie felt the stress building on her shoulders as Sasha's list of demands grew. At least Sasha's demands would keep her mind from wandering back to Scotland and overthinking Eve and Lachlan's proposal.

"Did you get Sasha's email?" Lucas appeared out of nowhere as Carrie slipped through the staff entrance of the hotel. His shirt was half untucked, and he fought a yawn.

"Yeah, she called me at three o'clock this morning and then emailed confirming what we'd discussed." Carrie rolled her shoulders. "I need a coffee. Can we walk and talk?" She didn't wait for an answer but continued walking towards the staffroom.

"Carrie, you should turn your mobile off outside of work hours." Lucas was following her.

"I keep it on in case you need anything," she whispered, keeping her back to him so he couldn't see her expression. Carrie knew he'd be able to read the desire in her eyes. She busied herself with the coffee machine.

"Carrie," he whispered, stepping closer to her. His hot breath tickled the back of her neck. "Have dinner with me tonight? I'll even give you my personal number. Why haven't we already done that?" he asked.

"We really should. You really want to have dinner together?" She kept her focus on the coffee streaming from the machine and into the pink porcelain cup she'd chosen.

"We have so much to go over for Sasha and Milo that we might as well do it over some dinner. Why don't you meet me in my office around seven? Do you like Chinese? I'll order something."

"Takeaway?" Carrie hissed as she reached for her cup and the hot coffee spilt over the edges.

"Sorry, do you want to choose what we order in?" he asked, handing her some tissues to wipe the hot sticky coffee from her hands.

Carrie took a deep breath, wondering how he could be so thoughtful and so obtuse at the same time. "You want me to have dinner with you, in your office, while we go over work?" she ground out between her teeth, throwing the used tissue into the bin with force.

"Yes?" Lucas's tone wavered.

"I'll be there at seven. You can choose the food." Carrie's tone was cold. She pushed past him with her coffee in hand. They had hardly seen each other all month and the first chance Lucas got to spend any time with her and he wanted to order a takeaway and discuss work.

Carrie let out a sigh as she thumped her coffee down on the worktop.

"You okay?" Camille stopped in her tracks, balancing a tray of drinks in one hand.

"Just stupid men." Carrie grabbed a tissue to wipe up the spilt coffee.

"I'm an expert on that topic! I need to get these out, but give me a shout in an hour if you want to talk about it." She gave Carrie a wave with her free hand and walked away.

Carrie plonked herself down on the stool. Between Sasha's demands, Lucas's hot and cold behaviour, and Eve and Lachlan's proposal, she felt as though she were losing her mind. She'd come to London to find herself, but she felt more lost than ever. How was she supposed to decide what she wanted when so many people wanted something from her? They were all chipping away at her, leaving a hollowed shell of a woman behind.

"Carrie?" Lily's timid voice called.

Carrie lifted her head from her hands and pasted her best fake smile across her face. "Morning, Lily. How're you?" she asked.

"I need to make a birthday cake," Lily announced. She walked over to her apron and pulled it on.

"Okay. Do you need any help?" Carrie asked, already jumping up to put her own apron on.

"Yes, please. Maria's picking me up today and

it's her birthday." Lily had already started pulling every bowl and cake tin from the cupboard, littering the surfaces with items they didn't need.

"Right. Well, let's start from the beginning. For a start, we don't need that doughnut tray." Carrie followed Lily around the kitchen, putting away everything they didn't need. Eventually, they had just a mixing bowl and two large round cake tins.

"What flavours does Maria like?" asked Carrie, grabbing a basket to take with them to the cold storage so they could get their ingredients.

"Chocolate cake and caramel buttercream," Lily replied without even a second thought. She had a bounce in her step as she walked along beside Carrie.

"Lily, that's your favourite." Carrie reminded her.

"Maria will love it." She assured her.

Over the next couple of hours, Carrie's worries melted away as she helped Lily measure, mix, and bake the ingredients to create a mouthwatering chocolate sponge with a vanilla buttercream with homemade caramel running through it. They'd each got a spoon and scraped the leftover buttercream out of the bowl and into their mouths. Lily had carefully piped a flower in the middle of the cake and they'd sprinkled gold glitter over it. There was a homemade feeling to the cake, something Carrie considered to be underrated. She loved the beautiful creations that she poured hours of her time into, but cakes like this looked as though someone had poured hours of love and treasured memories into them. Once they were happy with the cake, they carefully lifted it into a cake box just in time for Maria to pick Lily up. Carrie helped Lily carry the box to the staff entrance, and she wished Maria a happy birthday before waving them off.

The afternoon with Lily had been a welcome break from the endless thoughts and worries weaving their way around Carrie's head. Lily was a whirlwind, keeping her on her toes. But it had also meant Carrie had got none of her own work done. She had two hours until she was supposed to be meeting Lucas in his office, so she got her notepad and went up to her room.

"No. That doesn't work." Carrie frowned at her reflection in the mirror. She'd planned to spend an hour and a half sketching, then having a quick shower before meeting Lucas. Instead, she'd spent an hour showering, preening her hair, and covering her body with floral-scented moisturisers. Then she'd glanced at her wardrobe, wondering what to wear. He'd made it very clear it was just a business meeting between them, but that didn't mean she couldn't show him what he was missing. The problem was, most of Carrie's wardrobe was thick-knitted jumpers. She pulled off the cropped green T-shirt and threw it onto the bed, leaving her standing in just her flared white-washed high-waisted jeans and black lacy bra. With a sigh, she gave up and pulled on a plain v-neck white T-shirt to tuck into the jeans. It was seven o'clock, so she was already running late. Without checking her outfit in the mirror, she collected her notepad, laptop, and work phone and made her way down to Lucas's office, making a mental note to order some summer clothes.

Carrie knocked on the door and held her breath. After a few seconds, the door swung open and Lucas stood, blinking. His shirt was now completely untucked and his hair was sticking out in all directions. Carrie's eyes wandered across his sleepy expression as he continued to blink at her, his eyes slowly filling with recognition.

"Did I wake you?" she asked, pushing past him.

"It's not seven already, is it? I was supposed to meet Lily and Maria at five." He groaned and walked back round to his desk, slumping down in the big leather chair.

"It's gone seven. I'm late." Carrie started setting her laptop and notepad out on the desk.

"Right. I need a coffee."

"You can't have caffeine at this time of night. Are you working tonight?"

"No. My shift ended at five, but I have too much to do."

"I'll make you a coffee. You order food. I'll be back in five minutes." Carrie left his office and went down to the staff room to use the coffee machine. She made them both decaf cappuccinos and carried them back to Lucas's office on a tray, with a couple of plates for when their food arrived.

"Thank you. Food should be here in half an hour," he commented, taking the coffee from Carrie and gulping it down.

"So, shall we get started while we wait for the food?" Carrie suggested.

The next half an hour flew by as they waded through countless emails from Sasha. She'd demand something, then ten minutes later send a new email changing her mind and demanding something else. By the time a kitchen porter knocked on the door with their takeaway, they'd created a one-page plan of Sasha's updated instructions for the wedding.

"We need to email the florist and tell her about the change of colour scheme," commented Carrie.

"I'll do it tonight. Carrie, can we just put all this work to one side for a moment and talk?"

Carrie swallowed her mouthful and put her plate down, giving him her full attention. "What do you want to talk about?" she asked. Her voice was no louder than a whisper.

"I know this sounds ridiculous, but I miss you. We've both been so busy the last few weeks, I feel as though I've not seen you. And when I do see you, all we do is talk about work." He pushed rice around on his plate with the plastic chopsticks that had been delivered with their meal.

"It's just a very busy time and you're so understaffed." Carrie did her best to reassure him, but everything he said was true. "I understand what you're saying, Lucas. I miss you too." She reached across his desk and clasped his hand in hers, never wanting to let go of it.

"I know we have lots to do, but I'd like to take you out tomorrow evening. The work will still be there in the morning. I can't stay the night, though. I wish I could." He rubbed his thumb over her knuckles. The disappointment on his face was obvious to her. From the way his mouth drooped to the sadness in his eyes.

"At least it's still time together."

"I wish I could come upstairs with you now."

"We could continue this meeting in my room," whispered Carrie. Her voice was husky as her fingers trailed up his arm. His eyes flickered closed from her touch and Carrie knew she'd convinced him. Her fingers intertwined with his and she stood up, guiding him to follow her.

"The staff lift goes up to your floor," he said, allowing her to lead him to his office's door. "You look amazing," he whispered, staring at her figure-hugging jeans and low-neck top. He was behind her now as he wrapped an arm around her waist and kissed down her neck. Carrie felt her heart rate quicken as she gasped for breath.

"Come on, let's go upstairs," she gasped out, moving slightly to allow some space between them so she could coordinate her hands to unlock the door. As Carrie's hand wrapped around the door handle, somebody knocked from the other side. She immediately dropped Lucas's hand from her grip and stepped back. Lucas cursed under his breath and pointed to her to sit back down at the desk.

"What is it? I'm in a meeting," he grumbled, opening the door.

"Sorry, sir. One of the guests is complaining about their room service. Apparently, they were very specific about their allergies, but there's been a mixup." Jamal's voice floated in through the open door.

"Have they eaten anything? Do we need to call an ambulance?" Lucas frantically stepped back into his office and reached for his blazer from the back of his chair. "I'm going to have to see to this. I'm sorry, Carrie, but our, um… meeting, will have to be cut short."

Carrie nodded at him, unable to force any words from her mouth. Jamal stood against the door as Lucas grabbed his phone. Carrie caught Jamal's eye and immediately wished she hadn't. He raised his eyebrows at her, followed by a wink.

"I'll leave you to it." Carrie scrambled to gather her belongings, ignoring the half-eaten takeaway strewn across Lucas's desk.

"I'll see you tomorrow?" asked Lucas, already walking out the door.

"Text me," Carrie called after him.

She made her way up to her room with the takeaway sitting heavy in her stomach. They'd been so close to having some time together. If Jamal hadn't turned up, she would have stumbled through her bedroom door with Lucas hot on her heels, tearing at her clothes, and trailing hot kisses down the back of her neck. Instead, she walked through the door alone and dumped her laptop and notebooks down on the hall table. Carrie changed into her pyjamas, wrapped the duvet around her and sat in the chair overlooking London. Her body was tense and ached for Lucas. Meanwhile, her mind was confused and yearned for rest. Carrie's phone bleeped from on her lap. It was a text from Lucas.

Sorry about this evening. Emergency with a mango. One of the waiters didn't realise a mango allergy extends to mango chutney. Wish I was with you. Are we still on for dinner tomorrow? X

Carrie let out a little chuckle at the waiter's stupidity. Their overnight team comprised all new employees, most of whom hadn't ever worked in hospitality before. Many of them were school leavers and so had a lot to learn. They would run poor Lucas off his feet, correcting their mistakes if they didn't bring on some more experienced members of staff soon.

CHAPTER EIGHTEEN

The hotel reception was buzzing with activity as Carrie walked through it. She loved this time of day when the guests were tucked up in their silk sheets while the staff busied themselves preparing for the day ahead. Staff dressed in smart trousers and shirts scurried around with vases of fresh flowers, perfectly pressed linen, and trays filled with cleaned and buffed silver ready for the breakfast service. Housekeeping polished every surface in sight until the light twinkled on it. The front doors were open to allow the fresh morning air to filter in, while the stale air escaped. There was a sense of excitement as the day readied itself. Carrie's eyes wandered over to everyone. Despite them all having a common goal, they would each have a very different day. She forced her feet to keep moving. There weren't enough hours in the day to allow herself to get lost in her thoughts and daydreams about what everyone's day would bring.

"Morning!" called Camille as Carrie walked into the kitchen.

"What are you doing here so early?" asked Carrie. The breakfast team was preparing the continental buffet for the guests, so she picked up a pair of tongs and filled a plate with fruit and yoghurt. Jamal rolled his eyes at her but didn't say anything.

"Lucas texted me last night and asked me to come in to cover the breakfast service. Apparently, one of our waiters went rogue last night and tried to poison a guest." Camille frowned. Jamal cleared his throat in the background, clearly eavesdropping on their conversation.

"It wasn't quite that dramatic," explained Carrie, spearing a cube of mango on her fork and popping it into her mouth.

"No, it wasn't," Jamal confirmed. He'd given up pretending he was preparing the buffet and joined them. "I'm sorry about ruining your evening with Lucas." He glanced down at his freshly painted nails. They were a beautiful pastel yellow with small daisies on his pointer finger.

"It was just a work meeting." Carrie shrugged, staring down at her own nails. They were bare.

"Mmhmm." Jamal looked her up and down as his eyebrows flew up.

"What have I missed out on?" asked Camille, looking between them.

Carrie cried, "Nothing," at the same time Jamal offered his explanation. "Carrie and Lucas looked very comfortable with each other over a takeaway in Lucas's office."

"We were having a work meeting over dinner." Carrie stared down at her plate as her mind flashed back to the previous evening. They'd wanted it to be more than just a meeting, but then Jamal knocked on the door. He might as well have doused them in cold water.

"Okay, I'll believe you. Some wouldn't." Camille winked at her.

"Don't you two have work to do?" asked Carrie, forcing herself to eat another mouthful of her breakfast.

They each took one look at her and mumbled their excuses before scurrying away in separate directions. Carrie put her plate down so she could rub her eyes. They felt like sandpaper from lack of sleep. Thoughts of 'what-ifs?' whirled around her head. What would have happened if Jamal hadn't knocked on Lucas's office door?

Carrie scooped up the last of the yoghurt and fruit on her plate and popped the empty plate into the industrial dishwasher on her way to her workspace. While tossing and turning in bed, she'd decided to do a trial run of the macarons Sasha had requested. First, she needed to decide how to make them gold. Carrie switched the kettle on and scrolled through Google to find out how other people had achieved it. To her utter horror, she discovered she'd have to paint each shell. She pulled up a message and quickly texted Eve, telling her they were never offering gold macarons at the castle. The kettle boiled, and Carrie poured the boiling water onto the horrible instant coffee granules. She should have thought to make herself a coffee in her room, but she'd been too focused on getting into the kitchen.

Her phone beeped from her pocket and she pulled it out to find a text from Lucas saying he wouldn't be able to take her out for dinner that evening. With a sigh, she sipped the scalding hot coffee and scrunched up her nose as the temperature burned her mouth. A glance at the clock told her Lily would be there in the next couple of hours, so Carrie started making the macarons, and then Lily could help her paint each one.

"We have to paint each one?" Lily frowned at the rows of macaron shells Carrie had set out on the work surface.

"I'm afraid so. And this is just a trial. We'll have to do it all again for the wedding." Carrie poured some edible gold powder into a jug, and with a steady hand, she added a couple of drops of white rum to it. Everywhere online had told her water would soak straight through the shell, leaving her with a soggy macaron.

"Can I try some?" asked Lily, pointing to the bottle.

"No! Lily, we're at work. We can't drink rum." Carrie handed the jug to Lily to mix while she returned the rum to the bar. She only hoped she didn't return to Lily scooping the gold paint out of the jug with her finger in to taste the alcohol.

When Carrie returned, Lily was checking the consistency of the paint by running it off of a spoon. "How does it look?" asked Carrie.

"Like paint," said Lily.

Carrie bit her lip to suppress a smile. "Perfect. Here's a pastry brush. Let's get painting!"

The radio played in the background, and the usual clanging and raised voices of the kitchen swirled around them as they lost themselves in the task at hand.

An hour later, they'd finished. Carrie's hand ached, and she kept getting cramp.

"They look like gold coins," said Lily, her eyes wide with wonder.

"Come on, let's treat ourselves to a break before we ice these." It was only nine, so Carrie had plenty of time to take a break before she had to ice the macarons for the afternoon tea service.

"Can we go out for coffee?" asked Lily, her eyes shining. Carrie didn't know if she had *that* much time, but she couldn't say no to Lily when she looked so hopeful.

"Grab your coat, but I'm not buying you one of those ridiculously sugary drinks again. I saw how many shells you ate when you thought I wasn't looking. I'm making a raspberry and cream filling for the macarons this afternoon, and I know you'll want to taste some." Carrie had linked her arm through Lily's and was guiding her to the staff exit.

"Fine," huffed Lily.

Carrie ordered herself a flat white with an extra shot, and Lily got a cup of tea with a splash of milk. She'd voiced her thoughts on how vanilla syrup would taste in tea, but Carrie refused to allow her any sugar on their trip out. They slowly walked back with their drinks and strolled through the Burlington Arcade.

"Carrie, my brother and I would like to invite you to dinner tomorrow night." Lily had stood up straighter, and her tone had slipped into something formal and unlike her.

"Is this an official invitation?" Carrie teased her.

"It is. Would you like it in writing?" Lily raised her eyebrows, matching Carrie's teasing.

Carrie giggled and linked her arm back through Lily's. "I'd love to. Will you get your brother to text me your address and to let me know what time you want me round for?"

"Of course." Lily smiled at her and did a little skip, causing her tea to spill onto her hand and soak the sleeve of her coat. "It's hot," she cried, shaking her hand and causing more tea to spill. Carrie reached forward and took the cup from Lily, placing both of their drinks on the floor. She then pulled

Lily's coat from her shoulders so the soaked fabric wasn't against her skin. One of the security guards had witnessed the events and had come over with some tissues.

"Thank you." Carrie took them from him and helped Lily dry herself. "Are you burnt?" she asked. Carrie held her breath as she waited for an answer.

Lily flexed her fingers and looked down at her hand. "It's fine," she said, shrugging her shoulders and picking her damp cup up from the floor before taking another sip.

Carrie suppressed a chuckle at how blasé Lily was over the events. "I'm sorry for the mess. Would you like me to mop it up?" Carrie asked the security guard as she glanced down at the puddle of tea that Lily had left in her wake.

"No, it's fine, Ma'am. Are you sure your friend is okay?" He'd already pulled out a phone. Probably to call someone to clear up the mess.

"She'll be fine. I'll get her back to work and check her over properly. Thank you for the tissues." Carrie held up the bundle of soggy tissues.

"You're welcome. Would you like me to dispose of those for you?"

"Oh, no, it's fine," Carrie replied before she could think through her answer. She hadn't wanted to burden the man any further, but now she was left walking through central London with tea-drenched tissues which were slowly disintegrating in her hands. Lily had already started walking off, so Carrie gave the security guard a last smile before picking up her own coffee and jogging to catch up with her.

"Why didn't you give him the tissues?" Lily asked, clearly having overheard the conversation.

"I panicked!" Carrie replied.

She followed Lily back to the hotel, looking forward to spending the next couple of hours icing the macarons. They walked through the staff entrance, and Carrie went straight to the bin to dump the tissues and then walked over to the sink to wash her hands.

"What happened?" Jamal asked. He was sitting in the staff room eating a late breakfast, having just finished the breakfast service. Lily had wandered off to sit next to him and was in the middle of pinching a sausage off his plate while he was distracted watching Carrie.

"Carrie panicked," said Lily, taking a bite of the food.

Jamal frowned at her before turning his attention back to Carrie. "Are you okay?" he asked.

"I'm fine. Someone spilt their drink." She looked pointedly over at Lily. "A security guard came to help with some tissues. He asked if I wanted him to throw them away, and I panicked and said no. In my head, I was thinking he'd already helped enough." She dried her hands on a tea towel before downing the cold dregs of her coffee.

"So you just walked home holding a lot of soggy tissues?" Jamal smirked at her.

"Yes."

"Didn't you think of putting them in a bin?"

"That's a really good idea. Why didn't you put them in a bin?" Lily chimed in.

"I didn't see one." Carrie huffed, refusing to admit that it hadn't crossed her mind.

"Anyway, Lily, I'm making soup after this. Would you like to help me?" asked Jamal. He shot Carrie a quick wink, understanding that she needed a moment to collect herself after the morning's events.

"Lily, before you go, I need to check if you burnt yourself." Carrie's senses returned to her and she went to grab the first aid box under the sink.

The tea hadn't scalded Lily, so Carrie just wiped the area before leaving Lily and Jamal to discuss the soup they were going to make. She was annoyed at herself for letting a small incident overwhelm her. Carrie returned to her workspace and pulled out her phone to see a text from Eve, asking why she was texting about gold macarons at six in the morning.

"Hello?" Eve answered on the second ring.

"Eve, it's me."

"Carrie, I know it's you. I have this brilliant invention known as caller I.D.. In fact, I think you have it, too."

"Don't tease me, Eve. I'm not in the mood."

"What's wrong?"

"I can't seem to get a moment alone with Lucas." Carrie lowered her voice to make sure nobody in the kitchen could hear her.

"You're calling me because you can't get a

moment alone with Lucas?"

"No," groaned Carrie. She should have known that Eve would see right through her. "Well, yes, but it's more than that. I feel overwhelmed, Eve, and it's not like me."

"I wish I could give you a hug."

"So do I. I want nothing more than to be sitting in the kitchen with you and Gran, eating shortbread, drinking tea, and having a good natter."

"Why are you overwhelmed?"

"I really like him, Eve. And I have so much to do for this wedding. And on top of it all, I'm coming home soon."

"Carrie, you know you don't have to come home, right?"

There was silence as Carrie allowed Eve's words to sink in. Not go home. Could she? Carrie hadn't ever allowed herself to think of a scenario where she didn't go home. She wanted to go home, but she felt herself being torn in two. Now Eve had suggested it, she could see her future here in London. She could continue working at *Hotel Mayfair* with Lucas by her side. Perhaps eventually they could find a small flat nearby to rent and move in together. She'd wake up each day and look out at the London skyline with a steaming coffee in her hands and Lucas's arms wrapped around her waist. All of her friends she'd made at the hotel could stay a part of her life. Friday nights would be filled with evenings out in fancy wine bars until the early hours of the morning when they stumbled onto the tube.

She'd sleep for a few hours before waking up for another day of work. In her mind, it was so clear. She could almost touch it.

"Carrie, are you still there?" Eve's voice pulled Carrie from the dream world she had conjured.

"Yeah, sorry." Guilt formed in the pit of her stomach as she realised she'd allowed the idea of staying in London to sweep her off her feet. The reality of that future was leaving her friends and family behind. Leaving her home behind. As much as the idea of living in London with Lucas filled her heart with joy, she knew it was an empty joy. The idea of waking up in the castle and looking out to the rugged landscape of the Scottish Highlands, with a steaming coffee in hand and Lucas's arms wrapped around her, was what really made her heart soar. But what if she could have both? Lucas couldn't move to Scotland with her now, so what if she made the sacrifice to move to London until he could go home with her?

"Carrie!" Eve's voice screeched down the phone, and she realised she'd lost herself in her head again.

"Sorry, Eve. My mind is scrambled."

"Carrie, do you think you'll come home?" Eve's tone had dipped, and Carrie could hear the sadness in her voice. She couldn't allow Eve's emotions to sway her decision. Carrie had to do what was right for her.

"Eve, I'll always come home, eventually. I should go. I have a mountain of macarons to pipe."

Without waiting for a reply from Eve, Carrie ended the call and put the phone down on the worktop as though it would burn her if she held it for much longer.

The piping bag was almost overflowing with bright red icing that she'd infused with raspberry coulis. Pushing all thoughts from her mind, Carrie concentrated on the macarons in front of her. She'd pulled up a picture from Pinterest, from Sasha's wedding board. The ones Sasha had saved were pastel-coloured, with pretty roses and daisies piped between the shells. However, the ones she had requested were much more gaudy, so Carrie set about to create something in the middle. Carrie piped delicate red roses in between the golden shells, before mixing up a green icing and piping little leaves to break up the red. Once they were finished, she stepped back to admire her work. They looked spectacular. She took a picture and sent it to Sasha to ask if they were what she wanted, and then she took some pictures for her own social media and for *Hotel Mayfair's*.

"They are stunning," Lucas said. He'd walked over while she was busy trying to get the perfect angle for her photo.

"Thank you." Carrie smiled, her mood immediately lifted by his presence.

"Carrie, I'm really sorry about last night," he whispered, glancing around to make sure nobody was in earshot of their conversation.

"You couldn't help it." Carrie shrugged. She'd

gone to say it was okay, but it wasn't. There was always something.

"I know, but perhaps if I was a better manager, then I could have avoided that."

"Lucas, you're a fantastic manager. You're just having to deal with rubbish owners. Look at you. Since Rachel left, you've stepped up and become the hotel's events planner. That's no easy feat. I'm proud of you." She smiled at him and reached out to give him a macaron.

"Thank you. I'm sorry I can't take you out tonight. The owners have scheduled a Zoom meeting, and with the time difference, it would be right in the middle of dinner. So, did Lily invite you to dinner tomorrow night?" he turned the macaron in his hand before taking a bite of it.

"She did. It was very formal." Carrie chuckled at the memory.

"You're lucky you didn't get a paper invite. I caught her writing you one this morning over breakfast."

Carrie's brow furrowed.

"I'll text you our address. I'm only working until lunchtime tomorrow, otherwise, I'd say just come home with us. Are you okay to get to us for about five? Lily likes to have dinner early."

Carrie's mouth opened and closed, but she couldn't form any words.

"Carrie?" Lucas asked. He'd finished the macaron and was wiping his hands on a piece of kitchen towel.

"You're Lily's brother?" Carrie stuttered out. She cringed as she heard her Scottish accent flood the words.

"Yes? Carrie, I thought you knew. I've told you about my sister?" His words came out as a question.

Carrie thought back to all the conversations she'd had with Lucas about his sister. She hung her head and groaned. It was so obvious now she knew. Why had she never realised?

"I'm so sorry, Lucas. I've been so caught up with everything, I just didn't connect the dots." She felt the blush of embarrassment creep up her neck and across her cheeks to the tips of her ears.

"No, Carrie, it's my fault. I like to give Lily as much independence as I can. I'm an overbearing, worrisome brother, and she doesn't need that at work. When she started at the hotel, we agreed we wouldn't make a big deal of our relationship. We've only told a handful of people and because we're running with lots of temporary staff, it's probably got lost in translation. We only refer to each other by our names inside the hotel." He stepped forward, so he was within touching distance of her.

"It's okay," she whispered.

"It's not," he said, staring down at her.

"It is. Now, I don't know about you, but I have work to do. Will you text me your address later today so I can work out the journey?" She sidestepped out of his way and made her way over to the sink to wash up the piping bags.

"Carrie?" His voice echoed across the room.

She didn't answer. Instead, she kept her attention firmly on the sink and watched as the soap bubbles formed underneath the hot running water. "I'll text you the address."

Carrie held her breath until she heard his footsteps retreat. She switched off the water and lent against the work surface. How had she not realised that Lily was Lucas's sister? Of course, he could never leave London. Lily loved her life here, and he would never take that away from her.

"Carrie, are you okay?" Camille poked her head around the corner. "I just saw Lucas walking away, and he didn't look very happy."

"It's nothing." Carrie wiped her hands on the tea towel and turned to give Camille her full attention.

"Carrie?" Camille pushed.

"I didn't realise Lily was Lucas's sister." Her voice sounded small against the backdrop of the busy kitchen.

"I'm so sorry, Carrie. I assumed Lucas had told you. When I started at *Hotel Mayfair*, my predecessor told me Lily was Lucas's sister, but they didn't want to draw any attention to it. Actually, Lily told him that if he ever acted like her brother at work, then she would bring in his baby photos."

"I feel like such an idiot, Camille. I've been daydreaming about Lucas coming up to Scotland with me. If I'd have known, I would never have allowed myself to dream. It all makes sense now. He could never move. He has to put Lily first."

"Camille?" called a voice from the other side of the kitchen.

"Sorry, it's lunch service. Why don't we go out for a drink tonight?"

"First round's on me. What do you want?" Camille called above the hum of the All Bar One they'd gone to. Tonight wasn't about fancy drinks, seeing somewhere new, or appreciating the atmosphere. All Carrie needed tonight was someone to listen to her with a few cocktails thrown in along the way. She'd called Eve before leaving the hotel and with a shaky voice, relayed the day's events. There was only so much support Eve could offer on the other end of the phone, so Carrie was very grateful to have tonight with Camille.

"Could I have an espresso martini? I'll go see if there're any seats free upstairs." Carrie left Camille fighting her way to the front of the crush at the bar.

Upstairs wasn't as busy. Carrie walked past the first few empty tables, heading to the back of the bar, where it was quieter. There were only a handful of tables filled. Carrie made her way over to an empty one in the back corner and sat down, pulling off her light trench coat and folding it onto the seat next to her. As she waited for Camille to get their drinks, Carrie drummed her fingers on the sticky tabletop in front of her. She wondered what Lily and Lucas were up to now. Perhaps they'd just got off the train together and were heading home to cook dinner. Carrie shook her head. How had she missed it? Now she knew it was obvious. From having the same hair and eye colour to similar mannerisms.

"You look deep in thought," Camille commented, putting a cocktail down in front of her.

"Thanks." Carrie smiled up at her and took a sip, allowing the caffeine and alcohol to flood her system.

"So, you really didn't know Lucas was Lily's brother?"

"No!"

"But she talks about him all the time?" Camille was sipping her mojito.

"She talks about her brother lots, but I don't remember her ever using his name."

"Carrie, I'm sorry. I should have made sure you realised."

"It wasn't your job to explain everyone's relationship." Carrie used her straw to prod the coffee bean that was floating on the surface of her drink.

"Does it really change anything?"

"I love London, Camille, but one day I want to go home. Whether that's at the end of this contract or some point further in the future. I thought maybe I could stay in London for a while and then, eventually, perhaps Lucas would follow me back to Scotland. That was when I thought his sister would move out in the next year or so and he'd feel more comfortable putting himself first. But now I understand why he can't move. Not that I'd ever ask him to. Lily is in her element at *Hotel Mayfair,* and everyone is so incredibly supportive of her. You've created an environment for her to blossom in. I could never disrupt that. From the start, I've known there was no future for Lucas and me, but learning Lily is his sister has made it real. That tiny part of me that hoped we might figure out a way to make it work has been crushed."

"I wish I could say something to help or to find a solution for you. It's an impossible situation."

"It is. But I'll be okay. Eve and Lachlan have plans back home that will keep me busy until I've long forgotten Lucas's name."

"You don't have to be brave with me, Carrie." Camille reached across the table and squeezed her hand.

"Do you want another?" asked Carrie, draining her cocktail. Carrie watched Camille glance down at her mojito and realised she'd hardly drunk any of it.

"I'll have another, please. Better drink this one while you're fighting your way to the bar." She winked at Carrie.

CHAPTER NINETEEN

"Be brave," Carrie muttered to herself. She needed caffeine, and she couldn't face the acidic hot water that was instant coffee. There were no pods left in her room. She needed to have a chat with housekeeping to get some more, so she was left with no other option than to use the coffee machine in the staff room. Carrie reminded herself that it would be less awkward to bump into Lucas at work than on his doorstep this evening.

The staffroom was blissfully empty. Probably because it was five o'clock in the morning and there was just a skeleton team of staff who were busy tending to the early risers. Revelling in the silence, Carrie made her coffee and sat down to take a sip. She really ought to head into the kitchen to make a start on the day, but she didn't want to allow the quietness of the moment to pass her by. A yawn escaped her, and she sipped her coffee. It hadn't been a late night with Camille. After two cocktails, they'd called it a night and treated themselves to a McDonald's. But Carrie had tossed and turned most of the night, unable to silence her mind.

"Morning," called Lucas, walking into the room.

Carrie watched as he glanced her way and then stopped and turned to face her.

"Sorry, I didn't realise it was you," he said.

"It's okay. I've just been enjoying a few moments of silence."

"Am I disturbing you?" He was still standing in the same spot.

"No. It's okay. I should really get on with baking. The macarons were a real hit yesterday. I'm going to make some more today but with less gold!"

"They were delicious." His eyes glazed over.

"I'm going to bake something to bring with me later. If I'm still invited to dinner?" Carrie stumbled over her words.

"Of course you are. We're really looking forward to it. Lily is going food shopping with Maria this morning before she comes into work."

"Well, I'll see you later." Carrie gave him a wave and walked out with her half-drunk coffee still clasped in her hands. Lucas had texted her their address shortly after their conversation yesterday, and Carrie had checked the route last night.

Actually, she'd checked it multiple times. She wasn't sure whether it was because she wanted to be certain of where she was going or if she just needed to keep her mind occupied.

Before Carrie knew it, she was standing in front of the mirror in her bedroom, trying to decide what to wear. The evenings were light and warm, so she could wear a dress. Was a dress too much for a casual dinner with Lucas and his sister? Carrie let out a groan and threw herself down on the bed. She needed to leave in ten minutes. There wasn't enough time for her indecisiveness. Her eyes kept wandering towards a discarded parcel on her bedroom floor. Eve had ordered her a present after hearing how down she was. It was a beautiful white lace tunic-style dress, but it was much shorter than anything Carrie would normally wear. But it would look lovely with her new knee-high brown boots with a block heel. Time was running out, so she opted to try the dress on to see whether it worked.

The bottom of the lace ended mid-thigh, making Carrie's legs look much longer than they were. She tried not to focus on how pale her legs were. Living in Scotland and spending the summer working in a kitchen had done little for her complexion. She pulled on her new boots and put on her brown leather jacket. As she looked at her reflection in the mirror, she hardly recognised the woman looking back at her. A mass of curls tumbled around her shoulders and her eyes were wide, staring back at her with a sparkle in them. Without giving herself the chance to doubt her choice, she threw her handbag over her shoulder, picked up the pie she'd prepared earlier in the day, and left.

As the London overground trundled along the tracks, she watched as the city passed her by. It was rush hour, which in itself was a lie. Rush hour lasted for hours. Carrie was squeezed into a corner with her arms wrapped around the dish she was carrying. The stale stench of sweat lingered in the stuffy carriage. Carrie kept her attention on the window, watching as they passed each station and counting down until she got off. It was just a twenty-minute journey, but it felt much longer. With every jolt, someone almost stumbled into the dish.

It was a relief to step off the train and onto the platform. Lucas had included instructions on what exit to take from the station, so Carrie took a left and went down a flight of stairs, moving with the flow of the crowd. It was a short walk to their flat, and they were on the fourth floor. As Carrie stood outside number ten, her hand shook as she reached out to knock on the door. Before her knuckles could connect with the shiny surface, the door swung open and Lily stood beaming at her.

"Welcome to dinner," she announced, stepping to the side and making a sweeping gesture with her arm to allow Carrie to cross the threshold.

"Thank you." A rush of relief overcame Carrie as she instantly felt at ease in Lily's company.

"Dinner will be served in approximately twelve minutes," Lily informed her.

"That's very specific." Carrie looked around the small hallway. The walls were white and there was a beautiful wood floor, but it was ruined by shoes everywhere. Coats were piled on a chair in the corner and an umbrella was half open, leaning against a small cluttered console table.

"Lily, have you offered our guest a drink?" Lucas's voice came from another room.

"Oops. Would you like some water?"

"Lily, we have more than water. What's that sparkling grape stuff you bought?"

"But I like that."

"Lily!" Lucas sounded harassed.

"Why don't you show me to the kitchen, Lily? I've brought a pie so we can put it in the fridge for later." Carrie thought she ought to step in before she witnessed an argument between the siblings.

Without answering, Lily walked off and went through a door to the right. Carrie followed her into another hallway. This one was thin and had two doors leading off of it. Lily took the door on the right and they stepped through to the kitchen, where Lucas was standing in front of a hob, stirring something.

"Thanks for having me," Carrie said, not knowing what else to say. There was still so much unsaid between them, but now wasn't the time to discuss it.

"Thank you for coming." He turned to smile at her before the pan on the hob overflowed. The water sizzled on the electric hob.

"Do you want some help?" asked Carrie. Lily had wandered over to a cupboard and got two glasses out. She filled one with water from the tap and the other with what Carrie guessed to be the sparkling grape stuff.

"Here's your water." She handed Carrie the glass with tap water.

"Thank you, Lily."

"No, I'm fine. Why don't you go sit in the sitting room with Lily?"

Carrie popped the pie in the fridge and then followed Lily through to the sitting room. The evening sun was shining through the windows at the far end of the room. A small beige sofa was pushed against the wall with a wooden coffee table in front of it on a Moroccan-style rug. In the corner was a sideboard that looked as though it had been pulled straight from the 70s, with a television perched on top of it. The room was basic and yet it looked lived-in and inviting.

"Have you lived here long?" Carrie asked, sitting down beside Lily.

"I was born here," replied Lily.

Carrie cast her eyes around the room again. Now she knew this was the flat Lucas had once lived in as a child when his parents were still alive. There was very little sign of them. Actually, there was very little sign of anyone living there. No pictures cluttered the surfaces and no happy memories hung on the walls. The flat was devoid of memories and yet it still looked like a happy place to live.

"Would you like to see my bedroom?" asked Lily.

"I'd love to." Carrie placed her water on a coaster on the coffee table and followed Lily as she led her to another hallway with three rooms leading off of it.

"The bathroom's there." Lily pointed to the first door they passed. Carrie's eyes lingered on the other two rooms. One was Lily's bedroom, the other was Lucas's. As Lily led her to one door, Carrie stopped her gaze from falling on Lucas's bedroom door. Lily's bedroom had the same wood floor and white walls as the rest of the flat, but her walls were covered with magazine cuttings, photographs, and a lifetime of birthday cards. There was a bed in the middle of the room with a purple throw over it and a teddy bear sat on top of it.

"Lucas made me tidy up before you came," Lily explained.

"You've got a lovely room, Lily." Carrie walked over to a desk below a window and glanced out at the view. In the distance, you could still see the London skyline.

"This card was from my best friend, Zara." Lily was pointing to a bright pink card in the middle of her display. She talked Carrie through each card and told her about the people they were from.

"Dinner's ready!" Lucas called, interrupting Lily's story about the time Maria had taken her to feed the ducks when Lucas joined them and was chased into the pond by an angry swan. Carrie felt her face aching from all the laughing and smiling.

In the kitchen, Lucas had dished up three plates of pasta with a side of garlic bread.

"I'm no chef," he said as he caught Carrie staring at the plates.

"I'm sure it's lovely."

Lily grabbed a plate and left the room.

"We usually eat in the sitting room," explained Lucas.

"Perfect." Carrie took the smaller of the two plates and followed Lily. She took a seat next to Lily on the sofa, who was piling her fork with steaming hot pasta.

Carrie watched Lily lift the fork to her mouth. "It's hot!" she cried at the same time Lucas shouted her name. Lily dropped the fork, which clattered down onto her plate. Her eyes immediately filled with tears, and Carrie saw her bottom lip wobble. She took Lily's plate and put it down on the coffee table with her own, not worrying about a coaster. Without thinking, she pulled Lily into her arms.

"It's okay, Lily. We just don't want you to burn yourself." Lucas had crouched down on the other side of Lily and had taken her hand in his.

"Come on, Lily, cheer up. There's chocolate pie for afters," Carrie reminded her.

At the mention of pie, Lily perked up and

decided she could finish her dinner. Lily and Carrie settled themselves on the sofa, while Lucas sat on the floor using the coffee table to rest his food. Carrie had offered to move up to make room for him on the sofa, but he'd declined. The food was surprisingly good. Lucas had confessed it was just a fresh pasta sauce that Lilly and Maria had picked up earlier in the day, but it was still bursting with flavour.

"What kind of chocolate pie did you make?" Lily asked as soon as she'd finished her last mouthful of pasta.

"It's a chocolate espresso pie. I made a pie case and filled it with a chocolate mousse that I'd flavoured with a shot of coffee." Carrie turned and mouthed "decaf" at Lucas, who visibly relaxed.

"It sounds like something people would have at a dinner party," commented Lily.

"Well, it's a good job we're having a dinner party!" Carrie chuckled.

Lucas took their empty plates and went to dish up the pie. Carrie had offered to help, but he'd told her to sit and enjoy herself.

"Are we making more macarons tomorrow?" asked Lily, suppressing a yawn.

"No, we're starting the preparation for Sasha and Milo's wedding cake." Carrie had left the dessert team with pages of instructions on how to recreate her patisserie masterpieces. She'd stayed late last week helping them to perfect their icing skills. There was room for improvement, but Carrie was happy with what the kitchen would be putting out.

It meant that she could focus completely on the wedding of the season. Tomorrow she'd bake the sponges and freeze them so they were ready to decorate the day before.

"Maria said her birthday cake was the best cake she's ever eaten."

"I'm so glad she enjoyed it. Did you tell her you made it?"

"She was very proud of me."

"You should be very proud of yourself, Lily. You're amazing in the kitchen." Lily was getting better at accurately measuring out her ingredients and baking some delicious cakes.

"I'm going to miss you when you leave." Lily sighed and turned to look out of the window.

"Pie's served!" Lucas walked in balancing three bowls in his hands with a dollop of squirty cream on each slice of pie.

They ate the pie in silence with just the odd noise signalling how good it tasted. Lily was yawning around each mouthful of food. Carrie was surprised to see it was already seven o'clock. The sun was slowly setting outside the window and the light in the room was dimming.

"That was amazing. Thank you, Carrie." Lucas smiled at her. For the first time that evening, his entire attention was on her and she felt a fizz run through her body.

"I'm tired." Lilly slumped back into the sofa with her empty bowl balancing on her lap. Carrie took it and stacked it underneath hers.

"Do you want to go to bed?" Lucas asked Lily, who nodded in response. "Okay, let me get your toothbrush ready. Then I'll pop your teddy bear in the microwave to warm it up." Lucas put his bowl on the coffee table and went to get things ready.

"It's like a hot water bottle, but it doesn't have water inside it," explained Lily. She closed her eyes and her breathing slowed as she fell asleep.

"Is she asleep?" Lucas asked, walking back into the room.

"I'm afraid so."

"Lily, come on, wake up. You need to brush your teeth, especially after all that sugar." Lucas shook her shoulder and Lily mumbled something in response.

"Maybe I shouldn't have bothered with decaf. Shall I take our bowls into the kitchen while you wake Lily?"

"Yes, please. There's a bottle of red on the side if you'd like to pour us both a glass?"

"Perfect." Carrie left Lucas arguing with Lily about brushing her teeth before bed.

The kitchen was sparse. There were a few cupboards, a small work surface, most of which was taken up by a bulky microwave, and an oven. A fridge was on the opposite wall, with a small table and two chairs next to it. At the end of the room was a door. Carrie peered out to see a small balcony on the other side. Another table and two chairs sat out there, alongside a poorly looking plant.

Hearing the sound of a door closing, Carrie

turned back to the kitchen and undid the bottle of wine, thankful it was a screw top, so she didn't have to go through the drawers looking for a bottle opener.

"The glasses are in that cupboard to your right," said Lucas, walking into the room. Without replying, Carrie reached up and took two glasses out of the cupboard. As she reached, she felt the hem of her dress rising and heard Lucas's sharp intake of breath.

"Shall we take these outside? I don't want to wake Lily. She was out early with Maria and then came into work with me."

"Sure." Carrie handed him a glass and followed him outside onto the balcony. The brick walls of the building radiated heat from the day's sunshine. He'd picked up her leather jacket she'd left in the hallway and hung it on the back of her chair for when she needed it.

"You've got a lovely home," Carrie commented once they were both seated.

"Thank you. My parents bought it shortly after they married, and then Lilly and I inherited it when they passed away. It was too small for all of us and my parents used to sleep in the living room. They couldn't afford to move, so we made the best of it." He sipped his wine.

"Is it strange living here when there are so many memories?" Carrie couldn't help but ask the question. She'd never had the chance to keep her parent's home. They'd lived on the McLeod estate and after they passed away, the McLeods rented it out again. Not that her parents had really lived there. She had a few happy memories as a young child when they'd come home for a few weeks and pretend to be a happy family. When she thought of home, Carrie thought of her grandmother.

"It is, but I'm not here very often. Usually, I'm busy at work. On days like today, I'd usually leave work, pick Lily up from one of her groups and then take her out for food, and then we might go see a film if we're not too tired. By the time we get home, I fall into bed, ready to get up and do it all over again."

Carrie studied him as he took another sip of his wine. He looked tired. The dark circles under his eyes were growing darker by the day. His jaw had stubble, which was a few days old. It suited him, but Carrie knew it wasn't a conscious style decision. He looked as though he was caring for everyone but himself. She reached out and intertwined their fingers.

"Are you happy?" she asked. As soon as the words left her lips, she regretted them.

"My happiness doesn't really matter. As long as Lily is happy, then I'm okay."

"You really love her."

"We almost lost her when she was a baby. At thirteen weeks pregnant, my mum came home from a doctor's appointment and I knew she'd been crying. She sent me to bed with a bowl of chocolate ice cream so she and my father could speak. That was the day the doctor told her Lily had

Down's syndrome. I remember that night like it was yesterday. I got up to use the bathroom, and I heard my parents still awake and talking. The following day, they sat me down and told me my sibling would have Down's syndrome. Of course, I wasn't old enough to understand what that meant." He paused and took another gulp of his wine, draining the glass. "The day Lily was born, a friend of the family looked after me and that evening they took me to the hospital to meet my baby sister. Only I couldn't meet her. My parents had shielded me from the truth, but all along they had known Lily would be born with a heart condition. She was very sick and my parents didn't want me to see her. Instead, I climbed onto my mum's hospital bed and she cuddled me. I could feel her silent tears trickling onto the top of my head, but neither of us said anything."

"Lily's very lucky to have you as her brother." Carrie leant forward and wiped his tears away.

"Every day with her is precious. My parents aren't here to love her and look after her, so I have to make up for it. The pain of losing my parents was so great, I wasn't sure I'd survive it. But I had to because I had Lily to look after. She got me through those dark days without even knowing. The thought of losing her, Carrie, I don't think I'd make it through a loss like that." He took a deep breath. "Would you like a refill?" Carrie had hardly taken two sips from her glass, but he didn't wait for her reply and went inside to fetch the bottle. She looked out at London, not seeing anything that was in front of her. She understood why Lucas could never leave London and why he was so intent on making sure Lily had the best life possible. He'd already lost his parents, and he knew one day he'd have to say goodbye to his beloved sister. Just thinking about it broke Carrie's heart.

When he returned, he seemed different. He'd wiped his eyes, and the vulnerability had left him. He refilled his glass and put the bottle down on the table for Carrie to refill hers when she was ready.

"Your pie was amazing. Thank you for bringing it. Lily did get dessert, but she got her favourite yoghurts." He raised his eyebrows. "Are you prepared for the wedding this weekend?"

Carrie took a sip of her wine to give herself a moment before she replied. He'd turned the conversation back to work. Perhaps it was for the best.

"I'm going to start baking the cake tomorrow so I can freeze the sponges. Then I just need to become superhuman to bake and decorate all the extras Sasha has asked for."

"Your contract ends the day after the wedding." Lucas's words hung in the air as they both let it sink in. She had just another week in London before she would leave for Scotland.

"Eve and Lachlan have offered me shares in the castle. They want me as part of the team, helping them to make decisions and run the place." She didn't know why she was telling him this. Maybe she wanted him to beg her not to accept it and to ask her not to go home.

He didn't. Instead, he congratulated her. "You'll be amazing, Carrie. I'm so happy for you. I can't wait to read about how amazing you're all doing."

Carrie bit back the sob that was rising in her chest. He was happy for her.

"Thank you," she choked out, turning to look out at the view. Soon, this would all be a distant memory. She wondered if Lucas would be out on his balcony drinking wine and thinking of her. "I should leave. Sorry, I'm keeping you up. You probably would have gone to bed at the same time as Lily if I wasn't here." She reached for her leather jacket from the back of her chair and started pulling it on, but Lucas reached over to stop her.

"Don't go, Carrie." His eyes met hers, and she saw a flicker of his earlier vulnerability. He stood up and pulled her into his arms. Carrie looked up at him. As their eyes met, she felt an explosion of fireworks inside her. He brought his thumb up to stroke her cheek. Carrie didn't know who moved first, but their lips were soon pressed together as his fingers weaved their way through her hair. His other hand ran down her back to the hem of her dress. Carrie let out an impatient moan against his lips.

"Come on, let's go to bed." He took her hand and led her to his bedroom.

CHAPTER TWENTY

Carrie woke feeling sick. From the moment she opened her eyes, she knew exactly where she was. Her stomach churned. The signature white walls and wood floor were a reminder that she was in Lucas's home. In his bed. After their heart-to-heart last night, he'd led her to his bedroom, and she had been more than happy to follow. Now, in the cold light of the day, she realised what a mistake it had been. It would only make saying goodbye to him harder. Carrie glanced over at Lucas. His arm was thrown above his head, pushing his unruly hair across his forehead. Her fingers itched to reach over and push the hair from his face, but she couldn't because it would wake him. She was on the side of the bed by the door, so she slipped out of bed, pulled her dress over her head, scooped up her underwear and held her breath as she undid his bedroom door. Silently, she tiptoed out of the room and to the bathroom to get dressed. She splashed water on her face and scrubbed last night's makeup off. Her hair was an unruly mass of curls, but she ran her fingers through them and managed to tame it into something presentable. Her leather jacket was still outside on the balcony. She picked up the empty bottle of wine and their glasses, leaving them on the kitchen counter.

The air outside was chilly, and Carrie regretted not putting tights on the night before. She retraced her footsteps back to the train station and let out a sigh of relief as the train pulled in as she reached the platform. It was much emptier than the night before, so she took a seat near the door. She focused her attention on the scenery passing them by to stop her mind from wandering to Lucas. It was too fresh and too painful to think about. They could never allow another night like that to happen. Saying goodbye to him was already difficult enough. Another night like that would only complicate matters. She needed to put some space between them in the buildup to the wedding. Surely they'd both be so busy that it wouldn't be a problem.

Carrie slipped through the staff entrance of the hotel and took the lift to her floor. She only saw a few members of staff but didn't recognise any of them. Once in her room, she headed straight for the shower, where she allowed the tears to fall and mix with the water cascading down her.

Once showered and re-dressed, Carrie opted to make herself a coffee from the pod machine in her room. Housekeeping had topped up her drawer of pods, so she didn't need to risk bumping into Lucas yet. As the coffee trickled into her cup, she unwrapped the fresh packet of biscuits that she'd left on the side. She wasn't in the least bit hungry, but she needed to keep herself distracted.

The kitchen was buzzing by the time Carrie walked in.

"You're late!" Camille called, already piling up used plates for the dishwasher.

"I had a lie-in as a treat before the chaos of the next few days." The lie slid effortlessly from the tip of her tongue. She wasn't planning on telling Camille where she spent last night.

"How was your dinner with Lucas?" she asked, her shrewd eyes assessing Carrie's expression.

"It was good." Carrie shrugged her shoulders and crossed her fingers behind her back, hoping Camille wouldn't ask any more questions. She should have known better.

"Good? Is that why you look as though someone is holding your puppy at gunpoint?"

"Don't be so dramatic, Camille." Carrie rolled her eyes to play it off.

"Come on. What happened?"

"We had a lovely meal, a heart-to-heart, and said goodbye to each other. Then I got home this morning and cried to myself in the shower," Carrie whispered to make sure nobody could hear her above the buzz of the kitchen. Her resolve had crumbled. She needed to talk to someone about it.

"This morning?" Camille shrieked.

"Shh!" Carrie grabbed her hand and pulled her down the corridor to the cold storage, yanking open the door and shoving her inside.

"It's freezing!" Camille complained, but Carrie was too busy checking there was nobody else in there before they spoke any further.

"We won't be long. I don't have much to say."

"So you slept with him?" Camille asked.

"Yes, but it won't happen again. Lily is his entire world. It's not just that he would never move her. There's just not any room in his life for anyone else. He's so scared of losing her that he won't take any risks. It's okay, Camille. I mean, it's not, but it will be. I just have to get through the next few days, then I'll be going home. There's so much for me to do at home. I'll just throw myself into it. Then we can make plans for when you're going to come and visit." Carrie did her best to paste a smile across her face. Camille saw straight through it and pulled her into her arms.

"You deserve to be happy, Carrie," she whispered, hugging her tightly.

"I will be. I might not be at the moment, but

one day I'm sure I will be."

Carrie left Camille to go back to breakfast service and disappeared further into the cold storage to gather the ingredients for the wedding cake.

As Carrie mixed the ingredients for the cake, she was certain there was some sort of magic hidden within baking. It was a form of therapy for her. Her mind cleared as her hands did the work. By now, she could judge the weights of dry ingredients by eye, but she did still check them on the scales. For a bake this important, everything had to be exact. Once the tins were in the oven, she pulled out her notepad and made a list of everything she needed to create over the next few days.

"Carrie?" She heard Lucas's voice before she saw him. He was walking towards her, his shirt half un-tucked and his hair looking the same as it had in bed that morning.

"What's wrong?" She jumped off her stool and placed her hand on his arm in an attempt to calm him down.

"The florist called. There's been a fire at her shop and all the flowers have been destroyed. She had all the flowers for the wedding stored in her cold storage and they've all been burnt to a pile of ash." His eyes were bloodshot.

"Okay, calm down. She's a florist. Surely she knows what to do in a situation like this?"

"She told me as an events planner I would have to sort it out. She's busy sorting the insurance.

I've got the number for another florist who might store the flowers for us and a warehouse where we can buy them from."

The cake timer went off, and Carrie went to check them. They were cooked, so she pulled them out and put them to one side.

"So we have to pick up fresh flowers and take them to the new cold storage? Will this new florist do the arrangements for us on the day?" The enormity of the situation was weighing down on Carrie.

"No, the original florist said she'd come in on Saturday morning to set everything up," explained Lucas.

"So if we can get the new flowers, we should be okay?" Carrie asked, trying to get everything straight in her head.

"Yes." Lucas nodded. His eyes held a frenzied edge.

"Well, go get them!"

"Will you come with me, Carrie? I don't know what I'm doing. How am I supposed to know if I'm picking up the right thing?" His eyes pleaded with her.

"I've got to cool these cakes and get them put away," Carrie said, glancing behind her at the cakes cooling in the tins.

"Camille can stand over them until they've cooled enough to go in the freezer. Please?"

Half an hour later, Carrie was sitting in the cab of one of the hotel's vans. Lucas was driving, and they were heading out of London to a flower market on the outskirts of the city. The florist had pulled some strings, and the owner would meet them there in an hour. Then they had to rush back into London to get them into storage so they wouldn't spoil before the big day.

"Is Lily not at work with you today?" asked Carrie. She attempted to keep the conversation away from anything that could make the morning any more awkward than it already was. Neither of them had mentioned how she'd left him alone in bed this morning before he had even woken.

"She's still very tired after hosting her first dinner party last night." Lucas smiled, but his eyes stayed firmly on the road in front of them.

"Thank you for a lovely dinner," Carrie replied, allowing her eyes to wander to the scenery flying past the passenger window.

"You're very welcome. Even if it was just pasta. Carrie, I wish..." he tailed off.

"Lucas, you don't need to say it. I understand. Let's just enjoy the short time we have left. We always knew there was no future. I've had an amazing time with you. Don't spoil it now." She reached over and squeezed his hand, which was resting on the gear stick. He shot her a quick smile before turning his attention back to the road.

The journey passed in silence as they left the bustle of central London behind them. Carrie's phone bleeped with a text from Eve saying her grandmother was already making preparations for her welcome-home dinner. A warmth filled Carrie's chest at the thought of Alice preparing her favourite dishes to welcome her back. At that moment, Carrie knew, however strongly she felt for Lucas, nothing would keep her from going home. As the motorway filtered into a built-up area, Carrie felt a pang of sadness. She felt so far away from her home. Lucas signalled to turn right, and they made their way onto an industrial estate.

"You okay?" he asked. He'd turned to watch her as her eyes flitted around the barren landscape ahead of them.

"Yes, sorry. It still shocks me that these factories and warehouses exist. I'm used to just popping to neighbours to buy food and other supplies." She shrugged her shoulders, resisting the urge to pull her knees up and hug them to her chest.

"I forget you're not from around here."

"It's all very different from where I'm from. My grandparents mostly brought me up. They were always busy working at the castle, so for me, there was very little outside the grandeur of a castle nestled amongst the rugged Highlands." Carrie's eyes had glazed over as memories of home crashed through the barrier she'd put up.

"It sounds wonderful."

"It is. But it can also be the loneliest place on earth."

"We're here." Lucas had parked outside one of the various warehouses. The signage above read *'Fancy Florals'* in big pink letters.

"Do you have the list the florist emailed over?" asked Carrie. She followed Lucas's lead and climbed out of the van.

The florist had called ahead, so they were expecting them. Lucas pulled up the email with the list on it and the receptionist took a note of what they needed. "Take a seat and I'll get someone to fulfil the order. Can I get you both a drink?" asked the woman.

"Coffee, please," they both said at the same time.

"I'll be right back." She disappeared, leaving them in the waiting room.

"Shall we sit?" Carrie suggested, pointing to the uncomfortable-looking black sofa in the corner. Vases of vibrant flowers improved the tired reception area. A floral scent permeated the air, and Carrie instantly felt her mood lifted.

"I'm sorry you felt you had to leave like that this morning," whispered Lucas. They'd sat next to each other on the sofa, which was as uncomfortable as it had looked.

"You didn't make me feel like I had to leave, Lucas. I left because I thought it would be less painful for me."

"I wanted the chance to wake up next to you in my bed." He was so close to her she could feel his breath caress the top of her head.

"Lucas," she warned him.

"Sorry."

"Last night was the perfect goodbye. I didn't

want to ruin it by hanging around. There's nothing more to say between us. Before I knew Lily was your sister, I had dreams of me moving down here with you and then, eventually, we could go to Scotland together. You could manage the hotel at Lachlan's castle and I'd slip back into my role as patisserie chef. I saw us spending weekends walking hand in hand through the grounds and having a Sunday roast with my grandmother in her cottage. Then I realised Lily was your sister, and I understood why you could never leave her and why you couldn't take her away from her home. Lily is the kindest person I've met. Just being in her presence makes me want to smile. She's been more than I ever could have wished for in a kitchen assistant, and I'm happy to be leaving London with her as a friend. I also understand why you have to put her first."

"Carrie, if things were different, I'd be packing my suitcase to come back with you. It sounds like an adventure I would love, but my life isn't just my own to think about. I appreciate how much you think of Lily and how you understand why I need to prioritise her."

"Lucas, you wouldn't be the caring man I've fallen for if you didn't priorities her."

"Why don't we take these flowers back into London and then I'll take you out for dinner? You're still here and there's no reason why we can't enjoy our last couple of days together."

"I've got a better idea. Why don't I take you out for dinner?" Carrie raised her eyebrows at him.

"Sounds perfect." He reached across to hold her hand in his.

His touch sent a jumble of emotions through Carrie as she thought about having to really say goodbye to him. She didn't have long to ponder the thought as the receptionist returned with their coffees and took her seat back behind the desk, putting a stop to their conversation.

Shortly after they'd finished their drinks, a man walked through the double doors which led into the warehouse. He was pushing two trolleys. "There's five more behind me," he announced.

Carrie shared a worried look with Lucas.

It took a lot of manoeuvring, but eventually, they fitted all the flowers in the back of the van. It was a tight squeeze, but they knew they couldn't leave any behind; Sasha would know if anything was missing.

The drive back into London was slower as they fought the traffic. They pulled up outside the hotel, and Lucas dropped Carrie off to get ready for their dinner. He was going to take the flowers to the cold storage with the original florist.

Carrie ran to the kitchens to check Camille had put her cakes away. They all looked fine, and she breathed a sigh of relief. A glance at her watch told her she had a couple of hours until Lucas was picking her up, so she decided to get ahead of herself and bake a batch of choux pastry, which would keep for the wedding.

"I didn't realise you were back," said Camille,

making Carrie jump.

"Camille, don't creep up on me like that when I'm getting a hot tray out of the oven!" Carrie protested.

"Sorry. How was your trip out with Lucas?" Camille sat on a stool and picked at the choux casing of an éclair that was cooling.

"It was good. By some miracle, we got all the flowers. Lucas is just taking them to the cold storage now." Carrie busied herself transferring the fresh batch of éclairs onto the cooling rack.

"I wasn't asking after the flowers."

"It was good. We're going out for dinner together tonight."

"I thought you had decided there could be nothing between you?"

"There can't be, but that doesn't stop us from enjoying our last days together."

"Be careful, Carrie." Camille stepped off of the stool and pulled her into her arms.

"Thank you."

"Anyway, I came to tell you not to make any plans for your last night in London. The wedding is in two days, right? Then you have the following day here before heading home?"

"That's right."

"Good. I'm arranging a leaving party for you." Camille beamed at her and Carrie didn't have the heart to tell her she didn't want a leaving party.

"Sounds great. I should go get ready for dinner."

"You should. I'll see you tomorrow. I've shuffled the rotas, so I'll be free to help you with anything you need."

CHAPTER TWENTY-ONE

Before Lucas, Carrie had never worried so much about her appearance. With the upcoming wedding and Carrie's leaving party, this would be their last night together, and Carrie wanted him to take one glance at her and come undone. She pulled out a pair of emerald green tailored trousers, a black silk cami and a pair of black heels Eve had insisted she take. The trousers hugged her curves and the cami's neckline skimmed the top of her breasts. Her hair cascaded down her back in a furious cloud of curls. She ran some oil through them to tame them and applied her makeup. By the time she was ready, she was a few minutes late. Lucas had texted her to say he was waiting for her at reception.

Carrie watched as Lucas took a sharp intake

of breath as his eyes roamed over her. She swung her hips as she walked to him, her eyes not leaving his. Carrie's skin tingled as she could feel everyone's gaze on her.

"Hello," she said, coming to a stop in front of him.

"I want to kiss you, but I think we've already given everyone enough to gossip about. Come on, let's go." He placed his hand on the small of her back to guide her to the door, and Carrie felt a shiver run down her spine from his light touch. "Shall we get a taxi?" he asked, glancing down at her heels.

"It's only around the corner. Come on." As they walked away from the hotel, Carrie slipped her hand into his.

Carrie felt a warmth radiating in her chest. It was a beautiful evening, the sun still high in the sky, warming everything it touched. The city was buzzing with tourists and workers, all enjoying the balmy evening. Excitement filled the air as the city opened up for the evening. With Lucas's hand in hers, Carrie walked the familiar streets of Mayfair.

"Will you miss London?" Lucas broke the silence.

"Of course. It's an odd feeling to be in love with two homes that are so very different. Although I think Eve is planning to make it her mission to keep me busy when I get home, so I don't have a moment to miss London."

"What would you be doing on an evening like this in Scotland?"

"Where I'm living now, there's a beautiful walled garden next to the castle, so I'd probably finish work and go outside for some fresh air. There's a bench next to the greenhouse where I like to sit. I'd take my notepad with me and plan recipes. I know it sounds very idyllic, but it's not. Some days, the midges make going outside a nightmare. Lachlan is restoring the castle's library for the hotel guests, so during the winter I would make myself a hot chocolate and take it in there. Lachlan ordered lots of secondhand books from an auction house somewhere in England called Ivy Hatch. There's a handful of first editions, lots of classics, and even a handful of modern-day romances. We're cataloguing them and deciding how to set them on the shelves. Eve wants to colour-code them, but Lachlan wants to organise them by era. It's an ongoing argument." Carrie chuckled. They'd reached the restaurant and Lucas stepped ahead of her to open the door, holding it for her as she walked through.

The maître d' recognised Carrie and showed them to a secluded table. Carrie took her seat and watched as Lucas looked around, his eyes wide. There was an Earl Grey candle in the middle of the table. Its flame threw a glow across their menus. Someone had meticulously placed cutlery, wine glasses, water glasses, and napkins on the table. It was perfection.

"I can see you curled up in a library on a rainy day," Lucas commented. His gaze was focused on the menu in his hands, but his eyes had glazed over.

"With the sound of rain hammering against the windows. Ignore that menu, we'll both get the tasting menu. It's the only way to show you the utter brilliance of Lachlan's creations."

Carrie watched as Lucas's eyes skimmed the page, landing at the bottom of the menu where the tasting menu's price was. "It's very expensive." He gulped.

"It's my treat. Besides, I get a discount since the owner is one of my oldest friends and soon-to-be business partner."

"Have you decided to accept their offer?" He settled the menu back on the table and returned his attention to her. Carrie fought the blush that was threatening to spread across her face under the scrutiny of his gaze.

"Unofficially, yes. Eve has emailed me the contract to look over. Some light reading material for the journey home." Carrie tried to make light of the situation, but it fell flat as she watched a pang of pain shoot through Lucas's eyes as they continued to bore into hers.

"Let's not mention you going home."

The waiter came over to take their order, putting an end to the topic.

"What are your plans, Lucas?" asked Carrie, sipping the wine that had just been poured for her.

"My plans?" he echoed.

"Yes. Will you stay at *Hotel Mayfair* forever? What about Lily? Is she happy just being a kitchen assistant forever? You must have thought it through, Lucas. What are your plans for the future?"

"I haven't thought it through. Although Lily looks and acts well, she's more fragile than you realise. Every day that we have together is a blessing. I don't want to risk changing anything in our lives right now. She's doing well and is happy. Any kind of change could harm that. I suppose my plan for the future is to keep everything the same." He shrugged his shoulders. His gaze had travelled to the glass in front of him, refusing to meet her eyes.

"I think you treat Lily like she's too fragile." As soon as the words had escaped her, Carrie wished she could claw them back. It was insensitive of her to say such a thing. Lily was her friend, but how she lived her life was none of Carrie's business.

"Don't, Carrie. Lily is my responsibility." His mood had shifted from happy Lucas to brooding and moody.

"Sorry. I overstepped the mark."

"I appreciate your input, Carrie, but I know what it's like to almost lose Lily."

Carrie reached across the table and intertwined her fingers with his. She might never know how it felt to almost lose a sister, but she knew what it was like to lose a loved one. It left a gaping hole in your heart and left you living in fear that you'd lose others close to you. For all she disagreed, she could understand why Lucas was so protective of Lily and why he prioritised her needs and her health over his own life.

The tense atmosphere was interrupted as the first course of their taster menu arrived. "This looks amazing," commented Lucas as he let go of her hand and glanced down at the cutlery.

"It's that one." Carrie pointed.

The dish was scallop ceviche. The food was served on a scallop shell on a bed of ice. It looked stunning, and Carrie's mouth was watering at the thought of tasting it. Tiny cubes of cucumber, garlic, spring onions, tomatoes, and peppers had been chopped up and mixed with the scallops.

"That's amazing," Lucas said. His face turned from joy to concern in the space of seconds.

"Are you okay?" asked Carrie, watching him.

"Sorry, it's just my phone is going off in my pocket. Do you mind if I check it? I'm worried it could be Lily." He looked torn as he glanced between her and his pocket.

"Of course. Please, check it." Carrie put down her fork, unable to eat anymore until she knew Lily was okay.

Lucas pulled his phone from his pocket, and Carrie recognised the moment he saw who was calling. His entire body relaxed, and the crease between his eyebrows disappeared. "It's the hotel owner," he explained, pressing a few buttons on his phone. "I'll just turn it on silent."

"Does the owner often contact you outside of your working hours?" Carrie picked up her fork and returned to the food.

"If I don't wake up to at least five texts and

two missed calls, I know something's wrong. I'm pushing for permanent contracts with contractual hours. The hotel can't keep operating like it is."

"You're too good for that place."

"I know, but what can I do?" He turned his attention back to his food.

"So, tell me, what's the one food you would never eat, no matter how much money someone offered you?" Carrie was eager to change the subject before she got on her knees and begged Lucas to move him and Lily to Scotland and manage Lachlan's hotel.

Dishes kept coming, the wine kept flowing, and their conversation flowed naturally. The candle in the middle of the table had burned out, leaving a puddle of wax and a puff of smoke. The last plate was on its way over, and Carrie was looking forward to the dessert. Since her time at the restaurant, the menu had been revised, so she didn't know what to expect.

"Chef made you something special," said the waiter, placing their plates down in front of them. "You have a cocoa biscuit crumb, with a layer of chocolate orange mouse on top, then a caramel jelly. There's also an orange curd to cut through the sweetness of the dessert. Enjoy."

Carrie inspected the dish and its presentation. The orange curd was a smudge across the plate with mint leaves and candied peel scattered through it. Atop of the curd was the play on cheesecake. It had been created in a circular mould with sharp edges. Each layer sat on the other. It looked perfect, and she knew that as soon as she took a bite, the orange and chocolate flavours would burst in her mouth. She took her spoon and cut into the dessert with it, marvelling at the marbled effect inside the caramel jelly. As Carrie lifted the spoon to her mouth, she felt her own phone buzz in her pocket. Her mind immediately went to her grandmother.

"Sorry, my phone's going now. Do you mind if I check it?" Carrie asked, putting the spoon back down on her plate.

"Of course not." Lucas smiled at her and took a bite of his own dessert.

Carrie's brow furrowed as she pulled out her phone just as the call ended. She clicked on the missed call icon and saw the call was from Lily.

"Lily's trying to call me," she said.

Lucas pulled his phone out of his pocket, and Carrie watched as the blood drained from his face. "I've got fifty missed calls from Maria and Lily's numbers." He gulped. Lucas punched a few buttons on his phone before holding it up to his ear.

"Maria?" he gasped out as someone picked up on the other end.

Carrie looked down at the perfect dessert in front of her, no longer feeling excited about it. She could hear a voice on the other end of Lucas's phone, but she couldn't make out what they were saying. The sound of Lucas's chair scraping along the floor interrupted her thoughts. It echoed throughout the restaurant and heads turned to look at them, but Carrie only had eyes for Lucas. His face was ashen as he pulled his jacket from the back of his chair.

"Hospital? What hospital?" he shouted down the phone.

Carrie scooped up her clutch bag and followed Lucas out of the restaurant. "I'll pop by tomorrow to settle the bill," Carrie called over her shoulder. As she stepped out onto the street, Lucas was hailing a taxi. Instinctively, she followed him into it. He was still on the phone, nodding along to whatever the person on the other end was saying.

"Royal Brompton Hospital, please," Lucas instructed the taxi driver. "I'll be there as quickly as I can." Lucas put the phone down and turned to look out of the window.

"Lucas? What's wrong?" Carrie reached over to take his hand in hers, but he pulled it away.

"Lily's been rushed to hospital." His tone was clipped, and he'd balled his hands into fists.

"Oh, my…"

"They're taking Lily straight to the heart specialist unit."

Carrie felt as though the food in her stomach had turned to stone. They'd been sitting enjoying a fancy meal while poor Lily was being rushed into hospital.

"Is it her heart?" Carrie gulped and held her breath as she waited for an answer she was sure she didn't want to hear.

"They think so," he murmured, still looking

out of the window. His body was rigid, his hands balled up in his lap. In the silence of the taxi, Carrie could hear him grinding his teeth.

It was just a fifteen-minute drive to Royal Brompton Hospital, but it felt like a lifetime. Lucas spent the entire drive staring out of the window, keeping as far away from her as possible. Carrie wanted to wrap her arms around him and tell him everything would be okay. But she knew he didn't want her near him and she couldn't promise him it would be okay, because she didn't know if it would be.

"You go, I'll pay for the taxi and come find you," she insisted as they pulled up outside the entrance. Lucas grunted in response and opened his door before the car stopped moving.

Carrie threw a handful of notes at the driver and ran out the door before he could offer her the change. "Keep it as a tip!" she called, running through the hospital entrance. She could just make out Lucas in the distance, so she kept running to keep up with him. The shiny floor beneath her feet felt like an ice rink. With every step forward, Carrie felt as though she was being pushed five steps back. People surrounding her became blurred shapes as she fought to keep up with Lucas. He wound his way through corridors, up flights of stairs, and across the building, always leaving Carrie a few steps behind. She was out of breath and panting. Her calves burnt, but she pushed herself to keep going so she didn't lose him.

There was a set of closed doors ahead, and Carrie skidded to a halt behind Lucas. He'd buzzed an intercom on the wall and was waiting for a reply.

"Hello?" a crackled voice floated through the machine.

"It's Lucas Raven. I'm here to see my sister, Lily Raven." He was still struggling to catch his breath.

"Lucas, come in." There was a familiarity in the woman's voice that made Carrie's heart sink. This clearly wasn't the first time Lucas had been to this ward.

She followed him through the doors and up to the nurses' station, where an older nurse smiled at him.

"It's not as bad as it sounds," she reassured Lucas as he stepped up to the counter. Carrie felt a rush of air leave her and she stepped back against the far wall, leaving Lucas to talk to the nurse. She could still hear their conversation from where she was, and she watched as Lucas's entire body visibly relaxed as the woman talked through Lily's tests. He rested his outstretched palms on top of the counter and hung his head.

"She just overdid it?" he asked.

"Yes. That's all. Maria is in the waiting room. You can go through and see Lily in a minute. We're just getting her to take some medication. I'm afraid she'll be limited to one visitor at a time." The nurse glanced over in Carrie's direction.

"That's fine. I'll be through there. Give me a

shout when I can see her." He turned to face Carrie and pointed towards the doors they'd just walked through. They stepped through them, but Lucas kept his foot wedged in the door so they didn't get locked out.

"You can leave now." His voice was harsh as his eyes focused on a spot just above her eyes.

"I'm not leaving you. I'll wait in the waiting room if that's okay. If not, I can always sit in the hospital cafe. At least you'll know I'm close by. Lucas, I know how terrified you are of losing her. Please don't push me away. Let me be there for you." She reached forward to take his hand in hers, but he pulled it away as her fingertips brushed against his skin. His brow furrowed, and he crossed his arms, still refusing to meet her eyes.

"I don't want you close by, Carrie. Lily's overdone it. She's been helping with this stupid wedding. Then last night she got worked up over having you round for dinner. I've been an idiot. Nothing can change. Don't you see that? Just a new friend in her life has pushed her too far. I was with you tonight when I should have been at home looking after her." His eyes shone as he spat the words at her. For the first time, his eyes met hers, but they were cold. It was as though he was seeing right through her. "I'm sorry, Carrie, but I've made a terrible mistake letting you into our lives."

Carrie felt as though she'd been punched in the stomach. Unshed tears stung her eyes, but she fought against them, refusing to cry in front of him.

This was about Lily, not her. It would be selfish of her to cry in front of him. Her legs shook as she took a deep breath and looked up to meet his eyes. "I'm sorry," she whispered, before turning on her heel and walking away.

She heard the door to the ward snap shut behind her, but she didn't look back. Carrie focused on putting one foot in front of the other until she got out of the building. On autopilot, she hailed a taxi and reeled off the address for the hotel. As she watched London pass her by, Carrie bit back the tears. She'd always known her time with Lucas would end. She just hadn't expected it to be so abrupt. Guilt ate away at her insides as she thought about Lily lying in a hospital bed with wires attached to her. Lucas had been right. Lily had done too much. The unsaid implication was that she'd pushed Lily too much. With a sigh, Carrie fished out a tissue from the bottom of her bag. She blew her nose and wiped her eyes with the back of her hand. There was no time for self-pity or tears. She had caused pain for those she cared about, and there was nothing she could do to make it better. All she could do now was get through the next couple of days before she returned home.

CHAPTER TWENTY-TWO

Once back at the hotel, Carrie pulled out her phone and called Eve. She needed to hear a comforting voice, and she needed to be reminded of home.

"Carrie?" Eve answered the phone just as Carrie thought it was going to voicemail.

"Eve," she cried down the phone. Her resolve not to cry had gone out the window the second she heard Eve's voice.

"Carrie, what on earth is wrong?" asked Eve. The last thing Eve had heard was that Carrie was going out for dinner with Lucas at Lachlan's restaurant.

"Lily's in hospital and it's all my fault." Saying it out loud was like a knife piercing her heart. The pain was threatening to unleash a fresh wave of tears.

"Your fault? Carrie, what happened?"

"I made her overdo it and now she's in the hospital because of her heart. Lucas doesn't want me anywhere near them."

"This isn't your fault. Lucas is upset and worried, and he's lashed out at you. Please don't blame yourself for this."

"But it is all my fault. I should have ignored my feelings for Lucas and then none of us would be in this position. Lily would be well and I wouldn't be sitting in my room heartbroken over the handsome and caring man I've fallen for. He hates me, Eve. He blames me for Lily being rushed to hospital. It's all my fault."

"Oh, Carrie. I can't wait for you to get home."

"I can't wait to come home. What was I thinking coming to London? I was so much happier at home."

"You wanted an adventure."

"If I ever mention an adventure again, you have permission to lock me in the castle's dungeons."

"We don't have dungeons, Carrie."

"Well, that's the first thing I'm going to do when I become a shareholder. I'll build some dungeons."

"You're going to accept our offer?" Eve let out a little squeal of delight.

"Yes. I need something to tie me down in case I ever decide to leave Scotland again."

"Carrie, stop it. We have the final contract ready, so I'll email it to you. Give it a read on your way home, but please don't jump into anything, Carrie. We want you to join us because you're excited about the opportunity. Not because you're running away from heartbreak."

"I know," groaned Carrie. The problem with having a best friend that knew you so well was that, well, they knew you so well.

"Now, get to sleep. You've got some big days ahead of you. I love you."

"I love you," Carrie said. She was grateful Eve ended the call because she wasn't sure she would have had the courage to press the button.

Carrie barely slept that night. She kept tossing and turning and rolling over to check her phone. A small part of her hoped Lucas would message her, apologising for how he had spoken to her. But deep down, she knew he meant it. As much as he blamed himself for Lily's health scare, he also blamed Carrie. She'd led him astray, pulled him from his usual routine, and distracted him from rigidly keeping Lily to her schedule. At four o'clock, Carrie heard the first notes of bird songs outside her window and she decided to give up on any hope of sleep. She got ready and went down to the kitchen, relieved to see the nighttime shift still working. It would be a while until Camille came in. She breathed a sigh of relief as she put off Camille's interrogation.

Like a whirlwind, Carrie made choux pastry, mixed up macarons, and cooked them all in the huge industrial ovens. They'd changed the daytime menu to allow Carrie use of the ovens so she could bake everything for the wedding. By the time Camille walked in, there were four hundred éclair shells cooling on racks and six hundred macaron shells stacked on racks above them. There wasn't an empty surface in sight as Carrie had moved on to mixing up the buttercream to decorate the wedding cake.

"Carrie, have you done all of this yourself?" Camille gasped. She turned on the spot, her eyes wide at the sight of so many sweet treats.

"The wedding's tomorrow. I've got little choice but to do it all myself." It came out harsher than she'd intended, but Carrie shrugged her shoulders and continued to pour icing sugar into the buttery mixture inside the electric mixer.

"I'm going to help you in whatever way I can, but Lucas called to say he won't be in today, so I'm in charge." Camille's face paled.

"Did he say how Lily is?" Carrie's voice wobbled.

"She's being discharged later today, but he wants to get her settled in at home with Maria before he comes into work. Which means with the wedding tomorrow, we have a lot to do without a hotel manager or an events planner." Camille took a deep breath.

Carrie nodded. She felt her shoulders relax from the news that Lily was being discharged today. The brief moments of sleep she'd had were plagued with nightmares of Lily's condition worsening. She shook her head to rid it of those thoughts and refocused her attention back to the wedding they had to prepare for.

"He blames me," Carrie whispered.

"For what?"

"Lily being in hospital."

"Oh, Carrie, don't be so silly. He doesn't."

"He said it, Camille." Carrie checked the consistency of the buttercream. It was perfect, so she switched off the machine.

"Carrie, Lily often has trips to the hospital. It's nothing unusual."

"She was rushed to hospital in an ambulance while I was with Lucas."

"Carrie, Lily is fine. She'll be at home in her own bed by this afternoon. Please, you don't put yourself through this."

Carrie took a deep breath and squared her shoulders. "If I can borrow a couple of people from the dessert team, I'll be fine. I've been teaching them to pipe so they can help me with some of the decorating. Even if they just fill the éclairs for me, that'll be one less job." Carrie didn't mind having lots to do. She'd stay up all night and finish the piping if need be. There was little chance of her sleeping since her mind was replaying Lucas's parting words to her on repeat.

"Carrie, don't bury this," warned Camille.

"I'll deal with it once we have this wedding over with."

"Okay. I'm sorry I can't be with you to help.

I'm sure you could benefit from a shoulder to cry on." Camille squeezed her shoulder.

"I'll be fine, and if not, I'll be going home soon."

"I'm going to miss you."

"I know, but we can stay in touch. I'm also counting on you being one of our first guests once the hotel opens."

"Of course. I can't wait. Now, I need to get on. I'll get some members from the dessert team to come and give you a hand. Is there anything else you need?"

"Could you ask one of them to bring me a coffee from the staff machine? I can't stomach another cup of instant." Carrie sent a glare in the direction of the pot of instant coffee next to her kettle.

"Will do! I doubt either of us will eat today, so let's pencil in dinner together at eight. I'll get something from the chef and bring it over to your station."

"Sounds perfect. See you later." Carrie waved to Camille and watched as she walked off.

Carrie split the buttercream and added the colouring to each portion. With a fork, she whipped the buttercreams until they were the perfect shade. She could do it by machine, but she needed the monotonous activity to keep her thoughts at bay. Besides, she'd mixed so much buttercream over the years, she was almost as fast as the machine.

By eight o'clock, Carrie had cramp in both of her hands, three plasters on two fingers, and her head was pounding from the amount of caffeine she'd drunk. Sasha had texted her countless times throughout the day with various changes she wanted. Buttercream flavours and colours had seen last-minute changes. For the first time, Carrie had said no to Sasha. She'd asked whether Carrie could 'quickly whip up three hundred iced sugar cookies with her and Milo's names on them to put on guests' seats for the ceremony.' There was only so much Carrie could achieve before tomorrow, and three hundred iced sugar cookies did not fall within her scope.

"I got us pasta. Specifically carbonara. Jamal made it especially for us while he was on his break." Camille walked over, holding two bowls piled high with their dinner.

"That smells amazing. Please tell Jamal that he is my favourite person in the whole entire world." Carrie took a bowl from Camille and sat down. It was the first time she'd sat down since she'd got out of bed that morning and her feet were throbbing. The dessert team had gone home an hour ago, but Carrie still had one hundred macarons to pipe.

"How are you?" Camille sat beside her.

"Busy," Carrie mumbled before taking a bite of her food. "This is amazing. Do you think I could convince Jamal to move to Scotland so he can make me pasta every day?"

"Carrie, I appreciate Jamal's pasta is amazing, but you're changing the subject."

"I'm fine. Please, let's not go over it all again. My hand has cramp and I have another hundred macarons to pipe before I can even think about having a shower and going to bed. I'm getting up early tomorrow to make the finishing touches to the cake. How're you? Is everything in hand?"

"I feel as though I've aged ten years today. How Lucas has been doing this whilst also managing the hotel, I have no idea. I've spent all day on the phone with Sasha and arranging all the changes she's requesting."

"I'm surprised she's had time to call you!"

"Have you had her on the phone, too?"

"Yup. Last-minute changes to colours and gold leaf." Carrie yawned.

"Oh, to be rich with too much time on your hands." Camille scooped up the last mouthful of pasta. "Do you need anything?" she asked around the mouthful of food. There was no time for politeness.

"I'm fine. Just going to power through and finish these macarons. What about you?"

"I'm good. I've got some of the night shift team setting up the reception room while I eat, and then I'll go check it once I've finished. Then Lucas should be here at ten and I'll do a handover. He's going to come in and work through to the end of the wedding."

"What about Lily?"

"Maria is moving in for a couple of days, so Lily has someone there."

"Good. I wish Lily was well enough to see the wedding. She's been so excited about the lead-up and helping me with my piping designs." Carrie pushed a piece of pancetta around her bowl.

"So do I. We'll take lots of photos for her."

"Camille, I don't think I'll see her again." Carrie's voice wobbled as she admitted to her worries. The thought had been fermenting in her head for the last few hours and saying it out loud had hurt.

"I'll have a word with Lucas about your leaving party." She crossed her fingers before taking Carrie's empty bowl for her. "I'll give our compliments to the chef. See you tomorrow!"

CHAPTER TWENTY-THREE

Carrie woke the following morning to find texts from everyone back home wishing her luck for the wedding. They all knew how important it was to her. Carrie's time in London had been leading up to this day. Even her grandmother had sent her a text wishing her good luck. The multiple spaces and a few strange letters made Carrie think Alice had sent the text on her own. It was four in the morning, and technically, Carrie's job would be over very soon. She just had a few more adjustments to make to the wedding cake. However, with their staffing issues still unresolved, Carrie was working overtime as a waitress to help the day run smoothly. With a groan, she pushed herself out of bed to get ready for the day. It would be over before she knew it and she'd be hurtling back to Scotland. If she was honest with herself, it couldn't come quick enough.

Carrie made herself presentable, dressing in the hotel's uniform, and slicking her hair back into a somewhat neat bun. She ignored her makeup, which was scattered across her bathroom counter. The recent sunshine had brought out her freckles, and she liked how they looked. She made herself a coffee in the room and took it down to the kitchen with her.

"There you are! Lucas needs to know how you're going to transport all the macarons to the ballroom without damaging them?" Jamal was pacing around her workspace as she walked in.

"Jamal, it's half four in the morning. What are you still doing here?" asked Carrie, ignoring his question.

"I live too far away to go home and come back, so I'm drinking lots of Red Bull and coffee." He shrugged his shoulders.

"I'll sort the macarons. You need some sleep. Take my room card and go have a nap. Set your alarm for eight." Carrie watched as he opened his mouth to protest. "Just take the room key, Jamal. I don't have time to argue with you. We both know I'll win." She shot him a sickly sweet smile as he took the key card from her.

"Carrie, you're a star. Will you let Lucas know where I am?" He took off before Carrie could say no. She glared into her coffee cup. That was what she got for being nice.

She didn't go to find Lucas. Instead, she focused on getting the wedding cake ready. Besides trying to avoid the awkwardness of bumping into Lucas, Carrie didn't know how she was going to transport the macarons from the cold storage to the ballroom. The delicate shells of each macaron were sandwiched together with elegant floral buttercream piping. Just the slightest knock would ruin all of Carrie's hard work and turn the beautiful sweet treats into a pile of mush.

"Have you seen Jamal?" snapped Lucas, storming into her workspace. Ignoring him, Carrie finished the line of piping she was on before she looked up at him. "In your own time. It's not like I have a wedding today!" He huffed as she put the piping bag down and turned to look at him.

"You'll have a wedding with no cake if you continue to talk to me like that." Carrie put her hands on her hips and stared at Lucas. She watched him shrink under her gaze. He backed up to the work surface and slumped back against it.

"I'm sorry. It's been a stressful couple of days." For a brief moment, she saw him drop his defences as he looked up at her.

"How is Lily?" whispered Carrie.

"She's fine," he snapped, and just like that, his walls were up again.

"Good. You asked where Jamal was? I sent him up to my room to have a nap. Did you realise he hadn't gone home?"

"No." Lucas sighed, rubbing a hand across his

face.

"He'll be back at eight. I'm finishing the wedding cake and then will figure out how to get the macarons and éclairs to the ballroom before the guests turn up for the reception. Don't worry about that." Carrie sounded a lot more organised and capable than she felt.

"Thank you, Carrie." He smiled at her, but there was a hollowness behind it. "It's been a pleasure working with you." The finality of his words brought tears to Carrie's eyes. She looked down at her feet as she heard his footsteps retreating. With a deep breath, she forced her attention back to the wedding cake. There would be plenty of time to wallow in her emotions on her journey home. Until then, she just had to get through the next couple of days.

Somehow, the wedding went smoothly. Well, as smoothly as Sasha and Milo's wedding could have ever gone. The last-minute decision to release doves in the ballroom caused a bit of a stir. Lucas hadn't approved it and there were staff already handing out canapés. Carrie had held her breath as she watched the doves fly towards the front of the room where the wedding cake sat proudly on top of a gilded table. Thankfully, Jamal and some other members of the kitchen team threw open the doors to the courtyard and encouraged the birds outside. The team had transformed the ballroom into a floral paradise with enough hints of gold to make the setting look opulent and not tacky. Each table had a huge floral display in the centre with beautiful deep red blooming peonies nestled amongst pretty Baby's Breath and green foliage. The flowers were in round golden pots which made the red pop against them. They weren't the exact flowers Sasha had insisted on, but she hadn't seemed to notice. Freshly pressed white linen tablecloths covered each table. Each place setting had a gold table mat, gold cutlery, and a menu printed on deep-red paper with gold embossed letters. Scattered amongst the flowers and place settings were white candles in glass holders. It was a feast for Carrie's eyes and she'd been excited for her wedding cake to take centre stage.

After much deliberation, Carrie had opted to use a room service trolley to transport just fifty macarons at a time. She had to ensure they were evenly spaced so they wouldn't roll into one another and crush the delicate piping in the centre. As it was such an important job, Carrie didn't trust anyone but her to do it. The six trips took her much longer than anticipated, as she'd forgotten to factor in setting up the macarons at the other end. Sasha had insisted on a dessert table where Carrie's creations would be displayed before guests could be served them. Sasha, being Sasha, hadn't thought through all the implications of a dessert table. The éclairs had fresh cream in them and needed to be kept refrigerated. Meanwhile, the macarons needed to be brought to room temperature before eating, but couldn't risk being too warm or the piped floral display in the centre would melt. It had caused the engineering team a real problem, but eventually, they came up with a solution.

The table was modern with gold spindly legs and perspex domes above it. Somehow, the engineering team had created two separate temperature-controlled spaces. The table top had been spray-painted gold to hide the pipes underneath it. Carrie had taken a picture of it before she arranged the desserts. She wondered if they could create something similar at the castle so the guests could see her beautiful creations to tempt them into ordering them.

After countless trips back and forth, Carrie had transported both the macarons and the éclairs, and they were beautifully displayed under their individual domes. A small thermometer hidden behind the goodies confirmed the correct temperatures. The room was truly stunning, and the guests had commented on it as they stepped through the ballroom doors. The staff had all aged twenty years in the space of a day, but when Sasha and Milo made their exit with huge smiles on their faces, they knew they'd pulled it off.

As Carrie served meals, cut the cake into hundreds of portions, and served the macarons and éclairs to everyone, she was overwhelmed by the conversations she overheard. Everyone had something nice to say about the show-stopper wedding cake or the beautiful éclairs, and the stunning macarons. Hundreds, if not thousands, of pictures were taken of her creations alone. The magazine photographers all photographed Carrie's creations.

"Do you know who made the desserts?" a photographer had asked her around a mouthful of éclair.

"I did." She had beamed back at him.

"Here's my card. Drop me an email, as I'm sure my editor would be interested in running a piece on you."

"Oh, but I don't work here. I'm going back to Scotland the day after tomorrow." Her heart had sunk at the missed opportunity.

"What do you do in Scotland?" The photographer picked up another éclair and took a bite.

"I'm helping my friends set up a castle hotel and restaurant. It's Lachlan McLeod's project. You might have heard of him?"

The photographer's mouth had hung open, causing Carrie to flinch back at the sight. "You're Lachlan McLeod's protégé?" he gasped out.

"I wouldn't say I was his protégé, but I was trained in his kitchen by his pastry chef."

"Send me an email as soon as you're back in Scotland. We'd love to run a piece on you, and Lachlan's new hotel and restaurant. I look forward to seeing you again." He had waved at her and grabbed another éclair before wandering off to shoot some more pictures of the happy couple.

The photographer's business card was still in Carrie's back pocket as she stood next to Camille, watching as Lucas ushered the last handful of guests out of the ballroom. A glance at her watch told her it was two in the morning, meaning she'd been awake for twenty-two hours.

"We did it!" Camille cried and held up her hand for a high-five.

"I'm ready to sleep for a week." Carrie suppressed a yawn as she high-fived Camille.

"A week? I was thinking a month!" Jamal pulled them both into a hug.

"But what about Carrie's leaving party?" Camille reminded them. She stepped back from the hug and stared at them both with her hands on her hips.

"I wouldn't miss Carrie's leaving party." Jamal narrowed his eyes at Camille.

"And I couldn't possibly miss my own leaving party, so it looks like we're all settling for eight hours' sleep and a lot of concealer."

"What she said." Jamal nodded.

"That's a wrap!" Lucas called, gesturing for everyone to come together in the middle of the room. They were a combination of daytime staff, nighttime staff, and temps. Carrie wasn't sure who would be around to start the day shift, but she reminded herself that it was no longer her problem. Technically, her contract ended two hours ago.

They all gathered in front of Lucas. Carrie

fought the urge to reach out and take his hand. He looked utterly exhausted with dark circles under his eyes, stubble across his chin, and his hair in his eyes, although that may have had more to do with Sasha's grandmother combing her fingers through his hair rather than his lack of time to get it cut. Thankfully, Sasha had swiftly moved her grandmother on to her next unsuspecting victim.

"Thank you all for your hard work. This wedding wasn't without its difficulties, but we pulled through and look what we achieved. I'm happy to announce that we have a new events planner starting on Monday." The crowd erupted into cheers. "Yes, thank you." Lucas held up his hands, but the edges of his lips turned up as though he were fighting a smile. "We have also made the decision to offer many of you permanent contracts. It's something I've been pushing for and it's finally been signed off. I'm hoping to meet with you all over the next few days with the finalised contract."

Carrie tuned out as Lucas continued to tell the staff about upcoming events at the hotel. Her eyes were focused on him. She watched as his mouth moved and his eyes flickered across the crowd. Each time he reached the person beside her, Carrie saw his eyes flicker back and he would skip over her. She felt a cold rush go through her body each time.

"I won't keep you any longer, but I just wanted to remind you all that we have to say goodbye to the very talented Carrie. She'll be leaving us the day after tomorrow." He gestured towards her, but still, his eyes didn't settle on her.

"We're having a leaving party for Carrie tomorrow evening. Actually, it's past midnight so I suppose the leaving party is tonight. Meet in the staff room at seven. We'll be going out for dinner and drinks." Camille informed everyone.

"Goodnight everyone! See you all on Monday." With a last wave, Lucas set off towards the ballroom doors.

Carrie wanted to follow him and talk to him, but with news of her impending departure, everyone had crowded around her to say goodbye. By the time Carrie had smiled, hugged, and said goodbye to her well-wishers, Lucas was nowhere to be seen.

"Maybe he'll come to your leaving party tomorrow?" Camille suggested. She'd walked up to where Carrie stood at the ballroom doors.

"Perhaps," Carrie whispered. She couldn't allow herself to cling to the hope that she might see him again. He'd made it clear he would see everyone on Monday. Lucas wasn't coming to her leaving party.

"Come on, up to bed with you." Camille took her arm in hers and led Carrie to the lift. She pressed the button and waited with her until the lift came. Neither of them said anything until the lift pinged and the doors opened.

"Come over early and get ready with me?" asked Carrie. She suspected she'd need all the distractions she could get.

"Of course." Camille gave her a hug before pushing her towards the lift doors. "See you later." She waved as the doors closed.

Carrie covered her mouth as she yawned. The lift doors opened, and she stepped out, stilling as she saw a figure outside her bedroom. Her legs shook as she walked down the hallway. As she neared the end of the hallway, she saw it was Lucas waiting for her.

"I thought you'd gone," she whispered.

"I couldn't go without saying goodbye to you."

Carrie unlocked her door and held it open for him. "We don't want to wake anyone," she said as she saw his hesitation.

"I can't be long. Maria's waiting for me to get home so she can leave Lily."

"How is she?" Carrie lent her hip against the table in the hallway. She knew there was no point in asking him any further into the room.

"Recovering. I sent her a picture of the cake and she said it looked fit for a princess."

"I'm glad she's okay, Lucas. I didn't mean for any of this."

"Carrie, I'm sorry for what I said in the hospital. I don't even remember what I said. I was in such a state and wanted to blame someone."

"I understand. Lily is very lucky to have you, Lucas."

"I'm very lucky to have her."

"Be happy. Both of you. I know you want to protect Lily, but don't forget to live your lives."

"Goodbye, Carrie." He stepped forward and pressed a quick kiss to her lips.

Carrie held her arms by her sides, resisting the temptation to wrap them around him and hold him to her.

"Goodbye, Lucas," she whispered. The tears that filled her eyes threatened to fall. He turned one final time before leaving her room, closing the door behind him so it wouldn't slam.

CHAPTER TWENTY-FOUR

Carrie's leaving party was a whirlwind of laughter, delicious food, and many hugs. Somehow, Eve had got hold of Camille's number and had arranged for them to hold Carrie's leaving party at Lachlan's restaurant. It had been a huge surprise, and it felt somehow fitting to bring her two lives in London together before she left. For good this time. They'd closed the restaurant to the public, and the staff had decorated it with leaving banners and balloons. Tears had filled Carrie's eyes the second she'd walked in and seen how much effort everyone had gone to. It was truly something, to see a physical representation of how much people cared about you, and it was something Carrie desperately needed after yesterday.

They'd all been seated at a long table that ran the length of the restaurant. A waitress brought over a bottle of champagne with a tag on it and handed it to Carrie. She turned the tag over and read the words, '*Wish we were there. Love, Eve, Lachlan and Gran xxx*'. Carrie felt her heart pine for them. As much as she enjoyed her evening saying goodbye to London, she couldn't wait for the following day to be on the train hurtling home.

Despite the evening being everything and more than Carrie could have wished for, she still felt Lucas and Lily's absence. Last night's crushing guilt had eased, but she couldn't completely forgive herself. Even if she hadn't been responsible for Lily overdoing it, it was still her fault that Lucas was with her when Lily needed him. She must have been terrified when she was taken to the hospital by ambulance without him around.

"Don't think about him!" Camille had chastised her whenever she saw Carrie's eyes glaze over.

The evening had been the perfect goodbye to the city she had once loved so much. Camille had walked Carrie back to the hotel and hugged her goodbye.

"What time are you leaving in the morning?" she asked her.

"I'm leaving the hotel at about seven. My train is at eight-thirty from Kings Cross."

Eve had tried to convince Carrie to return home in style by booking herself on the Caledonian

Sleeper. She'd suggested Carrie might be as lucky as she had been and meet her own Scotsman on board. Carrie had declined. She didn't want her own Scotsman. All she wanted was Lucas, but she couldn't have him. Also, the Caledonian Sleeper left in the evening and she didn't want to spend any more time in London than necessary. Since it was Monday, the castle restaurant was closed, so Eve had suggested she get a direct train to Edinburgh and they would collect her from the station. Carrie had tried to argue, saying she didn't want them to go to that much effort for her, but it had been pointless. Eve had booked the train for her while she was on the phone.

"I don't start work until eight, but I'll try to get in early if I can. If not, I'll see you very soon," Camille said.

"Yes! Let me know when you can come and I'll make sure everything is ready for you to stay at the castle."

They hugged one last time before Camille left Carrie at the entrance of *Hotel Mayfair.*

Carrie left the hotel at six the following morning. When she told Camille last night that she wasn't leaving until seven, she hadn't been lying. However, when she woke, she realised she couldn't face any more goodbyes. And so, without even stopping to make herself a coffee, Carrie slipped out of her room and was grateful to see the night staff still milling around. She'd been dreading walking into reception and seeing Lucas at the counter, but her fears were quashed as she stepped out of the lift and saw a woman looking bored as she drummed her fingers on the countertop. It took just a few seconds for Carrie to hand over her key. She took one final glance around the reception area, smiled at a few people she recognised, and walked outside where the doorman hailed a taxi for her.

"Goodbye, London," she whispered as she closed the taxi door behind her.

Despite the early hour, the station was busy as Carrie wheeled her suitcases across the concourse. The only problem with leaving the hotel so early was that she was now in a busy train station with nothing to do for the next two hours. Carrie wheeled her bags to Pret and ordered herself a cappuccino and a mozzarella and tomato croissant. She took her order in a paper bag and went in search of a seat.

As she nibbled at the molten cheesy croissant, she wondered where everyone was heading off to. Each one of these people had their own story and their own heartbreak. Carrie would have been lying if she'd said a tiny part of her wasn't hoping for an emotional train station reunion with Lucas. Her mind drifted to a scenario where he would come frantically running through the station doors, pausing to look up at the departure screen as he tugged a hand through his hair. Then his eyes would scan the concourse and he'd find her. Their eyes would meet as he ran to her and told her he was so sorry and Lily would be there shortly with their suitcases to join her.

"Never going to happen, Carrie," she muttered to herself. Clearly, she'd read too many romance novels.

Between the food and the people watching, the time went by relatively fast and Carrie was soon hauling her suitcases onto the train and settling into her seat. She breathed a sigh of relief as the train pulled out of the station and nobody came to sit next to her. With her head resting against the window, she watched as they pulled out of London, leaving the bustling city behind. As the train put further distance between her and the city, she felt the weight on her chest lessen and she took in a deep breath.

There was one last thing Carrie wanted to do before she put the whole debacle behind her. She pulled out her phone and scrolled through her camera roll, choosing the best pictures from the wedding. Carrie pulled up a blank message and attached the photos to it. She spent a few minutes considering her message before she settled on keeping it short and friendly. Even if Lily replied, she knew she would have to ignore it. *'Lily, I hope you're feeling better. Thank you so much for all of your help. Here are some pictures from the wedding. Take care. Carrie xxx'.* She hit send and slid her phone into her handbag. Her hand brushed against the contract and she pulled it out. Before her leaving party, Carrie had used the hotel printer behind reception to print out the contract Eve had emailed her. She settled back into her seat and read the first page.

Including the delays, the train took six hours to reach Edinburgh. Carrie was starving by the time she dragged her suitcases off the train. She'd spent most of the journey reading through the contract. By the time the train pulled into Waverley, Carrie was ready to grab the first pen she saw and sign on the dotted line. There was no doubt in Carrie's mind that she wanted to be a part of what Eve and Lachlan were creating.

Lachlan was waiting for Carrie on the other side of the barriers.

"Hello, you!" he greeted her and pulled her into a quick hug before he took her suitcase.

"Hello! It's so good to see you." They still had another five hours to go in the car, but just being around Lachlan made Carrie feel as though she was home. "Where's Eve?" she asked, glancing around him.

"She's gone in search of food and your grandmother is in the car. I tried to talk her into coming with me, but she said she loved you, but she wasn't going to fight through the crowds when she could wait in the car."

Carrie fell into step beside Lachlan. That sounded just like her grandmother.

"How does it feel to be home?" asked Lachlan. Carrie saw the uneasy glance he sent her way. She knew Eve had been keeping him updated since he'd texted her last night, asking if she wanted him to drive down and pick her up. He also offered to play the big-brother role and have a chat with Lucas. Carrie had declined both his offers.

"It's good. I know the next few weeks won't be easy, but I'm ready to throw myself back into work. I've got so many ideas, Lachlan. I've also got a magazine interested in featuring us once we're properly open."

"Wow. You don't waste any time, do you?" He chuckled, leading her into the car park.

As promised, her grandmother was sitting in the car waiting for her. The passenger door opened and Alice climbed out to throw her arms around her only grandchild.

"You're not going back there again, do you hear me?" Alice said, squeezing her a little too hard.

"Don't worry, Gran. I don't want to. I'm home now." She smiled despite the pain of her ribs being slowly crushed under her grandmother's grip.

"Good. Let's get in, it's cold."

Carrie climbed into the back of the car and was relieved to find it toasty warm. The drop in temperature from London had been apparent the minute the train's doors had slid open.

"Eve's gone to get some food. Lord knows what she'll come back with. She mentioned something about greasy hamburgers, French fries, and, I think, she said apple pies, but I could be wrong." Her grandmother's fingers drummed against the centre armrest.

"She's gone to get McDonald's." Lachlan's nose scrunched up as he climbed into the driver's seat.

"I'd love a McDonald's!" Carrie clapped her hands together.

"You two are disgusting creatures." Lachlan sighed.

"Are you telling me you're going to go hungry rather than eat a Big Mac?" Carrie teased him.

"Of course not."

"Will you two ever grow up?" Alice rolled her eyes, but Carrie could see the smile across her face in the windscreen's reflection.

"Carrie!" The door swung open and Eve stood there holding two huge brown bags filled with greasy fast food.

"Eve!" Carrie threw herself across the backseat to throw her arms around her best friend.

"Be careful of the food!" Lachlan called, climbing back out of the driver's seat to retrieve the bags of food before they were crushed by Carrie and Eve.

"How are you? Are you okay?" Eve's arms were firmly clasped around Carrie.

"I will be." Carrie buried her face in Eve's shoulder. Now she was back with her best friend, she realised just how much she'd missed her. Being at the other end of a phone just wasn't the same.

"We'll have a cake and wine evening and you can tell me all about it," promised Eve.

"You call this an apple pie? It's in a cardboard

box!" Alice's voice screeched from the front seat. Carrie and Eve let go of each other and leaned forward to see Alice's reaction as she took a bite. The car was silent as Alice finished the mouthful and went straight in for another bite.

"What do you think?" asked Eve.

"It's not as nice as mine," said Alice, taking another bite.

"Not you as well, Alice." Lachlan sighed, pulling out boxes of food and distributing them around the car.

CHAPTER TWENTY-FIVE

Being home was a strange feeling. A foolish part of Carrie had expected everything to be the same. She thought she'd go home, go up to her bed, and fall asleep ready to resume normal life tomorrow morning. They'd dropped Alice off at the McLeod's castle, with promises to see her in a couple of days, and then they continued home. Eve had stayed sitting in the back with Carrie, earning a few grumbles from Lachlan about being a taxi service.

"How are you really?" asked Eve once Alice had left.

"I'm okay," replied Carrie, keeping her eyes studiously turned to the scenery.

"I'll be here when you're ready to talk." Eve reached over and squeezed Carrie's hand.

Carrie squeezed Eve's hand in reply as her vision blurred with unshed tears. Inside, Carrie's heart was soaring being back home, but she couldn't deny the sadness within her knowing she was so far away from Lucas. The fear of walking around a corner and bumping into him had been replaced by a longing to walk around the corner and bump into him. She watched as the scenery passed her by and reminded herself that this pain was temporary. This was her home. It had always been there to protect her during the most painful times of her life.

The following morning, Carrie realised temporary was a little more permanent than she'd hoped. Lucas's kind smile, sparkling eyes, and wandering hands had filled her dreams. She woke and rolled over to find an empty, cold space beside her. However, a glance out of her bedroom window lifted Carrie's mood. The sun had already risen and there was a haze on the ground, a sign that it would be a warm day. She threw on some leggings and a jumper, piling her curls on top of her head into a messy bun, and went in search of Eve and coffee.

"Good morning!" Eve greeted her as she walked into the kitchens. Eve had suggested Carrie take the rest of the week off to settle back in since the temp covering her would be there until the end of the month. However, Carrie needed the distraction of the bustling kitchen so she had thrown herself back into life at the castle.

"Morning!" Carrie smiled. Stepping into the kitchen was like no time had passed.

"I'll make coffee. There are some pastries in the store cupboard if you want to get them. We've had to order them in as the temp is much more accustomed to making sponge puddings than French pastries." Eve raised her eyebrows at her.

They quickly slotted back into their routine. With two coffees and a pile of pastries, Eve led Carrie to the conservatory that she'd been busy renovating while Carrie was away. It was in one of the private areas of the castle.

"It's beautiful, Eve." Carrie smiled as they walked into the sunlit room. Rattan sofas were pushed to the edges, a huge fluffy rug was in the middle with a table on top. Hanging baskets hung from the ceiling, with beautiful-smelling flowers cascading from them. It was simple but beautiful.

Carrie picked a croissant from the bowl and sat down on the sofa, basking in the sunshine. She took a bite and scrunched up her nose. It tasted mass-produced.

"You haven't been serving these to paying customers, have you?" she asked, putting the rest of it back.

"No. They've just been for staff. The temp is excellent at what she knows. It's just, she doesn't really know much." Eve's face clouded over with guilt.

"I'll make a batch later."

"You're supposed to be relaxing. Slowly settling back into life here."

"Eve, you are my bestest friend. We may only

have met later in life, but when have you ever known me to relax into anything?"

"Good point. You do throw yourself head first at speed into everything. You're doing it now with the castle to distract you. How are you?"

"I'm okay." Carrie shrugged and reached forward to pick at a pain au chocolat. It was no better than the croissant, but she needed a distraction while Eve grilled her.

"Carrie, we may not have been friends for very long, but I know you enough to recognise when you're not okay."

The sun was beating down on Carrie's skin and Eve's eyes were watching her intently.

"Fine, I'm not okay. But I have to be okay." She tore off a piece of the stale pastry and shoved it into her mouth.

"You don't have to be okay, Carrie. You're home now. We can drink a bottle of wine, eat a ridiculous amount of ice cream, and you can cry if you want to. Don't pretend to be okay for our sakes."

"I'm not pretending for you, Eve. I'm pretending for me. You know how desperately I want someone. I clung onto Rhys because I didn't think I'd ever find anyone. Then I found Lucas, and he's everything I've ever wanted. I can't imagine life without him. But we can't be together, Eve. Our lives are very different, and neither of us can compromise. To be with him would be to leave you all behind, and that would break my heart. There is no happy ending to my story, Eve, just heartbreak, and I have to learn to live with that."

"Don't talk like that, Carrie. There's still time for you to find someone to spend your life with."

"Lucas was my person, Eve."

"You don't know that."

"I'm certain. You have no doubts that Lachlan is your person, right?" Carrie didn't wait for an answer. "That's how I feel about Lucas." She stuffed another piece of stale pastry in her mouth, chewing through the bitterness of the chocolate.

"I'm sorry, Carrie." Eve moved to sit next to her and wrapped her arms around her.

"I'll be okay. I've got this place to throw myself into."

"Have you thought about our offer?" asked Eve, pulling back so she could see Carrie's face.

"I'd love to accept it. If you'll still have me."

"Of course! We're only doing lunchtime service today. Why don't we throw a little celebratory meal for the three of us?"

"Sounds wonderful." Despite the heavy feeling in her chest, Carrie was excited for what was to come. She was finally home and surrounded by those that loved her.

"I'll go tell Lachlan. We've got staff in prepping for tomorrow, but they finish at three so we can take over the kitchens. I think Lachlan has builders in the hotel today, but I'm sure he can make time for us." Eve started piling their empty cups onto the tray she'd brought with her.

"How's the hotel going?" asked Carrie, adding

the bowl of pastries to the tray.

"It looks amazing. I'll give you a tour later once the builders have left. I need your opinion on a few things. Lachlan has asked me to help decorate, but I don't know where to start. We can't afford an interior designer, so it's all on us."

"I'll start a Pinterest board!" Carrie called after her. Eve chuckled and carried on walking away.

Alone, Carrie tilted her head back and allowed the sun to shine through onto her face. In the distance, there was the faint sound of the building work going on, but other than that, it was silent. Carrie's skin tingled under the warmth of the sun. It felt as though it were slowly melting the ice cage around her heart. She'd always miss Lucas and there would always be a 'what if?' in the back of her mind, but she was slowly coming to terms with it. With each day, the pain would soften.

Dinner was delicious. Lachlan had made a simple risotto and Carrie had made a Cranachan cheesecake. It was a simple twist on the traditional Scottish dessert. Oat biscuits and butter formed the bottom layer. Carrie had whipped up a mix of cream cheese, cream, honey, and whisky for the middle layer. Then she'd added a layer of her grandmother's raspberry jam. They'd all hummed in sheer delight at the food as Eve kept topping up their glasses of wine.

"Not too much. We all have to be up bright and early for work tomorrow." Lachlan reminded them.

"You know, I thought you were grumpy when we first met, and I was right. You're a grade-A grump," Eve teased him.

Carrie watched the happy couple as they teased one another. Their eyes glowed with their love for each other. A lump formed in Carrie's throat at the scene. "So, am I going to get this tour?" she asked, draining her wine glass and putting it down on the table beside her signed contract. "I need to see what I've officially signed up to!"

"Come on. I'll come with you both in case you fall over and need a shining knight in armour to save you." Lachlan pulled out both of their chairs as they stood.

"Do we have any suits of armour?" hiccuped Eve.

"No. We're lucky to have a staircase. This place was in such a state when I bought it."

The hotel was looking amazing. So far, five rooms were ready to be decorated and furnished. Each one had high ceilings, floor-to-ceiling windows, and a balcony overlooking the gardens. They would be truly breathtaking once they were decorated.

Carrie pulled out her phone and started showing Eve the pictures she'd saved on Pinterest. They wanted the rooms to feel modern and luxurious but with a nod to their surroundings.

"All we need now is a hotel manager." Lachlan was standing against the bedroom door as he watched Carrie and Eve turn around the room, imagining pieces of furniture in certain places. Holding up the phone to get an idea of how each piece would fit. His lips kept twitching as his eyebrows rose higher into his hairline.

"You still don't have anyone suitable?" asked Carrie, putting her phone back in her pocket.

"Nobody has enough experience in luxury service. If the restaurant is to get a Michelin-Star, then the hotel needs to reflect that."

"I'll message some friends from London and see if they have any contacts," promised Carrie. She wondered if Camille or Jamal had worked with any hotel managers that they'd recommend. Other than Lucas.

CHAPTER TWENTY-SIX

Despite being summer, Carrie's room was freezing when she woke the following morning. She shivered as she forced herself out of bed and into the shower. Last night had been filled with lots of laughter and plans for the future, and she was determined to continue today with the same level of excitement. Carrie dressed in a long-sleeved black top with the castle's logo on it and a pair of black trousers. They had customers in the restaurant today, so she had to dress appropriately.

The kitchen was in darkness as Carrie entered. Her footsteps echoed throughout it as she flicked on the overhead lights and turned the industrial ovens on. It was like she hadn't been away. A glance at the clock told her she only had about half an hour until Eve would join her, so she set about making the first batch of pastries.

"Everyone is going to love you! Actually, forget everyone. I love you!" Eve exclaimed as she walked into the kitchens and spotted Carrie baking.

"How're you feeling today?" Carrie asked, watching as Eve winced at the bright lights above.

"Don't. I need coffee. Would you like one?" She went over to the machine and got two coffee cups out before Carrie replied. Just like that, they were back in their routine. It was as if no time had passed. As if Carrie hadn't had her heart swept away and then trampled upon.

"Coffee would be wonderful." Carrie plastered a smile across her face and pushed all thoughts of her love life from her mind. Ignoring it was how she was dealing with it, and so far, it was working.

"Is that someone's phone?" Eve asked, stopping the milk frother so they could both listen.

"It's a phone vibrating. Oh, it's probably mine. I put it down by the door when I came into the kitchen." Carrie held up her dough-covered hands to show Eve she couldn't answer it.

"Got it!" Eve called as she picked up the phone. "I must have missed it. It's just stopped."

"Will you check who it was? I'm worried it's Gran."

"Of course. Let's see. Missed calls. It's from Lily. Is that *the* Lily?"

Carrie felt as though the dough had risen up and punched her in the stomach. What was Lily doing calling her? She couldn't answer.

"It's Lucas's sister. If she calls again, don't answer it."

Eve's mouth opened and closed as the phone in her hands vibrated again. "Are you sure?" she asked.

"Very. Lucas made it clear he doesn't want me to have anything more to do with Lily, and I intend to respect his decision." She turned her attention back to the dough she was preparing for their first afternoon tea service later in the day. They were hosting it for the staff as a trial sitting, but Carrie still wanted it to be perfect.

"Okay. No answering the phone to Lucas or Lily." Eve agreed and returned to making them coffee.

"I'll miss Lily." It had been nice having her own assistant at *Hotel Mayfair*. Even if she was incredibly unreliable and ate more than she baked.

"I'm sorry, Carrie." Eve handed her a coffee.

"I'll be fine. Right, any special requests for our afternoon tea extravaganza?"

Once the lunch service had finished, Carrie, Eve, and Lachlan sat down in the dining room with the staff and enjoyed afternoon tea. Eve had made two types of little sandwiches. There was smoked salmon from the river outside with horseradish grown in their own garden. A whisky-infused cheddar from one of the local farms and a pickle made by the farmer's wife. They were bursting with flavour.

Carrie had made petit fours like the ones she'd served in London. They were an array of pastel colours with floral piping on top. Beside them was a selection of miniature éclairs with elaborate swirls of raspberry cream piped atop them. There were lavender and Earl-Grey-infused biscuits, with the McLeod's coat of arms piped on the top, on the side of each cup and saucer. It looked wonderful.

"Have you taken pictures for your social media?" asked Eve, pausing with her hand outstretched before she took anything from the cake stand.

"Yes, already done," Carrie reassured her. She watched as Eve breathed a sigh of relief and reached out to take a sandwich, her eyes not leaving the sweet display.

"I'll add scones to it when we make the afternoon teas for guests."

"Sounds perfect."

The room was silent as everyone indulged in the food in front of them. Afternoon tea had been one of Carrie's suggestions. It would slot in between lunch service and dinner service and should be an extra stream of revenue. She would use her social media accounts to showcase the indulgent desserts and hopefully entice visitors from afar.

"I think it's fair to say this is a hit," Lachlan mumbled around a mouthful of petit four.

For the next week, Carrie was busy finalising her plans for afternoon tea. There was much more to do than she had anticipated. In London, the hotel had a social media manager, whereas here Carrie, Lachlan, and Eve were responsible for their online presence. They each had their own accounts and a joint account for the castle. After a few days of multiple posts, they'd worked out a schedule for the joint account. Eve had taken a backseat from the restaurant while she concentrated on decorating the rooms for the hotel's grand opening. When Carrie wasn't finalising menus, piping intricate designs on top of tiny creations, or taking artistic photographs of them, she was helping Eve decide on colour schemes for each bedroom.

Today, she could breathe a sigh of relief and take a step back from the busy goings-on at the castle. It was her first proper day off since she'd returned to Scotland and she was going to visit her grandmother. Alice had been just as busy, with the preparations for Alexander and Isla's wedding underway.

The sun was out, and the drive to the McLeod's castle was pleasant. Carrie unwound the windows in her beat-up Land Rover and sang along to an ancient cassette tape that had been in the glove box. Lachlan had offered to lend her his car for the drive, but she had refused.

Alice was working today as there was so much to do for the wedding, but she had suggested Carrie pop around to the castle for some lunch. The castle was peaceful as Carrie parked outside. It was a nice change from Lachlan's castle… her castle, where they had people milling around all the time. It would be even busier once the hotel opened. When Eve finished renovating the bedrooms, she was planning to renovate a handful of the cottages on the castle's land for staff to live in. She'd already told Carrie one would be for her. Carrie had tried to turn it down, but as Eve had pointed out, she couldn't continue to live in a bedroom without her own sitting room or kitchen.

"There you are!" Alice called as Carrie got out of the car.

"Sorry, I took a slow drive to enjoy the scenery." Carrie wrapped her arms around her grandmother.

"Well, you're here now. Come on, lunch is ready." Alice linked her arm through Carrie's and led her round the back of the castle to the staff entrance.

Alice had made Carrie sausage sandwiches with homemade bread and a thick layer of mustard. In the warm kitchen, with her grandmother's cooking in front of her, Carrie felt like a child again. There was a feeling of safety with the familiarity of her childhood surrounding her.

"How are you?" Alice asked as she sat down opposite Carrie. She'd made them both a cup of tea to go with their food.

"I'm happy to be home," Carrie replied around her mouthful of food.

"What about the man you met?"

Carrie hadn't told her grandmother much about Lucas, just that she had met someone and was enjoying spending time with them.

"We're not keeping in touch." Carrie focused on the food in front of her so her grandmother couldn't study her expression.

"That's a shame." Alice was watching her with her brow furrowed.

"I've signed the contract to be a shareholder in the castle." Carrie changed the subject.

She told Alice about her plans for the castle and the program she wanted to start to help young people find their passion for baking. Alice was interested in her plans and asked lots of questions and gave her some suggestions of people in the community to reach out to.

"You're going to do amazingly," Alice reassured her.

"Thank you, Gran." Carrie smiled and reached across the table to squeeze her grandmother's hand. For the first time in a long while, she felt content and at peace with where she was. Her time in London had confirmed to her that Scotland was her home, and it was where her soul felt at rest.

"I need your advice on the fondant for the wedding cake." Alice cleared her throat and Carrie bit back a laugh. Despite being professionally trained, Carrie had never given her grandmother advice on baking or decorating. Alice was far too proud to ask for help and, with a lifetime of experience, she rarely needed it.

"What do you need?" asked Carrie.

Carrie spent the next hour giving her grandmother a lesson on how to ice a cake in fondant. By the time they had finished, the kitchen was covered in icing sugar and they had tears running down their faces. Carrie had offered to make the wedding cake, but Isla had insisted on having Alice make it.

"When are you planning on icing the cake?" Carrie asked, looking at the mess in front of them.

"The day before. I want the icing to be as fresh as possible."

"I'll come over and help you ice it. We're closed for the long weekend over the wedding, so I'll be around."

"Thank you, my love. It's nice to have you home."

Carrie left Alice with a huge smile on both of their faces. The emails they'd shared during their time in London hadn't been enough, and spending the day together had been just what she needed. Despite the gaping hole inside her, Carrie was slowly regaining control of her life. At times, her eyes would wander to the landscape and she'd imagine walking hand-in-hand with Lucas to one of her favourite spots where they could sit and have a picnic. But as soon as those thoughts entered her mind, she pushed them away again. There was little point in making herself suffer any further by thinking of the future she wanted, but could not have.

When Carrie arrived back at the hotel, the dinner service had just started, so she slipped up to her bedroom and had a shower to wash out the icing sugar in her hair. Once clean and changed, she went down to the kitchens to see if she could find some dinner for herself.

"Carrie! I've been looking for you," Eve called as she walked into the bustling kitchen.

"Do you need some help?" Carrie asked. Her eyes flickered around the room and she noticed Lachlan wasn't at his usual station.

"Yes, please. Lachlan is showing our new hotel manager around, but I really need his help. Would you find him and take over from him?"

"Of course! Do you know where they are?"

"I think Lachlan was showing him around the bedrooms we're renovating."

"I'll find them!" Carrie jogged out of the kitchen and carefully slipped past the restaurant without any of the guests seeing her. She'd dressed in leggings and a baggy jumper, not expecting to see anyone. As she climbed the stairs, she pulled her hair into a bun in an attempt to look more professional.

The corridor was dimly lit, as they were still waiting for the builders to install all the lights. Carrie heard muffled voices coming from one of the rooms, so she headed towards it.

"Hi!" she called, pushing the door open. "Eve is looki—" Carrie's voice faltered as her eyes adjusted to the bright light inside the bedroom.

"Carrie?" Lachlan asked, waving a hand in

front of her eyes.

"Lucas?" she whispered, her eyes focused on the man standing beside Lachlan.

"Carrie," his voice was a whisper, just loud enough for her to hear.

"What are you doing here?" She stepped forward on shaking legs.

"I'll just…" Lachlan pointed to the door, but neither Carrie nor Lucas was paying any attention to him.

"What are you doing here?" Carrie repeated her question.

"I'm being given a tour of the hotel I'm about to manage." He stepped towards her.

"You're about to manage?" Carrie stuttered out the words. Her hands shook by her sides, so she wrapped her arms around her waist.

"I couldn't live with the idea of never seeing you again."

"But you said you didn't want me anywhere near Lily? Where is Lily?" Carrie glanced around the room as if she expected Lily to jump out and shout surprise.

"Lily and I have had a few conversations, and she's told me off a lot. Apparently, I can't wrap her in cotton wool and keep her from the world. She's back at home in London. I've paid Maria to spend the weekend with her while I come up to sort everything out. Lachlan gave me a rather generous advance. You were right, Carrie, we were forgetting to live. Lily is bored with the same routine every day.

If there's a chance her life might be cut short, then she's decided she wants to enjoy every second of it. Apparently, being with you and seeing me happy with you is Lily's idea of enjoying every second of it."

There was so much to process. Carrie shook her head, trying to arrange her thoughts. "What about Lily's health? It's a huge move for her. What if it's too much?" She started with the most important question.

"Lily's recent health scare was a panic attack. She's been having nightmares about her own health because of how overbearing I've been." Lucas rubbed a hand over his face, and Carrie looked at him properly for the first time. His sparkling eyes were dull and the purple marks under his eyes had deepened. "It was me that was making Lily sick. Not you. She confided in me about how worried she was for me. She thinks she's a burden and is stopping me from living my life." His shoulders had rounded, and his eyes had misted over.

"Oh, Lucas." Carrie couldn't bear the distance between them any longer. She stepped forward and his arms wrapped around her, pulling her close. They clung to each other.

"Do you still want us, Carrie?" asked Lucas.

"Of course I do. But are you sure? This is a huge move for both of you."

"We've spoken of nothing else since you left, and we're sure. Neither of us want to lose you, Carrie. When Lachlan called me and offered me the job, I didn't know what to say. I was at home and Lily had overheard the conversation. Before I'd even put the phone down, she'd started packing her clothes. Lachlan has offered us a cottage on the estate once it's been renovated. We'll keep the flat in London and let it out. That way, we'll have somewhere to go back to if things don't work out." He paused and dropped a kiss on the top of her head. "I think it will do Lily good to move somewhere like this. London is so fast-paced, she needs this. Lachlan told me about your initiative to work with young people, and I'm hoping Lily can be a part of it." He stepped back so he could see her face.

Carrie had a steady stream of happy tears rolling down her face. "Lily is coming straight in as my kitchen assistant. I've missed having her there chattering away to me, stealing biscuits, and doubling the chocolate in all my recipes."

"It won't be easy, Carrie. Lily's health won't improve."

"No, but you'll both have the support of everyone here. Any sign of anything wrong with her and Lachlan will call in the helicopter to take her to a specialist."

"Something tells me you're not exaggerating."

"I'm not. We're a close team here and we look after our own. How long are you here for?"

"I have to go home tomorrow. I've got two weeks left at *Hotel Mayfair,* then I'll need a couple of days to get packed up."

"Where are you staying?"

"I'm not sure. Lachlan had a car pick me up from the station and then he took me straight on a tour."

"Looks like you'll have to stay with me. Come on." Carrie slipped her hand into his and led him back to her bedroom.

EPILOGUE

"Carrie brought biscuits!" Lily's voice thundered. She reached out and took the plate from Carrie before she turned and walked into the cottage.

"Come in!" Lucas called from somewhere inside. He knew his sister well enough to know she wouldn't think to invite Carrie inside.

"Hello," greeted Carrie as she walked into the kitchen, where Lucas was hammering a nail into the wall.

"Sorry, I didn't think this would take me so long." He nodded towards the wall. They'd arranged to explore a local town today since they both had the day off.

"I'm happy to wait. Do you need any help?"

"Could you hand me the picture? I think this nail should hold it now."

Lucas and Lily had moved into their cottage a week ago after living in the castle for a month. It had been fun having them living in the rooms next to her, but all too often Lily would sneak down to the kitchens for a midnight snack. Eve had worked hard to get their cottage ready. She'd also surprised Carrie with the cottage next door to them.

"I think it's wonky." Carrie stepped back to look at Lucas's handy work.

"Don't say that. The last three I've put up have been wonky." He climbed down from the stepladder and let out a sigh.

Carrie wrapped her arms around his middle and rested her head against his chest. He pulled her into his embrace and held her. Having him and Lily here in Scotland was everything Carrie had dreamed of. They'd thrown them a welcome party a couple of days after they'd arrived, and Carrie had enjoyed introducing them to everyone. Lily and Alice had immediately hit it off and Alice promised to cook some traditional Scottish dishes that Lily had read about in her tourist books. When Lucas had returned to London, he'd told Lily the good news, and she'd immediately called Carrie and cried down the phone with happiness. She'd dragged Maria out the following day to buy a stack of books about Scotland.

"I can't believe we're finally here," Lucas whispered. He reached down and tilted her chin up. Carrie's eyes flickered up to his.

"I know," she whispered. As her eyes locked with his, she felt her stomach flip as the world around her melted away. His arms tightened around her waist so she was flush against his body.

"I love you, Carrie."

"I love you." Carrie only just had time to utter the three words before his lips met hers. Even though Carrie got to kiss him every day, her heart still thundered as her lips moved against his. She could feel him pressed against her. His aftershave filled her nose, and the taste of him was on the tip of her tongue. Her fingers tangled in his hair as he deepened the kiss.

They both broke apart as the sound of something falling echoed around the room. The picture Lucas had just hung had fallen.

"Do you want me to do it?" asked Carrie, stifling a giggle.

"Carrie, you've hung every picture in my home. I'm yet to successfully hang one."

"I'll do it for you when we get back. You can show me where you want the others. You're an excellent hotel manager, Lucas, but your DIY skills are rubbish." She reached up on her tiptoes and pecked his lips, stepping backwards before his arms could wrap around her and pull her to him again.

"Fine. Now, did Lily say you'd brought biscuits?"

"Yeah. Lily took them as I—" Realisation dawned on both of them at the same time. They both jumped into action and ran to the living room, where Lily was sitting on the sofa with an empty plate on her lap.

"Lily, did you eat all of those?" asked Carrie.

"Do you have any more?" she asked, grinning at Carrie. Lily had crumbs down her cream blouse.

"We're supposed to be having lunch in town! Oh, Lily, all that sugar." Lucas plonked down on the opposite sofa and held his head in his hands.

Carrie sat next to him and wrapped an arm around his shoulders. "Lucas, do you really think I'd leave Lily alone with an entire plate of biscuits?" She pulled a sandwich bag from her jacket pocket with the rest of the biscuits. She'd only put two on the plate, knowing Lily wouldn't be able to stop herself. "Also, they're sugar-free. I've been experimenting with recipes to improve Lily's diet and they seemed to have gone down okay."

Lily looked down at the empty plate in front of her with her mouth open and her eyes wide. "There was no sugar in them?" she asked.

"None." Carrie beamed back at her.

"You're a genius." Lucas laughed, his entire demeanour had relaxed.

"Right. Shall we go into town? There's an ice cream shop, and it looks like it's going to be a warm day." Carrie stood up, clapping her hands to spur them both into action.

"I love you." Lucas slipped his hand into hers.

"I love you, too." She squeezed his hand.

The End

Other books...

THE CORNISH VINTAGE SERIES

THE CORNISH VINTAGE DRESS SHOP

THE CORNISH VINTAGE JEWELLERY SHOP

THE PEACE, JOY AND LOVE SERIES

A MERRY CHRISTMAS AT THE CASTLE

A SPRING FLING AT HOTEL MAYFAIR

I HOPE YOU ENJOYED YOUR STAY AT HOTEL MAYFAIR

Please consider leaving a review.

Have you read A Merry Christmas at the Castle? If not, find the first chapter on the next page...

CHAPTER ONE

"Eve, I need to talk to you," Carlo's voice called from the other side of the restaurant.

Eve rolled her eyes. She'd just walked through the door. A glance at her watch told her she wasn't due to start work for another half an hour, and already her manager wanted to speak to her.

"I'll be right there," she called back. Eve dropped her bags on the closest table, careful to avoid the small fake pine trees wrapped in cheap tinsel. It was Carlo's budget attempt at making the backstreet Italian restaurant look Christmassy. After sweeping her hair back into a low bun, Eve walked through the kitchen to Carlo's office. When she applied for the job at Carlo's Calzones, Eve had expected the role to involve cooking. Instead, she was a glorified waitress who stepped in when the chef was ill. Three years studying Food Science at Reading University and this was all she'd amounted to.

"Morning, Eve." Eric, the chef, called to her as she walked past. He had swapped his chef's hat for a red velvet Father Christmas one. Eve stopped herself from rolling her eyes again.

The kitchen was already hot and stuffy,

despite it only being ten in the morning. *I Wish it Could be Christmas Everyday* blared out from the radio and Eve fought the urge to throw it out of the front door and into the Thames. Since the first of December, Eric had tuned the radio into Christmas FM and festive tunes had echoed around the kitchen.

"Morning, Eric." Eve waved but didn't stop to talk.

"Eve, come in." Carlo was sitting behind his desk in the office.

There was no seat for her and so Eve stood in front of the desk, clasping her hands in front of her as she waited for Carlo to speak. It wasn't unusual for him to call staff into the office. He had a very particular way of running the restaurant and liked everyone to know he was in charge. Even if that meant he did very little himself.

"I'm afraid I have to let you go." He took a drag from the vape he held in his hand. Eve winced as the sickly sweetness filled the air. She'd told him repeatedly that he shouldn't be vaping inside the premises.

"Let me go?" she gasped out.

"Yes. The last couple of years have been financially challenging and I've had to make cuts." He shrugged, refusing to meet her eye.

"It's three weeks before Christmas and you're firing me?" Eve raised her voice. She'd worked for Carlo since graduating from university five years ago.

"I'm sorry, Eve."

Without uttering another word, Eve stalked out of the office, back into the restaurant, and picked up her bags. This time she swung them at the stupid faux Christmas tree, knocking it onto the ground. She walked out of the restaurant and onto the icy street. Eve bit her lip to stop tears forming in her eyes. It would do no good to cry. She went to pull her phone from her pocket, wanting to call her boyfriend. His comforting voice would help. Her fingers wrapped around the phone just as it started vibrating. It was Rihanna, her neighbour and best friend.

"Hi Rhi," Eve answered. She took in a deep breath of the icy London air to stop her voice from wobbling.

"Michael's moving his stuff out of your flat."

The words echoed around Eve's brain as she tried to make sense of them. Moving his stuff out of the flat? The flat they shared together? Rhi must have been wrong. Michael would be at work by now. Eve had waved him off earlier that morning, kissing him goodbye, and wishing him a good day.

"I'm coming," she replied and put the phone down before Rhi could say anything more. It would all be a silly mistake and they'd laugh about it over a glass of wine and a takeaway tonight. The sickening feeling in her stomach knew the truth.

The tube journey back to her flat in Stratford felt never-ending. Eve stared out the window, watching as they passed each station. Her mind was threatening to cave in, but she was forcing herself to keep going. Just a few more steps to her building. She took the lift to the fifth floor, where the door to her flat was wide open.

"Michael?" she called. Her legs shook as she slowly entered the almost-empty flat.

"Eve, what are you doing here?" Michael whirled around to face her. His eyes were open wide.

"What are you doing?" Eve asked, ignoring his question.

"I thought it would be easier this way." He

shrugged.

"What would be easier?" she asked.

"Leaving you."

Eve stood open-mouthed, not knowing what to say.

"I think it's best if I go." He pointed towards the door and Eve nodded, unable to get any words out. Without a goodbye or a last hug, Michael walked out of the door.

"Eve?" Rhi was standing in the doorway peering in at the desolate flat. Most of the furniture had been Michael's.

"He's gone." Eve felt a sob rising in her throat.

"Oh, Eve. I'm so sorry." Her friend walked over and wrapped her arms around her.

"I lost my job, too." Eve needed to tell someone.

"Come back to mine. I'll make you a cup of tea."

Eve allowed herself to be guided into Rhi's flat across the hallway. She propped herself up against the kitchen cupboards whilst Rhi bustled around making tea.

"What happened?" Rhi asked.

"Carlo's struggling financially, so he had to let me go." Eve's voice sounded detached.

"What an ass." Rhi handed Eve a strong mug of tea and they made their way into the living room. "Hold on a minute. I saw something on Facebook this morning." Rhi grabbed her laptop from the coffee table and pulled up her internet history. "Here. Look!" She flung the laptop into Eve's lap.

Eve squinted at the screen, trying to read the tiny writing. It was an advert for a private chef.

"I'm not a chef." Eve went to hand the laptop back, but Rhi wouldn't accept it.

"No, but you can cook. We just need to tweak your CV."

Eve didn't have the energy to argue, and so, an hour later, Rhi had 'polished' Eve's CV for her and emailed it off with a cover letter.

"I can't believe you sent it." Eve shook her head and took a sip of the coffee she'd made while Rhi was drafting the letter.

"It's only two weeks' work. Do you want to spend Christmas alone? Or you could get this job and spend a wonderful Christmas up in the Scottish Highlands."

"The Scottish Highlands?" screeched Eve.

"Yes, didn't you read the advert?" Rhi chuckled.

"Rhi, I didn't think you were serious when you first showed it to me!"

"Oh." At least Rhi had the good nature to look a little guilty before a huge grin spread across her face. "You're going to Scotland!"

"I haven't got the job!" Eve argued.

"Oh, but you will. Your CV is very impressive."

"What do you mean?" Eve narrowed her eyes. She should have read it before she allowed Rhi to hit send.

"I embellished your role at Carlo's." Rhi shrugged.

"Rhi, what do you mean you embellished my role at Carlo's?" Eve spoke slowly, enunciating each word.

"I just tweaked your role at Carlo's slightly and possibly didn't mention that his restaurant is a backstreet Italian." Rhi shrugged and poured a handful of skittles into her mouth.

"Rhi," Eve grumbled. "Tell me exactly what you put on my CV."

"I said you were the head chef at an up-and-coming London restaurant which specialised in adding a modern twist to classic cuisine."

"Oh, Rhi." Eve hid her face in her hands. "Maybe we should email them and retract my application." Eve reached for the laptop.

"Absolutely not. I will not allow you to spend the festive period sitting in that flat feeling sorry for yourself."

"I'm okay. If I'm honest, I'm more upset about losing my job than losing Michael." Eve had been thinking while Rhi was lying on her job application. She and Michael had been drifting apart for a while now, but neither of them had wanted to confront it.

"I never thought you two suited each other," confessed Rhi.

"I know. It was just easy with him."

"Anyway, enough about Michael. We should go shopping. It's going to be freezing in Scotland at this time of year."

"I've not even got the job yet. Besides, I can't afford to go shopping. I've got no income and I'll have to cover Michael's half of the rent." Reality was dawning on Eve and she wanted to bury her head in the ground. Maybe escaping to Scotland was a good idea.

"Give your notice on the flat and move in with me. I've got a spare bedroom." Rhi's tone made it clear this was an instruction and not a suggestion.

"That would be perfect. Thank you, Rhi." As much as Eve treasured her independence and having her own space, she could hardly afford her half of the rent, let alone Michael's.

"Shall we email the agents now to let them know?" Rhi grabbed for the laptop again, and Eve agreed before she could change her mind and allow her pride to resurface.

"Oh look, you've got an email." Rhi had just hit send on the email to the letting agent. "It's from the job we applied to."

"Rhi, I think we should email them and retract my application. My CV is a lie and I can't cook for someone. My cooking isn't good enough."

"I think it might be too late to retract it," Rhi whispered, squinting at the screen.

"What do you mean?" Eve asked. It surprised her to find excitement bubbling away in the pit of her stomach.

"They want you to call them to arrange your transport. Oh my gosh, you got the job!"

Eve stared blankly at the screen in front of her. This morning she'd woken up ready for another day at work. With Christmas three weeks away, she had planned to nip out to the shops between lunch and dinner service to buy Michael's Christmas present. At least she hadn't wasted her money on a pointless gift. She glanced at the clock on Rhi's laptop. It was midday. Usually, she'd be flitting from table-to-table taking orders and bringing food out to hungry patrons. Instead, she was single and sitting in Rhi's flat, contemplating taking a job in the Scottish Highlands.

"Life can change in a matter of minutes," Eve muttered. She was still staring at the screen.

"Exactly. Do something a little crazy and accept this job. Eve, you're an amazing cook. It's just two weeks cooking for a posh family."

"Rhi, I can't do this. I've only ever cooked for friends and family. You can hardly call making a few pizzas and pasta dishes at Carlo's cooking."

"Come on, Eve! Your food is amazing. Besides, what's the worst that could happen?"

"I could make a mess of it and be forever blacklisted in the food industry."

"You're so dramatic. You'll be cooking for a family over Christmas. It'll just be lots of roast dinners and various cold meats."

"But I've lied, Rhi! Well, you've lied for me. They'll realise I can't cook and throw me out."

"But you can cook! Eve, remember last Christmas when my oven broke? Michael was away visiting his family so you were spending Christmas Day alone. Without a second thought, you took all my ingredients and told me to enjoy the morning with my parents and you'd bring lunch over at midday. We all loved your food, Eve. I'm not just saying this because you're my best friend. You're an amazing cook and I know you can do this!"

Eve thought about it. She was no stranger to throwing together last-minute meals, but that didn't mean they were restaurant quality. But perhaps Rhi had a point. What was the worst that could happen? After all, she was already unemployed. Without allowing herself another second to think, Eve grabbed her mobile from the table and dialled the number of the agency that was arranging the job.

"Hello, *Peace, Joy and Love Catering Company*. How may I help you?" The sound of a bored voice floated down the phone.

"Hello, It's Eve Merry. I applied for a role and I just received an email asking me to contact you to arrange transport."

"Oh, yes. Let me just pull up the information." The woman's tone remained flat. Eve could hardly believe she was making such an enormous change so close to Christmas, and yet this woman was acting as though it was nothing. "Here we go. The client has offered to pay for transport, so we can book you on a train on Friday. It'll be an overnight journey. You'll arrive Saturday lunchtime, staff will settle you in, and then you'll start work on Monday."

Eve reached out for a pen and paper. Thankfully, Rhi's job as a freelance writer meant there was an abundance of notepads and pens scattered throughout her flat. The conversation only lasted ten minutes and by the time Eve put the phone down, they had booked her on the Caledonian Sleeper to Fort William. Once she disembarked in Fort William, a driver would meet her and take her to The McLeod's Castle. She had almost choked on air at the mention of a castle. However, her nerves settled when the woman told her there would only be a party of seven in residence. Eve had covered Eric a handful of times so a party of seven should be easy.

Eve took a deep breath as she put the phone down. "I'm leaving on Friday," she whispered.

"Oh, my!" gasped Rhi.

"I can't believe I've said yes to this."

"I can. Carlo's Calzones was never enough for you, Eve. This is just the beginning for you. Perhaps this agency will keep you on. You could spend summer sailing around St-Tropez cooking on a luxury yacht!"

They were getting carried away, but Eve wondered whether it would be a possibility. She was single and unemployed, there was absolutely nothing stopping her from travelling the world and cooking. At eighteen, when she started university, Eve had big plans to cook on every continent. However, life had got a little too real when she graduated and had to find a job. It was a field where experience was everything and Eve had spent three years studying, when it seemed everybody else in the industry had spent three years working. It had felt like an answer to all her problems when Carlo offered her the job of waitressing and asked if she would be open to being trained up as cover for when Eric was off.

"Are you listening to me?" Rhi interrupted her thoughts.

"Sorry. What were you saying?"

"We need to pack!" Rhi stood up, grabbing Eve's keys from the coffee table.

"Rhi, it's only Monday." Eve laughed. She'd be in the kitchen for the entirety of her stay, so she wouldn't need to bring much with her. The agency had told her chef whites would be available for her at the property. She would work each day, but with breaks outside of mealtimes, so Eve only needed a few pairs of jeans and jumpers.

Rhi stood with her arms crossed and her steely gaze focused on Eve. "I'm not taking no for an answer."

Reluctantly, Eve followed Rhi back into her flat. She was shocked to discover Michael had even taken the chest of drawers, leaving all of her clothes on the mattress. He had bought the bed frame and so there was just a mattress left in the middle of the floor.

"He must have been planning this for ages," Rhi commented, looking around at the sparse flat.

"I know." Eve gulped. She'd been happily trundling on with life. Meanwhile, Michael was planning to leave. It was an eye-opener for her. She'd got too comfortable, and it was time for a change. Twenty-six was far too young to settle.

"Come on, let's move your stuff into my spare room. There's no point in delaying." Rhi grabbed Eve's suitcase and started piling her clothes into it. It didn't take long and the entirety of Eve's clothes fit in one case. She spent most of her life in chef whites or her waitressing uniform and had little time for clothes.

"I might have to lend you a few pieces," commented Rhi. It horrified her to see just how little Eve owned. Eve cringed at the idea. Their tastes were very different. Rhi was confident and had enviable curves. Eve was the polar opposite. She decided not to argue. So long as everything fit inside her suitcase, she didn't mind what Rhi put inside it. She glanced in the only mirror Michael had left behind and realised she didn't look like someone whose boyfriend had dumped them on the same day they'd lost their job. Instead, she looked like she was excited about the future. There was a sparkle back in her eyes. Food had saved her once before. It could do it again.

"Do you not own any makeup?" The horrified voice of Rhi echoed in the bathroom. Eve laughed and rolled her eyes. She owed a lot to her friend. Without her, she'd be sitting on the rug in the living room eating a gallon of ice cream, and contemplating how to pay the rent.

Printed in Great Britain
by Amazon

44112149R00209